NOV - 3 2014

W9-BAF-787

Praise for the Thrillers of
James Scott Bell

A master of the cliffhanger, creating scene after scene of mounting suspense and revelation . . . Heart-whamming.
- Publishers Weekly

A master of suspense. - Library Journal

One of the best writers out there, bar none.
- In the Library Review

A fresh take on the territory of Hammett and Chandler.
- Booklist

Scenes and characters jump off the page.
- Romantic Times

First-rate suspense with a fiery action-movie climax!
- CBD Reviews

Depth of characterization . . . redemptive ending.
- Clues Unlimited

Will leave you breathless to the unforeseen end.
- Novel Rocket

Readers will enjoy Bell's talent for description and character development. - Publishers Weekly

NOV - 3 2014

DON'T LEAVE ME

James Scott Bell

Compendium Press

Copyright © 2013 James Scott Bell

All rights reserved.

ISBN-13: 978-0-910355-04-9

Compendium Press
P.O. Box 705
Woodland Hills, CA 91365

Also by James Scott Bell

On Writing:

Plot & Structure
Revision & Self-Editing for Publication
The Art of War for Writers
Conflict & Suspense
Writing Fiction For All You're Worth
Fiction Attack!
Self-Publishing Attack!

Fiction:

One More Lie
Watch Your Back
Deceived
Try Dying
Try Darkness
Try Fear
Pay Me in Flesh (as K. Bennett)
The Year of Eating Dangerously (as K. Bennett)
I Ate the Sheriff (as K. Bennett)
City of Angels
Angels Flight
Angel of Mercy
A Greater Glory
A Higher Justice
A Certain Truth
Glimpses of Paradise
No Legal Grounds
The Whole Truth
Presumed Guilty
Sins of the Fathers
Breach of Promise
Deadlock
The Nephilim Seed
Blind Justice
Final Witness
Circumstantial Evidence
The Darwin Conspiracy

1

Chuck shot his arm across Stan's chest one second before impact.

Then came the sound of crushing and the jolt of a hard stop. Adrenaline laced Chuck Samson's nerves. And anger. Because it was the Escalade's fault, jamming on its brakes that way. Like the guy *wanted* to be rear ended.

"Oh God Oh God Oh God!" Stan's voice, high and scared.

"It's all right, Stan." Chuck kept his arm against his younger brother's wiry body. Feeling it tighten, no body fat, he'd always been this way, as a kid, as an adult. Stringy and ADD.

Stan writhed under Chuck's arm. "What happened? What!"

"Little accident is all," Chuck said. "You okay?"

"I'm all tingly!"

"Just take it easy now. Deep breaths. Can you do that for me, Stan? Deep. That's it. I've got to talk to the guy."

"Don't leave me!" It was what Stan used to say when he

3 0053
01072
6746

1

was scared as a kid. Chuck showing up whenever Stan got pushed or teased, putting a beatdown on the bullies. Or getting there afterward to wipe the tears off Stan's face and tell him he could be stronger, and Stan hugging his big brother and always saying *Don't leave me!* Stan hadn't said it in years. He was thirty now, and just starting to look it. But shouting the phrase made him seem ten again.

He knew he had his work cut out for him, keep his brother calm while he dealt with this crazy driver. "I'll be right outside the—"

Tap tap.

Chuck turned and recognized the face outside the window. Same guy. The one in front of his neighbor's house just five minutes earlier. The Escalade had seemed out place at Lucy Bowers' curb. She was single, new to the neighborhood. Driving by, Chuck had looked at the guy. The guy's face wasn't exactly friendly. Chuck nodded and drove on. What else could he do? He wasn't the sheriff of the neighborhood. People could park where they wanted.

But here the guy was again. Longish brown hair, unkempt but with a part down the middle. Beard stubble. Large, flat nose. Looked close to Chuck's age, thirty-four.

"You all right?" The guy's muffled voice, through the window, carried a slight accent of some kind. Russian?

Chuck said, "I think so." Suspicion gnawed him. Rear end insurance scams were common in Southern Cal. He wanted to give people the benefit of the doubt, but he knew too much about human nature.

Perfect setting for that scam, too. It was early morning and they were on a stretch of road on the other side of a new home development. One block north of Sherman Way, just before it turns into Platt.

2

And it didn't help that the adrenaline was bubbling up the PTSD soup that was sitting on the back burner of his brain. He'd just started to get more control over it, but something like this could set it off, spill it. Chuck took a deep breath.

"Insurance?" the guy said.

There it was. In a rear ender, boys and girls, the guy in back always loses. In all his years of driving, Chuck had three speeding tickets but never an accident. That this one could have been so easily avoided rankled him.

They guy opened Chuck's door. It groaned like a bored, metallic lion.

Chuck swiveled, put his feet on the street. His legs shook like he was in a ten-below wind. He felt duly embarrassed. He considered himself in good shape. Kept up his running, even a little of the kick boxing he'd learned in the Marine martial arts program. Not the usual training for a chaplain in Afghanistan, but it did teach a certain discipline. Which Chuck held onto now as he steadied himself.

Just stay calm and talk it through, the way Royce always told him to do it.

"Easy there, my friend," the guy said with a little scratch in his voice. Chuck decided Mad Russian would be a good name for him, the way he drove. And he thought he caught a whiff of whiskey breath. At this hour? Mad indeed.

He was about Chuck's height, a couple inches over six feet. Looked strong across the chest. A bar fight kind of guy. In high school Chuck had plenty of fights under the influence, and felt the familiar quiver of aggression shoot down to his fists. He told the quiver to shut it down, stay calm.

You were a man of God once, remember? A MOG . . .

"You okay?" Chuck said.

Mad Russian didn't say anything. Just stood there. Was that

3

a smirk on his face? What was up with that?

"So what happened?" Chuck said, keeping his voice steady. No need to get aggressive. Give the guy a chance.

"You look at me when you drive by," Mad Russian said.

"Excuse me?"

"You drive by, back there, looking at me."

"That? No, I wasn't looking at you. I was just—"

"You slow."

All right, simple misunderstanding. Chuck had learned to defuse emotional bombs. That had been a part of his work, his calling, after all. He said, "No, what happened is I'm driving to work, okay? So if—"

"Who is that?" Mad Russian nodded toward Stan, still in the passenger seat of Chuck's Sentra. Stan was sitting with his arms crossed in front of his chest, rocking back and forth. Keep things calm, Chuck told himself, so Stan doesn't freak.

"Look," Chuck said, "let's just—"

"I ask you question," Mad Russian said.

Okay, the guy did not want to be reasonable. Clean this up later. All business now. "Let's exchange information and I'm sure we—"

"You look at me and you study me."

"No—"

"You look like tough guy. You tough guy?"

"Listen, I told you, I didn't—"

A hand of iron shot up and clamped Chuck's throat. Mad Russian thrust his face within a hair of Chuck's and said, "You tell me why you look at me."

Chuck couldn't tell him anything, not with his air choked off. He looked into crazy, blue-ice eyes, rimmed red. Not with the buzzing of his brain now, kicking into survival mode, and the heat of it in his chest, that old and bad feeling when they'd cut his throat. It was back, all of it, in a fireball under his ribs.

Mad Russian tightened the neck vice.

Chuck heard Stan screaming inside the car.

Stay there Stan. Chuck tried to will the thought to his brother.

Chuck shot a fist at the guy's arm. No movement.

Blood pumping behind Chuck's eyes.

Stan screamed louder.

Chuck's mind shot to military mode. Thrusting up with his hands, he caught the guy flush under the chin with the heels of his palms. Mad Russian's head snapped back and he let go.

Chuck sucked for air, making a sound like a shovel scraping cement. His head was light and he thought for a second he'd pass out.

"Chuck!"

Stan was out of the car, racing around toward him.

Mad Russian was a couple of steps back. He just looked at the brothers, head cocked to one side.

Then he removed something from his pocket, as smoothly as a pool hustler pulls out a ten spot. With a flick of his wrist a blade flashed in the morning sun.

The half moon scar on Chuck's throat heated up. He knew what knives that size could do.

Chuck pushed his brother toward the sidewalk. "Run!"

Stan stumbled, kept his feet, but did not run.

Chuck stepped in front of his brother, ready for an attack, as much as you could be for a guy with a knife when you had nothing in your hands. But he did not think, he did not analyze, there was no time, it was a flash of knowing that he would never let Stan get hurt. He would take the cut if he had to, he would kill this guy if he had to, and he felt the blood rush to his face. And he knew then, too, in that blink of time, that he needed

Stan as much as Stan needed him. That the brother-blood tie was what was keeping him from sinking further down into the shadows.

And the Mad Russian just stood there. Smiling.

For a long moment no one moved.

Then a blue sedan came around the corner, off Platt, toward them.

Mad Russian watched it, holding the knife low against his thigh.

The blue sedan pulled to a stop.

As the driver's window came down Mad Russian flicked his wrist again. The knife blade disappeared into the handle. He slid the knife back in his pocket as if he'd just exchanged business cards with somebody.

Still smiling, he pointed his finger at Chuck, and then at Stan. Then he calmly walked to his Escalade, got in and drove off.

No license plate, Chuck noted.

"What was that?" the sedan driver yelled. "Was that a knife?"

Stan gripped Chuck's arm. "He had a knife, Chuck. Did you see the knife?"

"I'll call 911," the driver said. He was maybe fifty, short gray hair and glasses.

"Yeah, yeah," Chuck said. He looked to his brother. Stan was trembling. Chuck gently gripped Stan's shoulders. "It's okay now, bud."

"Why did he have a knife, Chuck?"

"I don't know. But he's gone."

"I have to go to work. The new specials are out!"

"We'll get you there. Don't worry. Don't—"

Chuck's phone vibrated. He fished it from his pocket. A

private number.

"Hello?"

A male voice, whispery, said, "Don't say a word."

"What?"

"You do and you're dead."

"Wait a—"

"She would not like that."

"Who—"

"She would not like it. She can see past the grave."

A cold, blue fire tore across his chest. Julia. He was talking about Julia.

The connection went dead.

2

"Chuck, I can't be late," Stan said. "I'm on door!"

"What? Oh yeah, sure." Chuck blinked a couple of times, like he was coming out of a dream. No, it couldn't have been Julia the guy meant, but it couldn't be anybody else—

The guy in the sedan was out of his car now, punching his phone. "Hey, what's your name?"

"What?" Chuck said.

"Name. Your name. I'll call."

"Chuck Samson. I work at the Raymond Hunt Academy, Calabasas."

She would not like it. She can see past the grave.

Who made that call? Not the guy in the Escalade. He couldn't have had Chuck's number.

Or could he?

But how?

. . . past the grave.

"Chuck!" Stan's face was etched with worry. Over-worry, as usual. Chuck's first reaction, ever since he could remember, was to calm Stan down. Stan shivered when things got tense. It started when they were kids, when their dad refused to accept Stan's autism and took out his own frustrations on both their skins.

"It's all right," Chuck said, touching Stan's arm. "Let's go."

Stan ran around and got in the Sentra. When Chuck got in, his door wouldn't fully close.

Great way to start the week. Rear ender. Guy with a knife. Guy choking you. Try that with your morning coffee, friends. Now your car needs body work. Your brother is freaking about being late, and you're not going to get to your class on time.

And how about that cryptic phone call about your dead wife, sports fan?

No, no way. A coincidence, it was just a whacked-out guy with too much drink in him, and then a wrong number and—

Chuck started the car and pulled tentatively into the lane.

The guy in the sedan shouted "Hey!"

Chuck didn't stop. The guy'd report it. Fine. Chuck had to get Stan to his job now or he'd be hysteria on stilts.

"Chuck, why'd he have a knife?"

"Stan?"

"Yes, Chuck?"

"Next time I tell you to run, you run."

"But Chuck—"

"Just do it," Chuck said. Then, from the distant reaches of his mind, it started again.

The shadow dance.

No. Not now. Please.

It hadn't happened in months, this series of visions all tied up with his tour in Afghanistan. Memory muddled by trauma, the VA docs said. You never knew when it would come and if it would ever get straight in his mind. He called it the shadow dance because the dark figures seemed to float in front of him. Distant explosions were the sound track —

"Look out!"

Chuck swerved just in time to avoid another rear ender, this time with a Mini Cooper.

"Chuck, you almost hit—"

"I know!"

"Don't hit anything, Chuck."

Stan, the voice of simple thought. Yes, little brother, I won't hit anything if I can help it. Thank you very much! Since Stan had come to live with him and Julia, over a year ago, it had been a difficult period of adjustment for all of them. Chuck was trying to get to know his wife again, after his return, and it was hard. His own psyche needed the most adjusting, but he wanted to get better, he wasn't one of those guys resisting it. Even though the VA was mucking up recently, denying him treatment. Still, he thought there was some daylight there, through the clouds, and then, then —

And then Julia's death, like a bad joke from Fate with a morning hangover. Only no joke, and it took him hours to believe it, and then it was like he'd been tied to a log in one of those silent movies, the log heading to the big buzz saw. Only he hadn't been rescued, he'd been sawed in half and even now, seven months since a drunk in a truck took his wife from him, he was barely stitched together with frayed thread.

Now he was looking after Stan, and he loved his brother, but he was a weight on him, too, and he wished Stan could be on his own somehow, and thinking that made Chuck feel like crud. He was on a merry-go-round of bad vibes and discordant music.

At least Stan was quiet the rest of the way to Ralphs Fresh Fare, the supermarket where he had a job greeting customers.

10

Chuck realized just how much he needed quiet now. In fact, he almost prayed. Which he found odd, given that he hadn't prayed once since Julia's death.

He got to the Ralphs lot and parked in front.

"You can't park here, Chuck," Stan said.

Chuck said, "Yeah, I'm a notorious criminal. Don't turn me in."

Stan smiled. "You're being funny."

Chuck fixed the collar on Stan's shirt, his Ralphs shirt, the black one with the red lettering. Stan didn't have many clothes in the shared closet, but this was his uniform and he always kept it apart from the other clothes.

"There," Chuck said. "Go make me proud."

"Chuck?"

"Yeah?"

"I don't like some people."

"I know," Chuck said. "Some people just don't act nice."

"Gimme five," Stan said, raising his right hand. Stan thought it was always the ultimate cool thing to do, give high fives, even now, even though high fives had gone out with the Clinton administration.

No matter, it was what Stan liked to do, a final gesture, a connection until he got picked up after work.

Chuck slapped Stan's hand. "Go get 'em, Tiger," he said.

"*Rrrrrr,*" Stan said. He tried to make a tiger sound but it was more like a loud purr. Or maybe something else, Chuck thought. Maybe the sound a tiger might make when wounded, lying on the ground.

3

Chuck pulled in to the Hunt Academy parking lot at seven-fifty eight. He got out and leaned on the trunk, downed a few sips of his Starbucks, noticed that his hands were wrapped around the cup like he was choking a man.

He put the cup on the trunk and took out his phone, looked at his call history again.

Of course he knew the other phone would be untraceable.

What was going on? How could the Mad Russian have called him that quick? If it was him at all. But if not, then somebody else was in on the whole thing. And then the Julia connection. They'd have to know all about Chuck's personal life.

He came back to the present when he saw one of his fifth graders emerging from a Lexus in the drop off zone. Joshua Faust. Neat kid. Was going to be the lead in the musical Chuck was writing for the class, titled *Moby!* It was a way for him to use his old high-school rock skills to introduce *Moby-Dick* to the kids, with song's like Ahab's lament, "You've Got Me Pegged."

Joshua was set to play Ahab.

Chuck picked up his coffee as a black Mustang pulled into the slot next to him. Wendy Tower. She was one of the high school teachers at Hunt, the private school carved into the hills of Calabasas. She herself seemed of the hills. She was thirty and always talked about hiking and biking and anything outdoors. She wore her buckskin-colored hair long and straight.

"Morning," Chuck said.

"Lock me up," Wendy said. She emerged with her own cup of coffee.

"Excuse me?"

"Put me away in a rubber room. Throw away the key." She slammed her door. "I'm at the counter, getting my drip, when a couple of guys, maybe twenty, get in this heated conversation, right? And the first guy says, 'You jerk. Louis Armstrong was the first man on the moon.' And the other guy says, 'You are so stupid. Louis Armstrong is that bike racer.' The first guy says, 'Okay, then who was the president when they landed on the moon?' And the second guy says, 'President of what?'"

She paused, took a slug of her coffee.

"Maybe you've had a little too much," Chuck said, playfully reaching for the cup.

Wendy snatched it away. "I wanted to turn around and slap them. I really did. Crack a book!"

"Are you sure you're ready to teach?"

"Chuck, we have to fight this thing. You have what, twenty-five kids? I have the whole high school tromping through my classroom at one time or another. This is it. The last stand. The OK Corral."

"Wasn't that a musical starring Gene Autry?"

Wendy socked him in the arm. "Just for that, I want you to try my paella. Tonight."

"Paella?" Oh right. Wendy Tower was an amateur chef. When she first told him that, Chuck said paella was the make or break dish. If you could make that, you could make anything. He was only half joking.

"Another time," Chuck said. "I'm going into rehearsals."

"For that *Moby-Dick* musical?"

"It's a hit in the making."

"A rock opera based on Melville." She shook her head. "You're either a genius or a . . ."

"Nut job?"

"I was going to say visionary."

"You just scored yourself a free ticket to opening night."

"Can't wait," Wendy said. "You know, I also do great cream puffs. What do you say?"

Part of him wanted to say yes, a small part. But it was drowned out by guilt, still fresh. The last words he and Julia had exchanged, before her death, were in anger. Despite what one VA shrink had told him, all that cognitive therapy mumbo jumbo, he couldn't just talk himself out of the guilt. His mind still sometimes whipped around irrationally.

"Bring your brother, of course," Wendy added.

"Maybe after the musical," Chuck said. "We artistic visionaries have to stay focused."

She smiled, and he wished he could get lost in it. But the memory of his failure with Julia pulled him back, the way a wrangler snaps a colt with a hard rope around the neck.

"Hey, what happened to your wheels?" she said, looking at the front of his car.

"A little thing. On the way over."

"You okay?"

"I'm here."

"Not what I asked."

His instinct was to cover it all in some throwaway line and walk to class. But he said, "I had a little run in with a guy. Just your typical rear ender, except this guy pulled a knife on me."

Wendy laughed. Then stopped. "You're not kidding."

"Stan was with me, too."

"What happened?"

"This guy was parked in front of my neighbor's house, in a black Escalade. I drove by and made eye contact. No big deal. I drove on and next thing I know, he's pulling in front of me and slamming on his brakes."

"And?"

"So I get out to talk to him, he's some wild haired guy with stink breath. He grabs my throat and—"

"Your *throat?*"

"—and Stan is all upset, and I get the guy off me and then he pulls out this knife."

"Chuck!"

"But a car pulls around the corner and the guy put the knife away and gets in his car and drives off."

"Did you get the license plate?"

"He didn't have one."

"Well that should tell the CHP something."

"This guy who stopped his car, he called 911. I should be getting a call myself."

"This is nuts. I mean, you never know anymore." She sighed. "But what I do know is we better get to class. We're cutting it close."

"Don't say *cutting,*" Chuck said.

"Good point."

"Don't say *point,* either."

She laughed, and this time it was fine and good and gave

Chuck a moment of relaxation in an otherwise crazy morning. For that he was grateful. Maybe dinner, yes. Maybe sometime soon.

4

Chuck took the perimeter walkway to class. He liked the edge of the campus, with its view of an undeveloped Calabasas hillside. There wasn't much ground left in LA. that didn't have asphalt or concrete poured over it. When he looked at this spot, it gave him a little slice of peace.

He ate that slice hungrily now.

Turning toward the playfield, he thought he heard a loud sniff behind a utility shed. He went to look and saw one of his fifth graders, Rachel, on her knees, drawing in the dirt with a stick.

"Rachel?"

She looked up, startled, her eyes red and wet.

"Hey." Chuck took a knee next to her. He knew what was wrong without even asking. Rachel was the tease magnet of the class. She wasn't one of the "pretty" ones, wasn't as well off financially as most kids at Hunt. Her single mom was getting a tuition break while working double duty. A receptionist for a CPA during the day, and as a fill in at the Cheesecake Factory at night, but only when there was a need.

Rachel looked back at the ground, making more lines in the dirt.

"What're you drawing?" One thing Rachel had going for her was that she could draw. She had that natural artistic gift, especially with pen and ink, and most especially when it came to rendering horses.

"Nothing," she said.

What a word to choose. Nothing, when there was obviously something. She must feel like that a lot of the time, Chuck thought. And then, with a twang in his stomach, he realized he and Rachel weren't so different in that regard.

"You want to know something?" he said. "A lot of artists get paid a lot of money for drawing nothing."

She looked at him quizzically.

"It's true, I've seen some of that art. Some of it in museums. And you do much better than they do."

Rachel shook her head.

"It's true," Chuck said, wanting her to believe it more than anything. "You just don't ever stop drawing, okay?"

She shrugged her shoulders.

Chuck went into a sitting position, cross-legged. "Hey, can you draw a whale?"

The girl paused, thought about it. "A whale?"

"Yeah. Can you do that?"

"I think so."

"I mean, a great big white whale, with his tail flapping and all that?"

"How come?"

"I want you to do the front cover of our program for the musical. Would you do that for me?"

"Really?"

"Think you can?"

Rachel nodded.

"Good," Chuck said. "How about we go to class now."

Rachel drooped at the shoulders, shook her head violently.

"Hey, none of that," Chuck said.

She looked at the dirt.

"You know, Rachel, I have a brother. He got teased a lot when he was a kid. I mean, a whole lot. And now he's the coolest guy, and he has a great job where he sees people every day, and everybody likes him."

Rachel appeared to be listening.

"When you have a job, as you know, as your mother knows, you work to get paid, right?"

She nodded.

"Well, I'm going to pay you to do this cover. But I'm going to pay you in ice cream."

Rachel looked at him.

"Cold Stone Creamery ice cream," Chuck said. "And I want you to tell your mom tonight, when you get home. You tell her about our deal, okay?"

She nodded again.

"But I have to have you in class to do it," Chuck said. "You come to class with me and we'll start off with a song. How about that?"

Rachel said, "Okay."

They walked to class together, and Rachel even skipped a little at the end. That tiniest bit of joy almost made Chuck bust out crying. Man, he was on edge. He needed to grab his guitar.

Which he did, the very second the bell rang.

Arash, in the front row, said, "Can we sing Moby's song?"

"You want Moby's song, huh?" Chuck said.

Amy raised her hand. "My dad says Moby-Dick is supposed

to be God."

"Your dad . . ." Now what? He just wanted the kids to enjoy a fish story. Okay, a mammal story. So how could he explain to them he felt just like Ishmael? Wandering. Perplexed about the nature of God. Which was why the book was so woven up in his own bones.

He didn't want the kids to see that in his face. Ever.

"Why don't we sing first?" Chuck said.

He sat on the edge of the desk, tuned his guitar.

"Remember now," he said. "I want you to sing this without laughing, can you do that?"

The class tittered, because they knew they couldn't. Chuck loved it when they giggled like this.

"Together," Chuck said. "*I got plenty o' blubber! And blubber's plenty for me!*"

The kids sang and Chuck almost laughed out loud himself. From thoughts of rock stardom to this. From a Tustin garage banging out licks full of euphoric hopes of someday touring, to a little private school classroom where you plunk strings to please little ones, the only fans you'll ever have.

Chuck worked the strings like he was in Yankee Stadium giving a concert for fifty thousand, even as he sang the silly song he'd written. In America, you never know what turns there'll be in the road, do you? You give up adolescent dreams when you survive a DUI crash, you start talking to God, and you think maybe you should serve your country for some greater purpose.

And then one day you look up and your wife is dead and you hate everything and God is silent and you're the only one who can take care of your brother. You start to think the future is nothing but darkness, then find yourself sold out to a bunch of kids, loving them more than you ever thought you could, wanting them—no, willing them—to believe happiness is possible in this world. Every kid deserves that.

So the children sang giddily, as if to believe, and Chuck tried to feel that way, too. He played hard and sang loud, but the guy with the knife kept popping up in his mind, ready to cut him.

5

After school was out Chuck sat in his empty classroom and called his aunt's house in Riverside. Aunt Jane was divorced and worked as an MRI technician at Kaiser. Chuck's mother had moved in with her a year ago.

"How you doing, Aunt Jane?" Chuck said.

"Living large," she said, which wasn't a lie. Aunt Jane loved to cook and eat what she cooked, and she did not skimp on the fat, the flour, the butter, or the sugar. "How about you?"

"Well, let me tell you, I've had better weeks."

"What's wrong, dear?"

"How about I tell you about it later? I just wanted to check in with Mom."

"You want me to put her on?"

"How's she doing?"

"So so."

"I'm sorry."

"What for?"

He paused. "That I couldn't take care of everybody the way

I wanted."

"Hey, Lucky, you're doing just fine." She'd called him Lucky ever since he could remember. He used to believe it was prophetic. Now it stung. "You're taking care of Stan, and that means the world to us."

"It's a laugh riot, that's for sure."

"You getting enough to eat?" That was her favorite question.

"I am. Stan keeps up on all the specials."

"That boy," Aunt Jane said with a laugh. "If we could harness that brain power we'd put men on Saturn."

"Sure," Chuck said. "I'll talk to Mom now."

He heard the sound of the phone being put down.

Then his mom's small voice squeaked, "Hello?"

"Hi Mom," Chuck said.

"Who is it?"

"Chuck."

"Chuck?"

"How you doing, darling?"

"Who is this?"

"It's Chuck, your son." He felt like an idiot, a stranger, a cold stranger who carried misery in a valise. Not a son who could make things happen. He wanted to make her right by willing it over the phone. She deserved it, the way the cards had been dealt.

"Is Stanley all right?" his mother said.

The mention of the name was a lifeline from past to present. Chuck grabbed it. "Yes. Yes, Stan is good. He's going to outlive us all. He's working steady and he's keeping tabs on all the customers. They love him."

Silence.

"We'll come out for a visit soon," Chuck said.

"Who is this?"

The chill of those words hit like a cold, Pacific wave, like when they were a family at the beach, a long ago November, the three of them. When his feet got cold in the ocean and his mother wrapped them up in a towel and rubbed them till they were warm again and now he could not make his mother warm or whole. He could not—

Aunt Jane came back on. "She's tired, Chuck."

"You're a saint, Aunt Jane," he said.

"Plaster," she said. "Do come see us when you can."

"Yes," he said.

After the call Chuck turned off the lights in the classroom and put his head in his hands and sat there until four-fifteen.

•

"Seven ninety-nine T-bone steak," Stan said the moment he got into Chuck's limping Sentra. "Oscar Mayer Deli Shaved Lunchmeat, two for six dollars."

"Good ones," Chuck said. It was four-thirty and he was picking up Stan from Ralphs. And this being Tuesday, Stan was eager to share the weekly specials. Sometimes that annoyed Chuck, but today, of all days, it was welcome and familiar. By the time they got home, Chuck told himself, we'll both be back on solid ground again. We can move on from the events of this one, crazy day.

"DiGiorno Pizza, two for nine dollars," Stan continued. "Chuck, can we have DiGiorno Pizza tonight?"

"Sounds good."

"And Coca-Cola, six pack, three for ten dollars."

"And Coca-Cola, kid."

Stan loved his job. Ralphs Fresh Fare hired a certain

number of the mentally challenged. The prime job was standing inside the doors, welcoming people and handing out the ad paper with the featured deals. Stan took his duties as seriously as a nuclear technician dispensing safety instructions. "I save people the big bucks," Stan liked to say.

Which was why he always replayed the ads, not reading them, but using the incredible memory that was part of his brain's circuitry. It was one of those inexplicable quirks of nature, like deaf kids who can play piano without a lesson.

"Chef Boyardee Microwave Cup," Stan said, "ten for ten dollars. Can we get ten of them?"

"Maybe," Chuck said.

"Are you going to get married?"

"What?" Sometimes Stan blurted the most random things.

"That teacher at school," Stan said. "Wendy Tower is her name. She has long hair and green eyes and her body is hubba—"

"Stan."

"She likes you."

"I know that."

"Does she make you gaga?"

"Gaga? Where do you come up with this stuff?"

Stan bobbed his eyebrows.

"If you want DiGiorno's," Chuck said, "you knock that off——" Chuck stopped when he saw a plume of black smoke in the sky a couple of blocks away.

"What's wrong?" Stan said.

"Looks like there's fire," Chuck said.

"Fire?"

"Maybe somebody's car."

"Can cars catch on fire?"

"Sometimes," Chuck said. But as he drove on, he knew this

was no car fire. It was too big.

And very close.

There was a police presence at the next turn, Chuck's street. No access. He stopped the car and got out, the door still groaning because of the morning's rear ender.

A young cop in sunglasses took two steps toward him. "Sir, you'll have to move your car."

Chuck didn't move. He stared. And reality hit. "That's my house," he said.

The cop gave a quick nod. "Let the fire department take care of this."

Stan ran up to Chuck, his eyes wide. "Is that our house, Chuck? What about all our stuff? What about my fish?"

Chuck put his hand up to get Stan quiet. "Stay with the policeman, Stan."

"Don't leave me!"

"Stay here!" Chuck didn't like the hurt look in Stan's eyes then, but this was a freaking fire. And though the heat of it wasn't near him, another heat was burning inside him, the conflagration of one very bad day.

"Sir," the cop said, "you need to stay here, too."

"So shoot me," Chuck said and ran down the sidewalk.

6

Up close the fire hoses seemed unreal, like somebody staging a giant Halloween prank.

But Chuck felt the heat and the spray slapping him like gloved hands. And the insane pumping of his heart. Orange and yellow flames shot out of the garage roof, and what was once painted beige was covered in soot streaks black as midnight.

And he knew, as clearly as he knew his own name, that this was the Mad Russian's work.

But *why?*

A firefighter nudged him and said something. Chuck didn't hear the words. Just looked at his house. Well, not his, technically. It was a rental, but it did not have his landlord's stuff in it. It had Chuck's. His life. And Stan's.

The firefighter pushed again. Chuck jerked away.

"Get back," the firefighter said. "We'll handle it."

Chuck heard a muffled scream as Stan ran up, arms flapping.

"Okay, okay, Stan. Easy."

Stan looked at the fire. Chuck felt Stan's finger slip into his rear pocket. "Don't leave me, please Chuck."

No, Stan, no, I won't leave you. But what about inside? In that ruin were the last vestiges of Julia's life with him. The scrapbooks she kept, her CD collection, her laptop from work. Gone. The last tokens of when things were good, before his deployment, before they began to look at each other like confused strangers.

When he first got back, she came to see him at the VA. She was there in the room and she looked like two women at the same time. She looked like the woman he loved more than anybody he'd ever loved, and she looked like some neighbor down the street, the one you wave to every now and then but never really get to know. She'd had some rough patches growing up, but she never wanted to talk about them. But that is exactly where he wanted to go with her, to help her get past all that, to heal her. Be something to her that she didn't have in her life. But now he was the damaged one, and the guilt ripped him like a clawing thing under his ribs.

Guilt he could never assuage now, because she was gone.

As the flames of the house licked upward, the shimmer of Julia's face in his memory was consumed by the heat, and he was powerless to stop it.

"Chuck!" It was his across-the-street neighbor, Belva, standing in her driveway.

Chuck gave her a quick nod. Belva Gilbert loved to talk, and he was in no mood.

"Chuck, come over here, please!"

Stan said, "Chuck, Belva wants you to—"

"I know, Stan."

"Right now, Chuck!" Belva said.

Well, it wasn't like he had any buckets of water to throw on the house. He crossed the street, Stan still hooked to his pocket.

"Are you two all right?" Belva put her robust hands on Stan's cheeks. Stan winced and nodded. Belva was sixty, with long white hair that befit a former hippy, which she happily admitted being. She still favored tie-dyed X-L tee shirts and didn't care about hiding her amplitude.

Chuck liked her, but she did play the earth mother role with a bit too much emphasis on *mother*. This was not the time. His house was *burning down*.

Chuck said, "You have any idea how this happened?"

Belva shook her head. "I was in the back, by the pool, absorbing my D. Next thing I hear sirens, and they came."

"Did you see anybody in the neighborhood today," Chuck said, "who looked like they didn't belong here?"

"I've been inside all day, except when I went out by the pool. That's my life now, you know, inside and the pool, ever since McSchmuck hit the road."

McSchmuck was Belva's ex, who, as she put it, had flown the coop for a spring chicken.

"Have you seen a black Escalade around here at all?" Chuck said.

A look of concern crinkled the corners of her eyes. "No, dear, no. What's the matter?"

"A guy with a knife!" Stan said. "He has brown hair and brown eyes and his knife was this long"—Stan showed with his fingers—"and it goes into a silver holder, and he put it in his black jeans and—"

"Okay, Stan," Chuck said.

"Knife?" Belva said. "Chuck, what on earth—"

"You wait with Belva," he said to Stan, and walked quickly to the corner, to Lucy Bowers' house. He knocked on the front door.

No answer.

He tried the doorbell, then knocked again. Checked the door. Locked.

He could hear Lucy's dog barking like mad in the back yard.

And yes, this was very much like madness, the whole thing. Stuff like this didn't happen here, in the nice part of the Valley. This was West Hills, safe and suburban, not Canoga Park where Latino gangs tagged signs, and businesses operated on asphalt shoestrings. No, this was supposed to be where you brought kids up and took dogs for walks in the evening, and maybe stopped off at the Starbucks on Victory, or quick shopped at Trader Joe's. No, it wasn't like it used to be, post World War II. Chuck knew that. That kind of close-knit neighborhood fizzled in the sixties and died in the seventies when transiency became the norm for American life.

But here, in this part of the 'burb, the houses still looked the same—Chuck's, what was left of it, was built in '64—and the people, aging Baby Boomers and a few young families starting out, were decent and community-minded.

So what were knives and thugs and fires doing here? More, what were they doing directed at *him*?

7

On his knees, Kovak prays before the icon. It is a cross, and it is made of knives. Two knives, one long blade, one short. And there is paint on the blades. The paint is red. Red spots and streaks, representing blood. Not the blood of Christ. His precious blood was shed for mercy. This red represents the blood of those who deserve to die.

"Almighty God," Kovak says, praying with eyes open, and looking at the knives, "Who delivered Your people from the bondage of the adversary, and through Your Son cast down Satan like lightning, deliver me also from every influence of unclean spirits. Command Satan to depart far from me by the power of Your only begotten Son. Rescue me from demonic imaginings and darkness. Give to me the power you have promised, and the will to see it through."

Kovak rises, crosses himself, picks up his phone. "Come in now," he says.

A moment later, the oak door opens and three of his soldiers enter. His best.

Vaso, of course, without whom he would be lost.

Antonije, the strong.

And reliable Simo.

They stand, shoulder to shoulder, arms behind them, at ease.

Kovak allows himself a moment of satisfied reflection. Here in the hills above Malibu he has constructed a compound, complete with this room that he calls his chapel, and has soldiers who have sworn allegiance. His new identity is well established, and his enterprise thrives.

"You know," Kovak says, "that it is only one week until it comes. You will all be enriched beyond dreaming, but only if nothing goes wrong. I am holding each one of you to account, is that clear?"

The three nod without hesitation.

"This business with the car, who is responsible?"

No answer, but the face of Vaso is telling.

"My son?" Kovak asks.

Vaso nods.

"Where is he?"

Vaso says, "He has not come home."

"Find him," Kovak says. He nods at Vaso, who leaves. To Simo he says, "You have the information?"

Simo steps forward and hands him one page.

Kovak looks it over. It is a fine summary, as always with Simo. Kovak demands nothing less than perfection, but knows some will fall short. Especially his son. But not Simo. Or Vaso. It is all about the team.

"A school teacher?" Kovak says.

"Yes, sir," Simo says.

Kovak shakes his head. "Stupid. So stupid." Kovak looks at Simo. "Get me all the information you can on this teacher."

"Yes, sir."
"As soon as possible."

8

"What happened to our house, Chuck?" Stan said.

"You saw it," Chuck said. They were driving away from the scene now, after two hours of watching and talking to both LAFD and LAPD. Chuck gave them as much as he could, then said he was through for the night. He had to get Stan settled down.

"But why, Chuck, why?"

"How the hell do I know? Why are you—" Chuck stopped when he saw the hurt look on Stan's face.

"You're upset, Chuck."

"Ya think?"

"You cussed."

"*Hell* is not a cuss word, Stan."

"Mom says."

"It's in the Bible. Hell is in the Bible."

"There's fire in hell," Stan said.

"Let's not talk about fire *or* hell," Chuck said. Because there's enough hell right here in this life, kid. You don't need to pile on anymore.

Chuck drove to the Outside Inn, the oh-so-cleverly named motel on Ventura, a block away from Ralphs. From here they could regroup, and Stan could walk to work.

Two anemic palm trees bracketed the driveway entrance, bending as if seeking to slink away from the place. The exterior of the joint was diffuse dull-orange stucco, like a couple of painters had slapped on a coat ten years ago then knocked off early and never came back.

After securing a room, Chuck showed Stan their new home away from home. Done up in American Plain Wrap. A queen bed, a table, small refrigerator, TV. On the wall hung a framed print, a rendering of a large, black bull looking straight out at them. Chuck thought the bull could be asking the question *How did I get stuck in a lousy dive like this?*

"Where'll I sleep?" Stan said.

"You can have the bed."

"You can sleep with me, Chuck."

"You flop around like a halibut, brother. I'll take the floor."

Stan said, "How long do we have to be here?"

"I don't know."

"Where will we live for the rest of our lives?"

Chuck guided Stan to the bed and sat him down. "Hey, you know how we've always talked about you getting a place of your own, a little apartment? Maybe now—"

"Don't make me!" Stan said. "Not yet. I want to stay with you."

"And you will, but if we just start to think—"

"Not yet! I'm scared."

"Well *stop* being scared!"

"Don't be mad at me, Chuck, please."

"I'm not mad at you."

"You sound mad."

"Sound! Yeah, I make sounds! You want to hear the sound of a chicken? *Buck buck buck.*"

Stan laughed. He could go from sad to laughter like a scared lizard from a rock to a hole.

"Do the fart one!" Stan said.

"You want farts? You got farts!" Chuck pulled up his shirt and put his hand under his arm and pumped out the farting sound middle school boys are known for. He had been the champion of that sound as a kid.

Blat blat blat. Chuck hit them hard, slapping at his side with his elbow, making it almost hurt. He could get rid of feelings when he hurt. He wanted to now, wanted to hurt and stop feeling.

Stan rolled back on the bed, laughing it up.

Blat blat blat.

More laughing from Stan, too much of course, he could get that way, but it was hard not to laugh along with him.

Chuck put his hands up in surrender and sat on the edge of the bed. It took Stan a minute to catch his breath.

Finally Stan sat up. "That was fun," he said. He looked around the room. "What'll we do now?"

Good question, brother! We just fell down an elevator shaft with no elevator. What *do* we do? How do I keep you from freaking out all the time? How do I keep myself from falling further down the shaft?

"What do you say we blow some bucks?" Chuck said.

"Huh?"

"We go out to a big old dinner and maybe a movie. We forget everything. How'd you like that?"

"Yeah! Can we have pizza?"

"We'll have two pizzas, one each, extra large. We'll tell 'em extra cheese—"

"Yes!"

"We'll tell 'em so much cheese it'll be big and gooey and melty—"

"Baby, oh baby!"

"Then we'll box up what's left and eat it for breakfast, too."

"Yeah!"

"And then we'll have ice cream after," Chuck said.

Stan let out a sound that was part rebel yell and part man sitting on cactus. *Yoweeee! Eee eee eee!*

"I guess you like that idea," Chuck said, "I guess you—"

His phone buzzed. Private number. A whisper of dread swept his mind.

"Yeah?" he answered.

A voice, low, said, "Don't be bad now."

Chuck's brain felt like it clenched, actually bunched up a like a fist at the base of his skull. He pushed hate through his teeth. "You like fire, do you?"

"Don't say anything to anybody. She would not have liked that."

"You listen now, I'm getting the cops on this, maybe the feds, so—"

"Oh no. Your brother. He could get hurt very badly if you do that."

Chuck looked at Stan. He was bouncing up and down on the bed with an ecstatic, ice cream-anticipation look.

The connection cut. Chuck looked at the phone like it was a dead animal, a dead thing sitting on top of his sweaty palm.

"Chuck, what's wrong?"

Chuck said nothing. Behind his eyes, shadows danced.

"Your face is funny, Chuck."

"That's me. Mr. Funny." Chuck wanted to throw his

37

phone through the window, shatter some glass. At least that would be something, instead of sitting around, helpless. Who was this person, or people? Why was he being singled out?

"Chuck?"

"What?"

"I'm sorry."

"Sorry? What for?"

"Cause I'm scared." Stan started clicking his left thumbnail with the nail of his right index finger. It was his front burner nervous tick, always had been. "'Cause I feel like the wolf man might come."

When they were kids they'd watched *Abbott and Costello Meet Frankenstein.* There was a scene where Lou was in a hotel room with Lon Chaney, Jr., who turned into the wolf man and stalked Lou, who was oblivious to the danger around the room. Chuck laughed but for some reason Stan got real scared. And starting having nightmares about the wolf man chasing him. It got better over the years, but every now and then he'd have the nightmare, intensely.

"No wolf men," Chuck said. "Not while I'm around."

"You mean that, or are you just saying?"

Chuck rubbed the top of Stan's head with his knuckles. A little too hard. Stan said, "Ow!"

Chuck said, "I guess you don't want ice cream, huh?"

"Do too, Chuck! You said!"

"Did I? Did I say that?"

"You said, Chuck. Pizza then ice cream!"

"Really? Did I swear on a stack of Bibles?"

"Aw, Chuck!"

"All right, kid brother," Chuck said. "Get your pig face on."

9

Detective Sandy Epperson pounded the table so hard she startled herself. The government-issue metal desk in the small interview room banged sharply, the sound quickly dying against the white insulation panels.

Why was she doing this? It was late, she should be home sipping wine. But right now she was here at the station, and all she could think about was the girl sitting in front of her.

"Look at me, Rosa. I mean *look*." Sandy strafed Rosa Renteria's sixteen-year-old brown eyes with a hard glare.

Rosa sent back the open-mouth silent look, challenging Sandy to try to make her talk.

"You saw it go down," Sandy said. There'd been a gang fight on Valerio the night before, one banger shot to death. "You saw the whole thing and you think you're being so cool and straight up. They're using you, Rosa, they always will."

"You don't know," Rosa said. Her voice was almost comically mousy, even for someone as small as she.

At least it was a response. That was something. A start. A

crack in the wall. Sandy knew these days you didn't get many of those. These *cholas* looked at any LAPD detective as *mierda*. Especially an African American female detective. The one thing Sandy Epperson had going for her was that she could relate to girls like Rosa Renteria. When she was Rosa's age she was around the gang element too, in Detroit. But she made it out. So could Rosa. So could any of them if you could just break through that crack.

"You're wrong about that," Sandy said. "I know *all* about it."

"Sure."

"How long you think you're gonna last with them?"

"You know what happen if I say something? Like that *chica* got shot down, that's what."

Sandy knew the case. It involved the big homey of the Westies, Jimmy Stone, and his white gang over in West Hills. Rich boys into drug running. And murder. Stone had been charged with first degree in the execution-style slaying of a Latino high school student. Two bullets to the head. But the only witness, a sixteen-year-old single mother named Esperanza Gomez, was gunned down in a park while strolling her baby. Without more, the prosecutor had to drop the case against Jimmy Stone. At least the baby had lived.

Which would be no consolation to Rosa.

"We can protect you," Sandy said.

Rosa laughed and turned her head. "Oh yeah."

Sandy felt like she was gripping the fingers of someone who was dangling over a cliff. "What's it going to take?"

"For what?" Rosa said.

"To get you out of the life once and for all?"

"Why you so interested?"

"I have to have a reason?"

"You're a cop."

"So I can't help you because I'm a cop?" The motto of the LAPD, *To protect and to serve,* flashed through Sandy's head. "You should be looking at your whole life, to school and college and—"

"School?" Rosa snorted. "I'm stupid. I can't be in no school."

"You're not stupid. I can tell."

Rosa's eyes sparked.

"You can tell when you talk to somebody," Sandy said.

"No way."

"I thought I was stupid."

"You?" Rosa said.

"Yeah. Me. My brother used to tell me that."

Rosa sat up. It was more than a crack now, Sandy thought. She had Rosa's attention. And for some reason Sandy needed to blast through it like a pile driver. She *had* to make this one understand.

"When I was four I almost drowned," Sandy said. "No oxygen to the brain for twenty minutes. I should've died. It was an ice cold lake. My dad fished me out. I made it, but my brother used to tell me all the time I was brain damaged. That's what he called me. BD for short. He made fun of me and I believed him. And when I was in school, I had a hard time. Until one day I found out I wasn't really stupid at all. I didn't have to believe it."

Rosa frowned. "How you find out?"

"A teacher gave me a book to read. It was called *A Wrinkle in Time.* I got so into that book, and then I knew I had to read and read and read, so I did. And what I read stayed with me. It'll stay with you, Rosa. You're not stupid. You just need to practice. But you'll never get practice hanging out with the gangs."

41

Rosa was silent for a long time.

Finally, Rosa shook her head. "No," she said. "I don't want to say nothing. I want to go home."

"I can't keep you here. I just would like you to stay and think about it. Let me get you something to eat."

"No. I want to go right now. I don't want to say nothing."

Rosa got up hard, like she was afraid of getting shot right there in the interview room. Sandy stood and put her hands up as a signal for Rosa to pause a moment. "If you change your mind, I want you to call me." Sandy handed Rosa her card. "Even if you're in trouble or you just want to talk. Okay? Would you do that?"

A tap at the door. It was Mark Mooney, Sandy's partner. "A second?" Mooney said.

Sandy put a finger up to tell Mooney to wait, then walked Rosa out to the front desk. "Remember," Sandy said to her. "Anytime."

Rosa put her head down, turned and left. Sandy did not allow herself to harbor any hopes. You got wrecked if you did.

When she got back inside she met Mooney standing by his desk. He said, "Lost kitty?"

"What is it you wanted?" Despite liking Mooney—he was junior, a Detective-I to her D-II—Sandy found his tongue a little too sharp at times. Like he was playing out some Raymond Chandler fantasy. It went with the square jawed, buzz cut, buffed out image he liked to present.

He motioned with his thumb to the computer monitor on his desk. Sandy saw a standard dispatch report. "911 call from this morning," Mooney said. "A guy pulled a knife on a driver off Platt."

"Road rage?"

"Don't know. The guy who called it in was named Grant

Nunn. The guy who got the threat, according to Nunn, was a guy named Samson, a school teacher."

"Is there a homicide lurking around this?" Sandy said.

"That's just it. Nunn never made it to work. They just found him in his car in back of Target. Bullet to the head."

Sandy said nothing.

"But get this," Mooney said. "This teacher, Samson, a few hours ago his house goes crispy. The whole thing. Boom. Up in smoke. That's a pretty big day for just one guy, don't you think?"

10

At six-forty-five Wednesday morning, Chuck called Ray Hunt.

"I've got a little problem," Chuck said. "As in, there was a fire at my house and I don't have any clothes or shaving gear or anything like that. In fact, I don't have a house."

"Fire!" Ray said.

"Long story, but I–"

"You all right? Your brother?"

"We're in a motel. I need to get some clothes and shave and all. I'll try to be in by nine. I may be a little late."

"Don't come in," Ray said. "I'll get somebody to cover for you. Not a problem."

"I want to," Chuck said. He almost added *I need to.*

"You sure?"

"Wal-Mart opens at seven. I'll grab a stunning new wardrobe and a razor and come back here for a shower, and be good to go."

"Chuck, this is terrible. Anything I can do, name it."

"Just make sure the whale costume comes in on time."

Chuck gathered Stan up and drove to Mickey D's for breakfast, then over to Wal-Mart. By eight-fifty they were back at the motel with enough clothes for a couple of days. As long as they weren't angling for GQ, they'd be fine. Chuck sped through a shower and shave. Stan was next and could walk to work.

Chuck did his best Jimmy Johnson, as much as he could in a dented Sentra, and made it to the Hunt school by nine-thirty-five.

And realized, getting out of the car, how much he truly did need this place. It was a safe haven, a healing zone. He'd been lucky to get the job last year. Ray Hunt's son, Raleigh, had been in the Marine expeditionary unit Chuck served as chaplain. Chuck reconnected with Raleigh stateside, and found out his father needed a fifth grade teacher for their spring semester. Chuck was about to run out of money. When he went in for the interview, he and Ray Hunt hit it off like they were the ones who were father and son.

It was Raleigh's drug problem, Chuck knew, that had put a veil between him and Ray. Ray Hunt was the proverbial straight arrow, and couldn't understand why Raleigh, who everybody called Rollo, couldn't lick the problem by sheer will.

Hunt agreed to hire Chuck for a probationary term, as long as Chuck pursued a full teaching credential. Chuck jumped at it, and dug in. The job became his life preserver.

It still was. And in a way, it was that for Ray Hunt, too. Because he hadn't heard from Rollo in half a year.

Chuck saw Ray striding—Ray never just *walked*—toward him in the parking lot, his full head of white hair topping a V-shaped body set in a crisp white shirt and gold tie. He was sixty-four and looked forty. A Viet Nam vet, he'd come back from the war and built up this prestigious private K-12 school with little more than moxie and eighteen-hour-days, alongside his wife, Astrid. Over the past thirty-plus years, the Hunts had become wealthy, respected, and active participants in the community.

He pumped Chuck's hand. "You're amazing for being here. You sure you're okay?"

"I'm fine. I should get to class."

"I have Miss Hayes running interference." Ray Hunt was old school. Women were *Miss* or *Mrs.* And the kids were never to use a teacher's first name. "How did your house—"

A thumping like Godzilla's foot hit Chuck's ears. He turned and saw a tricked-out pickup with fully amped gangsta blaring into the lot.

One of the high schoolers. Chuck knew about him. Tommy Stone was his name. He'd almost been suspended a couple of times. He had an older brother who'd gone here, Jimmy Stone. A very bad seed, Jimmy was, so they said.

Tommy drove by giving Ray and Chuck a look. A *look*.

Chuck turned and was about to speak when he saw something he never expected to see on the headmaster's face. But there it was, for a split second, before getting wiped off like a sheen of sweat.

It was a look of fear.

11

An hour before lunch Chuck was introducing the class to the battles of Lexington and Concord when Rene Hayes, the office assistant, stuck her head in the door.

Chuck said, "Can it wait? I'm about to fire the shot heard round the world."

Miss Hayes didn't smile. "I don't think it can."

Chuck went to the door.

"Mr. Hunt needs you at the office," she said, low so the kids couldn't hear. "It's the police."

"What?"

"I'll take class till lunch."

"Um, yeah, okay. Have them do the worksheet on page whatever it is."

To the class he said, "Miss Hayes is taking over for a bit. If you're good, we'll do the harpoon song this afternoon, *with* the props."

The kids cheered.

Ray was waiting with the cops in the teachers' lounge. He

introduced an African American woman, maybe mid–forties and on the hefty side, as Detective Epperson. The other one, younger, white, was named Mooney.

Then Ray excused himself, saying they wouldn't be disturbed.

"Thanks for your time," Epperson said. She had friendly brown eyes. "I'm very sorry for your loss."

It sounded like she could have meant Julia. "What's going on?"

"We'd just like to ask you a few questions."

"About my house?"

"The fire department handles that," Epperson said. "We're homicide detectives."

"Homicide?"

"Let's go to square one." Epperson seemed calm, understanding. Mooney kept his lips pursed as he jotted notes. If this had been an interrogation, it would have been a no brainer to see the good cop-bad cop routine playing out.

Epperson said, "Let's start with how you first learned your house was on fire."

"I thought this wasn't about the fire."

"This is about timing."

"Why is this important?"

"If you'll just bear with us for a few minutes," Epperson said, "we'll let you get back to teaching."

Fine. "I was driving home and I saw smoke, and that's when I saw the fire."

"Were you driving home from here?"

"No, I picked up my brother from work. He works at Ralphs."

Mooney said, "He was there from when to when?"

"What does my brother have to do with this?" Chuck said.

"You don't think he had anything to do with a fire."

Epperson spoke through Mooney's glare. "It's just background for us, Mr. Samson."

"He was at work all day, he always is. Check it. I pick him up after I'm done at school. Around four-thirty or so, usually. I did that, we were driving home, I saw the smoke, I thought it was close to our house. It *was* our house. That's how I found out."

Nodding, Epperson said, "Do you have any idea how it may have started?"

Chuck wondered how much to tell them. The voice on the phone had warned him not to talk to the police. But he knew he wasn't going to get very far on his own. He had to have help.

"All right," Chuck said. "Something weird happened to me yesterday. I was getting an early start, taking Stan in to the store, then I was going to go on to school. There was this black Escalade a little ways down from our house, with a guy in it. Sitting there. I looked at him, he looked at me. I drive on. Next thing I know, the guy pulls in front of me and jams on his brakes, and I hit him."

"A rear ender?" Mooney asked.

"A set up," Chuck said.

"Why would he set you up?" Mooney said.

"That's the thing. No idea. He had an accent, or it sounded like one, and he pulled a knife on me."

"Can you describe him?"

"About my age and height, long brown hair parted in the middle, blue eyes, a little red in them. He had something to drink, I'm pretty sure."

Epperson leaned in. "Go on."

"I got out to talk to him, and he starts saying I was looking at him on purpose. I was trying to tell him I wasn't, then he

49

grabs me by the throat." Chuck demonstrated with his left hand.

"How'd you get the scar?" Mooney asked.

"Afghanistan."

"Marine?"

"Navy chaplain."

"Chaplain?" Mooney said. "You look like a guy who could fight."

"So?" Chuck said.

"Just an observation. Where were you assigned?"

"A unit in the Helmand province, right before Operation Khanjar."

Epperson said, "How does the Navy get involved with the Marines?"

"Marines don't have their own chaplains," Chuck said.

"How do Navy chaplains get scars?" Mooney said.

"I was captured. I was cut. I don't really see how any of this is relevant."

"Just asking," Mooney said. "Go back to the guy grabbing your throat."

"I blasted his head back, like this." Chuck showed his palms up move.

"This guy had a knife?"

"Butterfly knife, you know, with the flip blade?"

Epperson said, "So this guy followed you and made you hit him, then grabbed you and threatened you with a knife?"

"That's right. Then a guy came along and stopped and the Russian put the knife away and drove off. And the guy in the car, he saw the knife, and called in a 911."

"Right," Mooney said.

"What do you mean *right?*" Chuck said.

Mooney said nothing. Epperson shot her partner a quick look.

"You guys know about this?" Chuck said.

"We do," Epperson said.

"Uh-huh. And you didn't want to share that little bit of information with me?"

"We wanted to hear it from you fresh," said Mooney.

"Next time, why don't you just tell me up front what you know," Chuck said. "Pretend we're all grown-ups."

Mooney started to say something, but Epperson cut in. "I'm sorry, Mr. Samson," she said. "This is not any reflection on you. It's how we gather information, that's all. Routine, as they used to say."

Chuck said, "Can we get on with it?"

"Tell us about your wife," Epperson said.

Chuck just looked at her.

"More background," Epperson said.

"You can tell me what this is really about now," Chuck said. "And I'll decide if I want to tell you anything else."

"That's fair," Epperson said. "We know your wife was killed in a hit-and-run in Beaman, up near the Grapevine."

"Then you know what I know."

"What was she doing in Beaman?"

"Working on a story. She wrote for a weekly covering Southern Cal."

"And Beaman meant what to her?"

"Why are you asking me all this?"

"Please, Mr. Samson."

"They have that alligator farm up there. She was doing a piece on the history of alligator farms in . . ." Chuck stopped, the words bunching in his throat.

"I'm sorry," Epperson said.

Chuck said nothing.

"Just a couple more things," Epperson said, "and we'll get

out of here. At 6:42 a.m., yesterday morning, the 911 call came in from a Mr. Grant Nunn. He reported the incident you've described."

"Yeah, sure," Chuck said. "I didn't know his name, though."

"Mr. Nunn was an administrator at DeVry University in Sherman Oaks."

"Was?"

Mooney said, "He never made it to work."

Chuck shook his head. He felt like they were lowering some sort of net on him. "And?"

"He never made it home, either," Epperson said. "He was found shot to death in his car in a store parking lot."

Chuck swallowed hard. It was like a fist of ice going down. "What does any of this have to do with me?"

"Let us ask the questions," Mooney said.

"I don't like your questions," Chuck said. "I don't know anything except what I've told you. Why should I know—"

"What about Lucy Bowers?" Mooney said.

Chuck eyed him. "I don't remember mentioning Lucy Bowers."

"We're mentioning her," Mooney said.

"What about her?"

Epperson said, "She's been reported missing, too."

Chuck stood. Too much information at once. He felt tight around his throat, like the Mad Russian had him in his grip again.

"I have to get back to class," Chuck said.

"Your boss said it's almost lunch time," Mooney said.

"Then I need to get to my sandwich," Chuck said. "You got an issue with that?"

"Maybe," Mooney said.

"Then deal with it on your own time," Chuck said.

Epperson handed him her card. "Will you just let us know if any thoughts on these matters occur to you? That's a direct number there. I'd appreciate it."

Sure, Chuck thought. The way you appreciate people putting ropes around their own necks. He slid the card in his back pocket and walked out.

Wendy Tower caught up with him just before he got to his classroom.

"I heard about your house," she said. "I'm so sorry."

Chuck nodded.

"Where are you staying?"

"The Ritz," Chuck said.

She smiled. "All you need now is a home cooked meal."

He was going to say no, as he had before. But maybe he needed this. Maybe he should take a chance. "Twist my arm," he said.

"Would you like—"

"What time?"

"Say six."

"Six."

"See you then." She turned and walked off toward the high school. She moved gracefully, like a dancer. It reminded him. The first time he met Julia, they'd done swing. He was the worst dancer ever, but in her arms that night he felt like Astaire.

12

He'd met Julia the night his chaplaincy was approved. Some of his high school friends, who were now older and unemployed, or marginally making money, wanted to have a party for him. They had it at Steve Manley's apartment in Westchester, by the airport.

It was almost the same, like being back in high school when drinking and getting high and playing rock with his band, Maniacal Fly, was all he ever wanted to do. He'd long since given up the binge drinking and the Mary Jane, though most of his friends were still hanging onto the residue of that life. Still, he liked hanging with them. Two—Steve Manly and Rob Pinnock—had been in his band.

Julia came to the party with Rob. She had short blond hair and cornflower blue eyes, and a brace of dimples. She might have walked out of a Norman Rockwell painting, except she had an edge to her that became apparent when he tried to charm her.

Steve and the others had convinced him to forget his

recent fortitude and do some tequila shooters for old times' sake. He succumbed. After the third he set his eyes on the blonde. He waited until Rob got distracted then caught up with her looking at the poster of Cobain on the wall near the bathroom.

"Are you Jamaican?" Chuck asked.

She turned around and looked at him like he was an escapee from the asylum.

Chuck finished, "'Cause Jamaican me crazy." He knew it was a corny line, but after three tequila shots he believed anything he said would sound like it came from George Clooney.

She rolled her eyes and started to walk away. Chuck grabbed her arm. "Wait a second," he said. "I'm here. What were your other two wishes?"

"Aren't you the guest of honor?" she said.

"I guess I am. It would be my honor to talk to you."

She pursed her lips, which were full and inviting. "Aren't you a Navy chaplain or something like that?"

"Something like that."

"Are you going over there to teach them how to drink and deliver bad lines?"

That tore it. The little glow of tequila charm melted into hot embarrassment.

"I'm just asking," she said, lightening the tone. "You want to start again?"

"I'm just trying in my own stupid way to meet you."

She looked at him for a long moment. "Why don't we grab a couple of Cokes and go sit in the backyard?"

Which is exactly what they did. And she told him about herself at his insistence. She was a journalist, working for an alternative weekly in LA, both print and Internet. She covered stories on City Hall and did the occasional offbeat profile of things in and around the city. Like the bacon hot dog vending underground. Chuck remembered reading that one, though he hadn't noticed the byline. It was about the vendors who operate like guerrilla warriors on the streets. And showed how the crackdown on this culinary practice was related to rich developers pressuring the mayor to clean up downtown so they could make it sterile for the tourists. It just wasn't LA without the smell of grilled bacon-wrapped hot dogs and onions, but that's what the money men wanted to do, suck the life out of the city.

It was an article that made Chuck happy. And that was *her* story. Here she was, talking to him now. It took him five minutes to fall in love.

His host was playing Nirvana and U2 CDs and piping the music outside. Then somebody threw a switch and Glenn Miller's "In the Mood," of all things, came on. The people in the backyard laughed, and so did Julia and she said she loved this kind of music and why don't they dance?

On the grass? Yes, on the grass, with the moon out and planes taking off and landing at LAX, their flickering lights like Christmas displays under the stars.

Chuck remembered the rudimentary swing step he'd learned in high school, and with her gentle prompts he started getting into it. And pretty soon several people were watching them and clapping and urging them on.

Yes, he thought then, I'm going to learn how to really dance. I want to keep up with this one.

And he went after Julia Rankin like a laser beam on steel.

When he went out on a limb and asked her to marry him after going out with her exactly three times, he was only partially amazed that she said yes. Because of the connection that was so obvious between them. He knew she would say yes. And they did one of those quickie weddings they used to do back in World War II, before the G.I. shipped off to France or England.

They said it would never last, his friends and hers. To be perfectly honest, he didn't know himself. But it did. For six great weeks.

It wasn't the same when he got back. How could it be? There was a distance between them now, as real as an unwelcome guest that refused to leave. Time was what they needed, a lot of it, to heal.

But they didn't get that time. The arguments started, and he knew it was his fault. He was messed up and had unrealistic expectations. He tried, God knew—if God was still hanging around this show somewhere—he tried to clean up the chaos in his mind. But when she said she had to move out for a time, he wasn't surprised.

Then they had that blowup, at the restaurant. He felt himself lose it, helplessly, and talked too loud and she left. The next day she went off to do her story, some stupid thing on an alligator farm.

He never got the chance to say another word to her.

And his life took the freefall he was still in, wondering if he would ever dance again.

13

"Could the guy look any more guilty?" Mooney said.

"Come on," Sandy Epperson said. "What's he guilty of, except not liking questions?"

They were in Mooney's Crown Vic driving up Topanga. Sandy looked at the sun-drenched rocky peaks of Chatsworth, straight ahead. The day was a lot clearer than the matter before them.

"He's a poster boy for tells," Mooney said. "What's he hiding?"

"Maybe he just doesn't like being Q'd at his place of work," Sandy said.

"Why'd he get threatened by a guy with a knife?"

"Does he have to know? Maybe it was random."

"It wasn't," Mooney said. "He saw the guy a few minutes before. Why'd that guy come after him?"

"That doesn't link him to Nunn's death. If anything, it links the other guy."

"That's what I'm saying. You put enough links together and you get back to Samson."

"A stretch," Sandy said.

"Then his house is on fire. Come on. I want to know what this guy's into."

"This is homicide, remember?" Sandy said, her tone mildly rebuking. Mooney had to remember who was senior, who called the shots. "Let's keep connected to our opens."

"What I'm doing," Mooney said, with more snap in his voice than Sandy cared for. "But maybe we connect up a lot more. Maybe that makes us look very good."

"Don't be so anxious to get down to RHD, Mark. You got time." RHD was Robbery-Homicide Division, the elite of LAPD detectives, working out of downtown.

"You could look good, too," Mooney said.

He gave her a sideward glance. Without him saying anything, Sandy knew what he meant by it. She was damaged goods and *needed* some rep polishing. She'd been sent to this far corner of the department after being on the Robbery-Homicide shortlist. Because they knew if she raised a stink about what her captain pulled on her at Central, she'd be seen as just another black shouting discrimination. They knew how to cover their collective butts, oh yes.

She could have sued for the groping and the slurs, the private threats. Even without extrinsic evidence, she could have scored a nice settlement and retired.

But she was a cop, and that's all she ever wanted to be. She'd outlast them, outwork them, out-detective them. She'd *show* them in a way that could not be denied.

Mooney was right, though. There were things Chuck Samson wasn't saying. And she would look good if they uncovered more. It would be nice to stick something right back up the brass's rectal canals.

"Let's talk about Jimmy Stone," she said.

"Oh yes, our little Westie," Mooney said. "You think he ordered the hit?"

"Don't you?"

Mooney shrugged. "Esperanza Gomez was into gangs deep. Who knows who did her?"

"Jimmy Stone did, but the prosecutors had to drop the case."

"We can keep beating the bushes for one," Mooney said.

"Which means working with the narco squad."

"Or we can squeeze the stones of Mr. Stone."

"Hard core," Sandy said.

"Don't get too excited."

"Please."

"Come on, admit it, working with me is—" Mooney tapped his Bluetooth earpiece. "Mooney . . . uh-huh . . ."

He gave another sideward glance at Sandy. This one was full of promise and a half smile. Mooney looked like a kid with a secret, about to tell.

When he clicked off he said nothing, but the smile grew wider.

"Well?" Sandy said.

"That was Friedman," Mooney said. Bart Friedman was another division detective, working drugs and gangs.

"And?"

"And you are not going to believe what Mr. Chuck Samson is into."

14

"Hello," Stan said.

The woman with the child nodded.

Stan liked it when they nodded.

He handed the woman a specials flyer.

She said, "Thank you."

Stan said, "You're welcome." He smiled. It was easy to smile at moms with kids. They were always friendly. Unless the kid had done something wrong and was crying.

A big man in a USC Trojans jersey came in. He was as big as a car. A very big car, if it was painted cardinal and gold. Cardinal and gold were the official colors of USC, the University of Southern California, located near the Los Angeles Memorial Coliseum, which was built in 1923. Stan knew that from a program when Chuck took him to a Trojans football game last year.

"Hello," Stan said, holding out a flyer.

The man did not smile. He walked by Stan without saying anything.

"Have a nice day," Stan said, and meant it. He wanted everyone to have nice days, because they should. If people had nice days they were more likely to be nicer to other people. If you had bad days, you were meaner. Stan had figured all this out by himself and who needed fancy psychology? People were pretty simple when you got right down to it.

He wanted Chuck to have good days for the rest of his life, because he deserved it. Chuck was the best person in the whole world. He was better than the President of the United States even. If he wasn't the best person in the whole world, he was the best big brother.

Stan smiled at the old man who came in with a cane. It was Mr. Manchester. He was always nice, Mr. Manchester was. He might have been the best old man in the whole world.

"How are you, Stan?"

"Fine, thank you, Mr. Manchester," Stan said. "Granny Smith apples, fifty-nine cents a pound." Mr. Manchester liked apples. "And Angel Soft bath tissue, five-ninety-nine."

"You mean toilet paper, don't you?" Mr. Manchester said, giving Stan a wink.

Stan laughed. "You're not gonna trick me, Mr. Manchester."

"Back in the day, when men were men, it was called toilet paper. We liked it rough, too. With wood chips in it."

Stan didn't know what to make of that, but he liked Mr. Manchester because he always joked with him. Stan gave him a flyer.

And that's when he noticed the man by the tomato paste. He was standing at the mouth of the aisle, like he was hiding almost. But he wasn't hiding. He was looking right at Stan. Right into his eyes. At least he thought so. He had sunglasses on. In the store. Stan didn't like that. He didn't like that one bit. It wasn't friendly.

People sometimes looked at him strangely when they heard him talk. He knew he talked funny, kind of from the nose, and it was because of his brain.

But this wasn't that kind of look. Not a funny look. It was a mean look. He wasn't very tall, this guy, and he looked younger than Stan. Older than a teenager, but not by much.

"Hey Stan."

Stan jerked around, as startled as if someone had popped a balloon behind him. It was Mr. Cambry. He was pointing at something. Stan looked and saw two women, maybe a mother and daughter, backs to him, walking away.

He'd missed them.

He hated that!

He started to follow them. Mr. Cambry caught his arm. "It's okay, Stan."

"But they won't know—"

"We'll let them be this time," he said. "You're doing a bang up job."

"I am?"

Stan looked over Mr. Cambry's shoulder, toward the tomato paste.

The mean looking man was gone.

For some reason that made Stan feel like the man was sneaking around. Like a spy. Like in the CIA. Once, when he was eleven, Stan told Chuck he wanted to go into the CIA. He wanted to be a spy. He thought that would be cool. He thought he could use his brain to remember things. Like secret maps and things. But he found out it was too hard to get into the CIA, especially for somebody like him. But he would have been a good spy.

"Just wanted you to know that," Mr. Cambry said, and

walked on toward the deli section. *A bang up job* he'd said. Stan wasn't a spy, but he was going to be the best on door there ever was at Ralphs Fresh Fare.

But he was spooked now. Even if that mean guy wasn't really a mean guy, there were lots of mean guys out there, and one of them had a knife and didn't like Chuck.

If Stan ever saw that man again he'd want to help Chuck. But he'd have to be brave to do that.

He wondered if he could be.

15

Wendy Tower's apartment was warm and filled with the smells of sea and spices. As she attended to final touches in the kitchen, Chuck and Stan sat in the living room. Stan had a smile on his face, a Cupid grin. With his eyes Chuck warned Stan not to say anything *or else.*

Stan's smile widened.

Keep it up, baby brother and I'll give you a wedgie. This whole thing didn't feel right, it was like a boat listing and it would keep on till it capsized. But Chuck was sick of things not feeling right. He had to get over what he couldn't change, namely the past. Now was as good a time as any. Grit your teeth and just do it, pal.

A Native American-style artwork—beads and feathers on a buff backdrop—hung on one wall, right over a small entertainment center with a TV, receiver, and set of small speakers. He remembered an old joke about Indians without electricity, having to watch TV by firelight. The joke did not make him smile. For some reason he felt the juxtaposition of the two images was just not right. Things were together that shouldn't be.

Or maybe he was just nervous. Standing outside Wendy's door, only a few short minutes ago, he felt like he was sixteen and going out for the first time with a pretty girl, hoping he wouldn't come off like a doofus with pimples and non-matching socks.

Now, inside, seated, he was still trying to work himself into fitting here, being comfortable. He knew it was the knife guy and the fire and the stirring up of his bruised and battered psyche, but come on! He couldn't let things outside him dictate his every move forever.

Wendy had music going from an iPod in a dock. Somebody that sounded like Nat King Cole was singing. And then Chuck reminded himself that no one sounded like Nat King Cole except Nat King Cole. He smiled at last.

On the coffee table was the big book *Baseball,* from the Ken Burns documentary. Chuck and Stan loved it when it first appeared, watching it together while eating popcorn and peanuts and even hot dogs. "You a baseball fan?" Chuck said toward the kitchen.

"Totally," Wendy said.

"Me, too," Stan said. "I'm Stan the Man."

Wendy appeared at the pass through. "That was Stan Musial's nickname."

"Yes!" Stan said.

"One of the greats," Wendy said.

"You know about Musial?" Chuck said.

"My grampa is a die-hard Cardinals fan. He told me so many Stan the Man stories I began to think he came from Mount Olympus."

"No!" Stan said. "Donora, Pennsylvania. Born November

21, 1920. Stanislaw Franciszek Musial. Career batting average .331. Hit total, three thousand, six hundred and thirty. Four hundred and seventy-five career home runs."

"Wow!" Wendy said.

"Ask me about Dizzy Dean," Stan said.

Chuck put a hand on his brother's arm. "Maybe after dinner—"

"Real name Jerome Herman Dean, or Jay Hanna Dean. Career Earned Run Average 3.02. Win-loss—"

"Thank you, Stan," Chuck said, squeezing the arm.

"Ow," Stan said. He took his arm back and rubbed it.

"I'll ask you more later, Stan," Wendy said. "You're amazing." She went back to the kitchen.

"I'm amazing," Stan whispered hard, in firm rebuke.

"So true," Chuck said.

"She likes you."

"Slow down, Stan the Man."

"I'll look away and you can kiss her."

"Almost ready," Wendy called from the kitchen.

"See?" Stan said.

"She meant the dinner," Chuck said.

Stan punched Chuck's shoulder, with a little extra oomph than usual. "I was just joking you. You think I'm stupid or something?"

What was no joke was the *paella de marisco*. In presentation and aroma and, most important, taste. As they all finally sat around the table, Chuck lifted his wine glass. "Here's to baseball, fine food, and good company."

Wendy smiled and joined the toast, as did Stan with his preferred drink, 7-Up.

Then Stan said, "Do the knife trick."

"What's that?" Wendy said.

"Nothing," Chuck said.

"Chuck does magic!"

"*Did* magic," Chuck said. "A long time ago."

"Oh please," said Wendy. "Do it."

He did not want to do it. He did not want to do any of those little magic tricks he'd done as a kid, then for awhile at a bar during the summer after college. He got to be pretty good, and the tricks rendered Julia open-mouthed the first time she saw them. To do them again was going to bring that last memory back in full color.

"I'd really like to see it," Wendy said. She wasn't to blame for anything in his life. And he was her guest. He could do it, sure, and maybe get past the memories. Maybe Julia would have wanted him to.

"All right," Chuck said. "Please notice that my hands will not leave my arms at any time."

"He *always* says that," Stan said.

Chuck placed both his hands over his knife, slid it toward him and off the table, into his lap. He kept the motion smooth and put his hands up to his mouth and pretended he was swallowing the knife.

But as he did the knife slid off his lap and hit the floor with a *clank.*

"Oops," Stan said.

Chuck had not blown that trick in twenty years. He looked at his hands like they were foreign objects who had betrayed him.

Wendy laughed good-naturedly. But when Chuck looked at her, she stopped laughing.

A cold blade was slicing through Chuck then. He had dishonored Julia's memory after all. Maybe she *wouldn't* have wanted this. Maybe her ghost knocked the knife off his lap. This was all just too soon. Only seven months since her death. He shouldn't have come. When was the last time he actually felt normal? He tried to recall it, and it was like searching for a box in a dark warehouse with all the fuses blown and the lights out. It was somewhere, in a corner maybe, but which one?

Everybody seemed to sense it, not talking, one of those lulls in a conversation that makes everyone think they're in an elevator with strangers.

Thankfully, there was a knock at the door.

"Excuse me," Wendy said, getting up from the table.

"She likes you," Stan whispered.

"Enough," Chuck said.

"She's a good cook," Stan said.

"Huh?"

"I could tell her about the specials, and she could cook them for you."

"Stan—"

"Fresh boneless, skinless chicken breasts, a dollar ninety-nine a pound."

"How about I skin you, Stan? And make you boneless?"

"Ha ha, jacky-daw." That was Stan's own phrase, had been ever since he'd read a bird book when he was ten and saw jackdaws and figured out the singular rhymed with *ha ha*. It drove Chuck crazy for awhile, everything was *ha ha jacky-daw* for months.

And then Wendy was in the room again. Behind here were the two detectives who'd questioned Chuck earlier at the school. Epperson and Mooney.

Epperson said, "Charles Samson?"

Just like his mother used to sound when he was in trouble. Chuck stood. Maybe they had some news about the house.

"I am placing you under arrest," she said.

Stan jumped so fast out of his chair he almost knocked the table over. Two water glasses fell.

Mooney came at Chuck with the bracelets. "Turn around," he said.

"What is this?" Chuck said.

"You are under arrest for the manufacture of methamphetamine," Epperson said.

"What?"

The next few moments were a haze of insane noise. Stan shouted, Chuck told Wendy to get Stan back to the motel, Wendy said she would, Mooney told everybody to be quiet. Chuck told Wendy to tell Ray Hunt he might miss school tomorrow. She said she'd do that, too. Mooney said be quiet again.

Then they were out the door, with Mooney squeezing Chuck's arm hard, pushing him toward the stairwell. Apartment doors opened and people peeked out, like a Whack-a-Mole game.

Stan's voice echoed down the hall. "You'll never get away with this, you dirty coppers! Never!"

16

In a Topanga station interview room, Chuck listened to Detective Epperson drone, "You've been advised of your rights. We cannot ask you any questions, and anything you say can be used against you in court. You can sign this waiver and talk to us, or you can wait to speak to an attorney."

Chuck said, "Tell me, honestly, if you think I am a guy who would be dealing drugs."

"I'm advising you not to say anything unless you sign this waiver."

Chuck paused, looked at the form. He snatched the pen off the desk and held it up to them, like he was showing them a magic wand. Then he signed his name. "All right," he said. "Now look at me and tell me that you think I'm a drug dealer."

"The fire was caused by an explosion in a propane tank in your garage," Epperson said.

"I don't have any propane tanks in my garage," Chuck said.

"How do you explain the presence of a propane tank, along with acetone, Freon, sodium hydroxide, sulfuric acid and paint thinner?"

Chuck stared at her. Pieces of a bizarre puzzle started flying around his brain. "I didn't have any of that stuff. So somebody must have put it there."

Mooney said, "And just a coincidence, I guess, that those are items used in the manufacture of methamphetamine."

"Right," Chuck said. "Which I sell to my fifth graders."

Epperson said, "I advise against sarcasm, Mr. Samson."

"I advise against any of this crap," Chuck said. "It's an obvious set up. Have you done any background on me? Why are you into this anyway? I thought you were homicide. You saying I killed somebody?"

"Who would go to all that trouble to set you up?" Mooney said. "What would be the purpose of that?"

"You're the detectives. You tell me." Chuck watched them both stiffen and didn't care if they did.

"If you're in the clear," Epperson said, "just answer a few questions for us."

"While I'm sitting here under arrest? Real friendly like?"

"Why not?"

"Then get on with it." Chuck was worried about Stan. Wendy would be with him but he knew his brother wouldn't be calm until they were together again. Maybe if he calmed down himself, got reasonable, they'd spring him.

Right. And pots of gold are sniffed by unicorns at the end of rainbows.

"You can just come clean about making the drugs," Mooney said. "I mean, your life hasn't exactly been a financial success."

Chuck shot him a look. Mooney shot one right back. It was a regular love fest around here, and Mooney was some sort of TV-cop wannabe.

Chuck said, "I've got a job, okay? I teach fifth grade. I like my job. I get along. I want to keep doing that. I'm not going to make meth in my freaking garage. I have a brother I take care of. I'm not going to do anything to mess that up."

"Real noble," Mooney said.

As Chuck's fists clenched, Epperson said, "Mr. Samson, are you still on call as a Navy chaplain?"

"No."

"Any reason why not?" Epperson asked.

"I don't need my head shrunk, okay? I didn't do what you think I did. That's all you need to know."

"That's a great defense," Mooney said.

Throwing up his hands, Chuck said, "Get me a lawyer."

"Uh-huh," Mooney said.

Epperson said, "You want private or the PD?"

Chuck had exactly $2,323 in combined checking and savings. He was not getting anything from Uncle Sam because of that paperwork snafu on his DD214 discharge form. He wasn't going to be getting any superstar attorney. But he was *not guilty of anything* and even a freshly scrubbed law grad should be able to clear things up.

"PD," Chuck said.

"Tomorrow morning," Epperson said.

"What about my phone call?"

"Yes, you can have one phone call."

Chuck called Royce Horne. He'd know what to do.

17

His given name is Dragoslav Zivkcovic, first name Serb for *glory,* but there has been no glory for him in his twenty-eight years. And so he prefers the name he was called since coming to America, Dag Kovak, and even what some others call him, The Dog. That would be a name of respect and fear, but he knows he has not truly earned either, not in the eyes of his father, the only eyes that matter to him.

The ones who work for his father will call him Dog to his face but behind his back he suspects they mock him. They fear him only because he is the son of Svetozar Zivkcovic, now Steven Kovak. A father who has killed more men and women than he ever will, because there is no honor in America, there is no ethnic cleansing. So he, The Dog, is the weak one, who drinks too much and is protected by his father's money. But it cannot buy honor or respect.

He hates the tears that sting his eyes and blur his vision, but he guns his Escalade through the canyon. Winding toward the ocean, windows down to smell the air, the scent of coastal sage and scrub oak, red shank and buckwheat, and his beloved Manzanita. It is a plant that is hard and twisted and sharp when dry, as he is hard and twisted, as he has made himself to be. But it is not enough and his tears shame him because his father knows that he is not as hard inside as he should be, but soft like the sand on the beaches of Malibu. There is nothing he can do to change his father's mind except to become like him and learn to kill without a thought, and that is why he carries the Manzanita branch in his car, it will teach him.

And so he drives. Down to Pacific Coast Highway, turning left, tears flowing faster, almost turning his SUV into headlights coming the other way, that would be a nice quick way to go, maybe a good heroic way to go, choosing his own destiny. He can see—no, it's more a sense—people laughing and eating and drinking in places that line the neon night. They are chasing dreams as he is running from nightmares and he hates them all. He can hate well.

Soon he pulls off the road and onto the shoulder, at a place where the beach is darkest. He has a place he comes to in the night to cleanse himself. With him he brings his twisted Manzanita branch, and with it he climbs over the rocks down to the sand and the branch stays with him as his companion as he whips it through the air, slashing the air as one would a fencing foil, hearing the sound.

When he reaches the spot where he will be alone he takes his clothes off carefully, ritually, this is his communion. His running shoes and white socks, his jeans and belt, his shirt, he is forming a pile. He slips off his underwear last and is naked in the cool breeze.

There is a moon out, a large mountain moon, and he looks up at it like a coyote and he is The Dog, but he does not howl. He weeps. And to stop the weeping he takes his branch of

Manzanita and whips his own legs and feet, and then his genitals. Then his back, over and over, the sound of the branch and crash of the waves making hymns.

When he is done and bleeding, he walks slowly to the water and into the brine, his whipped feet stinging, his legs feeling all the salt and cleansing of the Pacific, finally his back, and it burns in the cold of the water. For one brief moment he considers swimming out into the darkness, swimming until he cannot hold himself up, and then sinking to the bottom or maybe his blood will bring sharks and he will fight them before they kill him and that will be a heroic death.

He goes under the water fully, baptizing himself, and then he knows he will not die here, he is not ready to die. He comes back to shore, exhausted, still holding the branch.

He is sweeping the sand as he walks with the stick when he sees a form by his clothes, bent over the clothes, butt toward him. In the moonlight he sees the form stand up and turn around, and it looks like a skinny teenager who almost jumps when he sees The Dog. The kid freezes, looking at the naked man who is looking right back at him. The kid has something in his hand. The Dog cannot see what it is but it very clearly came out of his pocket and as the kid begins to run. The Dog knows already what the outcome will be.

The kid is fast but he is no match for Dragoslav Zivkcovic, who was graced with strong legs like his mother, his mother who was gunned down by Albanian soldiers when he was ten. He catches the teen by the back of the shirt and with one pull yanks him down on the sand. The boy cries out and says he is sorry, sorry, please don't do anything and The Dog puts his foot on the boy's throat and holds him down like a butcher might hold down a live chicken.

The boy squirms and cries and begs for mercy.

Up in the sky, over the mountains, the moon is bright and glorious.

"Thank you!" Dag says to the moon.

18

In his cell, Chuck realized this was his first forced absence from Stan since his brother had come to live with him.

As kids, Stan stuck to Chuck like cherry powder to a Lik-a-Stix. School had separated them—Stan needed special classes—but they both knew it was temporary. Even when Chuck went to Afghanistan, it wasn't like being ripped away from his brother. Stan, who was still living with their mom at that time, talked to him every day on the phone in the two weeks before Chuck left. He was proud of his joke—*You can't forget me, Chuck. It's AfghaniSTAN!*

Yes, it was. His brother was like a landscape for Chuck, a grounding. In the weeks after Julia's death, there was Stan. His presence was an odd comfort, but comfort it was. They knew without speaking how much they needed each other then. They cried and laughed. Stan peppered him with memorized trivia, things he'd find on the back of cereal boxes or in *The National Inquirer.*

More memories buzz-sawed in, but the one that stuck out

in full color and sound was the 7-Eleven incident. Chuck was twelve and Stan eight. It was raining that day and Chuck was walking Stan home from his special class at school. Chuck had his bike and the back tire was low, so he went to the Shell station to give it some air, while Stan went into the 7-Eleven.

When Chuck came in he saw Stan in tears, a store employee holding him by the shirt. Stan was struggling in the grip. He hated to be held like that.

"What's this?" Chuck said.

Another guy stepped around the counter wearing a 7-Eleven shirt. "He tried to steal some candy."

"Did not!" Stan cried. "I forgot I had it!"

"Look," Chuck said, "I know he didn't mean—"

"Forget it. The cops are coming."

"Come on, I'll pay for it. We won't come back."

The counter guy, who looked about forty, poked his finger in Chuck's chest. "You can leave. He can't."

Before Chuck could answer, Stan screamed and broke free of the other guy's grasp. He charged the counter guy and head-butted his stomach. It was a beautiful move, Chuck would reflect later, like a fierce lineman putting everything he had into a tackling dummy.

The guy let out an *oomph*, but caught the back of Stan's shirt. He sent Stan flying into the chips rack. Stan cried out and hit the floor, bags of Lays and Fritos tumbling on top of him.

Filled with instant rage, not thinking at all—except that they'd hurt Stan and he was going to hurt them—Chuck grabbed a pot of coffee off the burner next to him and threw it across the store. It shattered on the floor, hot coffee bursting out in a satisfying explosion.

The only other customer, an old Hispanic man, watched motionless from in front of the hot dog rollers.

There were three other pots on the coffee service. Chuck pushed them to the floor with a single motion.

The store employees came after him.

"Run, Stan! Run home and tell Mom!"

Chuck darted down the aisle, toward the drinks case, leading the counter jockeys away from Stan. He snatched bags of corn nuts and cashews along the way, then turned and faced the enemy.

Chuck had one of the best fastballs in the Tustin Little League. He showed his stuff.

By his later reckoning he threw four strikes and only two balls at the 7-Eleven All Stars. Two of the strikes got face. But it only delayed the inevitable by a few seconds.

When the two guys got to Chuck they tried to lay hands on him. Chuck got in a couple of good shin kicks and a back hand across one chest. But soon enough he was on the ground with the older of the two sitting on him.

But at least Stan was gone. He'd made it out. But when he came back to the store it wasn't with Mom. It was with Dad, and that was not good.

His dad had to sort it out with the cops, and apparently did, after he agreed to pay all the damages.

At home he took it out on Chuck's bare butt and legs with a nozzled hose. He laid on the stripes as if to transfer all the pain he held inside for being a failure as a father, for being out of work all the time, for having the burden of a son with special needs.

And Chuck knew then if he tried to whip Stan, Chuck would find his own rod and lay his father out. Then run away with Stan, hop a train, see the country.

Instead, a couple of days later, his father was gone for good. Last word was he was with a woman he met at a Reno casino and was riding off toward the east in her Mary Kay pink Caddy. They never heard from him again.

From then on it was only Mom and the two of them, in the little house in Tustin, where the end of the street looked like the beginning of all bad things.

And it was Chuck looking out for Stan, getting into more fights than he cared to think about, after every insult hurled at his little brother.

But now, in the 4 x 6 box, on the hard mattress, staring at the pea green ceiling, Chuck hoped Stan could make it through this night without him.

He hoped Stan wouldn't dream about the wolf man.

Then the shadow dance began again, and Chuck knew he would not sleep. Not for a long time, at least. The figures from the past, traceable only to that war, mocked his remembering, because he could not remember fully, could not see the faces.

One of them said something. It sounded like *Rushton Line.*

What was the Rushton Line? Where was it? Were these figures even real? Had he experienced this scene somehow? Was the VA doc right, that his very memories were traumatized and diffuse? Answers were always just beyond his grasp, and he knew that must be what insanity felt like. Maybe insanity, after all, would be the place he'd end up.

He fought back. He wouldn't go nuts, not with Stan to take care of. And not until he got some other answers—about why he was here, and who was after him.

The shadows danced, the distant booms sounded, and Chuck pounded the wall with his fist. Rhythmically, punching at phantoms, music for the dance.

19

Jimmy Stone realized his throat was as dry as microwaved cotton. He did not want to give into the fear, or even acknowledge it.

But the guy in front of him gave off the deadliest vibe he'd ever been around. Jimmy didn't want to be here. But it was business. No choice.

Jimmy was about to break to the top of the gangland mountain. A few years ago he was playing Pony League baseball and dealing a little weed on the side. Now here he was, at 22, on the verge of controlling the distribution of H in the Valley, and running the most powerful crew in Los Angeles. Because with the Serbs behind him and his boys, he had the fire power to back up any attempted incursions.

No white gang had been able to keep Bloods and Crips from biting off territory. That was going to change on Jimmy's watch.

But it meant taking orders from the Serbs, and they put this one called Vaso right up in his grill. Jimmy hated him, hated his voice, hated always having to meet him at night in places like this.

At least the darkness covered his own twitching muscles.

He was here with Ryan Malik, his right-hand guy, in this spot in the unincorporated hills between LA and Ventura counties. Officially it was the Ahmanson Ranch, but at this hour it felt like a graveyard. The smell of tumble brush in the night wind was strong. Jimmy never liked it. It smelled like camping, and he hated camping. Better to be where there was cement and asphalt and concrete and his boys and girls.

Vaso flashed a penlight at Jimmy's face, making it impossible to see his expression.

"Come on, man," Jimmy said.

"Speak only when you are spoken to," Vaso said. His voice was low and scratchy and all out creepy. Jimmy knew he had to respect him, but he wasn't going to be walked on. If anybody else had talked to him that way, they'd be buried right now. But this was Vaso, and you did what he said.

"Sure," Jimmy said, but with a little edge, just to let him know.

"You ordered the hit on the girl?"

He was talking about Esperanza Gomez. "Yeah, she was gonna testify against me."

"You didn't ask."

"That don't got nothin' to do with distribution—"

"You didn't *ask*."

"I gotta ask every time?"

"Do you know what happens to those who do not ask?"

Ryan spoke. "We took care of it, clean." Jimmy heard a little waver in Ryan's normally hardcore voice.

"You don't talk at all," Vaso said.

83

"Come on, man, enough of this," Ryan said.

Jimmy saw a movement behind the pen light and then a *whump* sound. Ryan screamed and went down.

For a moment Jimmy froze between rage and fear.

"My leg!" Ryan cried.

Jimmy dropped to his knees, put his arm around Ryan.

"Did you have to do that?" Jimmy said.

"No," Vaso said. "I could have done this."

Whump.

Jimmy felt Ryan's head snap back. Ryan made no more noise. Blood gushed out onto Jimmy's shirt. He opened his mouth, it was dry, no sound came out of it.

"Next time, you ask," Vaso said.

20

Early Thursday morning they shackled Chuck, herded him onto a bus with the other criminal masterminds, and took him to the Van Nuys courthouse. They stuffed everyone into a holding cell where Chuck got to hear about cops planting evidence or kicking in doors, and a hundred other complaints.

Chuck said nothing. He was still trying to sort out what was real and what was dream in the last twenty-four hours of his life. Like a drowsiness that will not fade, his sense of being captive in a nightmare—one that was only just beginning—refused to drop from his head.

He didn't know what time it was when the voice called his name. He went to the bars of the holding cell and saw a young woman with auburn hair and a serious look and an arm full of file folders. "My name is Carrie Stratton from the Public Defender's office," she said. "I'll be representing you today. You know that you're being charged with the attempted manufacture of a controlled substance, right?"

"That's what they told me," Chuck said. "But—"

"Health and Safety Code section 11379.6, sub a, and Penal Code section—"

"I don't need—"

"—section 664. Any questions?"

"Yeah," Chuck said. "How can they possibly be doing this to me?"

"I'm here to help with your initial appearance. I haven't seen the police report yet."

"Will they let me out on bail?"

"Do you have a prior record?"

"No," Chuck said.

Carrie opened a folder and glanced at some papers inside. "You apparently have a friend in the courtroom who said he'd post if you needed it."

"That would be Royce."

"He spoke to me. You know him how?"

"We met at the VA."

"You're a veteran?"

"I was a chaplain."

"And you were at the VA hospital?"

"For awhile."

Carrie looked at his neck. "You were wounded?"

"Not exactly," Chuck said.

"How'd you get that scar?"

"Is that relevant?"

Carrie shrugged. "If it's war related, might hold sway with the judge."

"Then leave it at that."

"War related?"

"Yeah."

"Good," Carrie said, and pulled a pen from her coat pocket and scribbled something on one of the papers. "That's very good. I'll argue you have no record, you served your country, and maybe we can get the judge to give you a get out of jail free card."

"What else do I have to do?" Chuck said.

"Plead not guilty and we'll ask for a continuance and you can figure out whether you're going to be represented by private counsel or qualify for the public defender's services."

"Anything else?"

"Yes," Carrie said. "Keep your mouth shut."

•

Rodney "The Terror" Terrell loved this time of the morning, especially when the beach was closed in by fog. It gave him the wonderful sense of being alone in the world, which is what he was anyway, and preferred it that way. He did not like people much. He liked fish.

For a few weeks in 1967 The Terror had been the number three middleweight in the world. But that was many dollars and many blows to the head ago. Now he lived alone in a motor home and caught his dinner in the early morning before the beaches got crowded. The crowds reminded him too much of the fight game, and he never liked fighting in front of people. It was all about the boxing for Terrell, the art of it. Not satisfying the blood lust of the frenzied masses.

But the returns for his boxing career were not so great. He was on welfare now and his head didn't work so good. He couldn't get his thoughts to pull together very often.

And when he got around people and got too excited, he was liable to punch somebody just to stop the confusion.

Which is why he liked being alone, and today looked like a good day for it. He carried his bucket of bait and his pole, his jeans rolled up, the cool sand between his toes. He got to his favorite spot. But somebody else was there. A somebody who was sleeping where he liked to set up shop.

Which was fine. He didn't own the beach. But it was a little strange for a guy to be sleeping there at this hour without a blanket. It was cold-fog wet.

Then Terrell saw the blood. It was soaked in the sand around the guy's head. Terrell bent over for a closer look—and saw it was just a kid, and somebody had jammed a mean-looking stick of red wood under the boy's chin. In the red-black hole of the skin, milling around in the dead flesh, were a couple of wasps.

Rodney "The Terror" Terrell dropped his bucket and his pole and tossed his breakfast onto the beach. Then he ran up to the road to try to flag somebody down. He didn't have a phone, and his thoughts were really jumbled, but he knew one thing for sure—the police ought to know about this.

21

Chuck kept his mouth shut. It was all over in a matter of minutes. And the lawyer, Carrie Stratton, was very good. She convinced the judge to let him out on his own recognizance and an hour after that he was standing with Royce Horne just outside the Van Nuys courthouse doors.

"So, Dillinger, you want to tell me what this is about?" Royce said. He was everyone's picture of a tough soldier—square jawed with beard stubble you could strike a match on. Marine tat on his left deltoid, avenging angel on his right. They'd connected at the VA a year after Chuck got back, in a PTSD group. Royce, a couple years Chuck's senior, had served in Iraq. He ran a little gardening business now. He also ran interference for Chuck with the VA, like he did with a lot of the guys who were having trouble getting what they needed.

"Let's get out of here," Chuck said.

"Let me buy you a Quiznos. I'll spare no expense."

"How's Stan?"

"Don't worry about your brother," Royce said. "I did like

you said and talked to him and that teacher, what's her name again?"

"Wendy Tower."

"I like her, Chuck," Royce said. "Stan says you like her, too."

"Just tell me if he's okay."

Royce nodded. "I told him I was going to get you, and he said that was good because he had a plan to come bust you out if they didn't let you go. I think he meant it."

"No doubt. Why don't we—" Chuck stopped when he saw Detective Sandy Epperson striding toward them.

"Mr. Samson," she said.

"What is this?" Chuck said.

"I'd like to talk to you. With your attorney present, of course. I've cleared it with Ms. Stratton. Court is in recess, and we can meet in the PD's office. This is not related to the current charges."

"Fantastic. You have more you want to lay on me?"

"Not at all. I do think you'll find it to be important."

Royce stepped between them. "Can't you give him a break here, detective?"

"And you are?" Epperson asked.

"A friend," Royce said.

"Would you mind waiting for a few minutes?"

Royce turned to Chuck. "You don't have to do this."

No, and Chuck didn't want to, either. Yet there was something in Epperson's face. She didn't look like a detective out to set traps. And as long as his lawyer was there . . .

"All right," Chuck said.

"I'll be right here waiting for you," Royce said.

22

"I am recording this interview," Detective Epperson said within the confines of Carrie Stratton's cubicle. Epperson placed a digital recorder on the corner of Carrie's desk. "It is 10:43 a.m., and Charles Samson is present with his attorney, Carrie Stratton of the Los Angeles County Public Defender's Office. Mr. Samson, how much do you know about Edward Hillary?"

The name was a spike to Chuck's chest. It was a name he'd been trying to forget for seven months. "I know he was the guy who killed my wife.

Epperson opened the file folder sitting on the desk. "A retired cop. Clean record."

"So they say. What do—"

"Moved to Beaman a year and a half ago."

"And I should care about this why?"

Epperson scanned the sheets. "His blood alcohol level, according to the toxicology report, was point-two-two at the time of the hit-and-run. That's a lot of alcohol."

"Yeah it is, but what's all this got to do with what I'm charged with?"

"Bear with me. I've been looking over the accident report. The local police questioned a bartender at a place called the Tall T. He said Hillary came into the bar that night at approximately 7:15, and left at approximately 9:30. The accident happened at or around 10:12."

Chuck said nothing.

"The bartender also said he served Hillary three beers while he was at the bar. Hillary spoke to the bartender, a man named Renner, and other patrons."

"Detective, please get to the point of all this."

Carrie Stratton put her hand on Chuck's arm. She had a look on her face that indicated he should be patient. Like she knew where this was leading.

"Just a few more facts, Mr. Samson," Epperson said. "Edward Hillary was six feet, three inches tall, and weighed two-hundred-and-sixty pounds. He was not a small man. There is no way that three beers in the span of two hours-plus could have given him a point-two-two, even if he came into the bar with some drinks in him. So the question is, how did he get so tanked before the accident?"

Chuck looked at her a long moment. "What are you saying?"

"I'm just asking questions," Epperson said.

"Well I don't have any answers." He was starting to feel tongs gripping his temples. "Just tell me why you're talking to me."

"What was your wife doing in Beaman?" Epperson asked.

"I told you, some stupid alligator farm story."

"I find that strange," Epperson said. "I checked. There aren't any alligator farms in Beaman. Never have been."

Little sparklers snapped at the corners of Chuck's vision. He closed his eyes and tried to shake them away.

"Are you all right, Mr. Samson?"

"Do I look all right? What the hell are you saying to me? That my wife was lying to me?"

"I'm trying, believe it or not, to help you, and help myself," Epperson said, her voice calm yet firm. "I have a murder on my hands, Grant Nunn. The man who killed him may be the same man who threatened you with the knife. There's probably a connection. And when I started looking into your background, I found your wife's death, and this report, and now I have more questions. I want to know what you're into, Mr. Samson. And maybe it's not something you started. But here you are."

Carrie Stratton said, "You don't have to say anything else. I advise you not to."

Chuck looked back and forth between his lawyer and the cop. "I'm not into anything," he said, standing. "That's all you need to know. Nothing. The sooner you drop this the better for everybody, especially you."

Blindingly, unthinkingly, Chuck swept the back of his hand at the file in front of Detective Epperson. The contents went fluttering to the floor.

Epperson did not react like Chuck expected. She didn't clench her jaw, point her finger, or answer immediately. Instead she gave him a lingering glance and nodded slowly. Like she understood. She said, "Thanks for your time, Mr. Samson. You know how to reach me. Advise your lawyer if you ever want to talk."

23

Royce was still in the spot where Chuck had left him.

"So what did she want?" Royce said.

Chuck let out a long breath. He felt like he hadn't slept in weeks. And like he wanted to punch a tree, any tree. "Something about Julia's death."

"Like what?"

"Like I don't know! I don't even know what day it is anymore."

"Thursday."

"Well that's just great. What do I get on the weekend? A murder indictment?"

Royce said, "You need to regroup, bud. You need some help in this. I'll call Shel."

Shel Simpson was an investigator of the Los Angeles District Attorney's office, a Gulf War vet. He was part of a regular poker group at Royce's apartment, a group Chuck sometimes joined. Shel knew all the best defense lawyers in town because he'd seen them operate in court.

"I'm not rolling in dough," Chuck said.

"We'll get some together. The Wild Bills will kick in." The Wild Bills was what the poker group called themselves.

"I can't ask you to do that," Chuck said. "This Stratton seems competent."

"You don't want just competent, Chuck."

Chuck looked at the sky. It was slate gray. The kind of LA sky that doesn't threaten rain, just shuts out the sun.

He felt his phone vibrate. A text message.

Samson. Smrt.

"Bad news?" Royce said.

"What is this?" He showed Royce the text.

"You're smart?" Royce asked.

"Apparently."

"Who sent it?"

Chuck swallowed hard. Private number.

He felt Royce's hand on his shoulder. "You feel your triggers coming on?"

Chuck shook his head.

"Don't hold out on me," Royce said.

"I won't."

"Let's get that sandwich."

"Just take me to the motel," Chuck said.

"I think you need—"

"Let's go."

They got Royce's car in the lot on Sylmar and fought traffic down Van Nuys Boulevard.

"Know what let's do?" Royce said. "Let's you, me, and Stan go out on my boat again. Go out to Catalina. Remember the dolphins?"

Chuck wasn't remembering anything. He was breaking out in cold sweats. And shaking.

"Hey, man," Royce said. He pulled into a Mobil station and parked in the air and water bay. Chuck was starting to feel sucked into the dark memories again. He jammed himself back against the seat, as if doing so would keep him grounded in reality.

"Breathe easy," Royce said. "I'm right here." He clutched Chuck's arm, and Chuck tried to take in more air. Noises reverbed in Chuck's head, the sound of explosions getting closer.

Royce said, "Try to get it out."

"It's bad. I don't know why it's happening now."

"Confront it, like the doc said."

Chuck winced, like he was having a tooth pulled. "Let's just go."

"What do you see?"

Figures. Three of them. Indistinct. "It's the same," Chuck said. "It never gets clearer."

"Sounds?"

"Booming. Exploding."

"You're on the battlefield."

"No. I think it's coming from somewhere else." Chuck grabbed his head, squeezed. "I just want it to stop."

"If you can get one picture or voice, that can open it all up, " Royce said. "That's what they say. It's like lancing a boil and all that puss comes out."

"Wow, I'm hungry. When's lunch?"

"Come on. Try to see one thing."

Chuck clenched his mind. He wanted his brain to gush it out, like Royce said. "All I see is Dylan Bly, and the explosion. Three shadows."

"Wait a minute, wait a minute! That's new. Who is Dylan Bly?"

"He came to me, had something he wanted to tell me. The night before the patrol."

"The one where you got captured?"

"Yeah." And the one where the concussive blast of the RPG had knocked him senseless before he could get to the dying Dylan Bly.

"What else?" Royce said.

"It's still fuzzy, dammit. I see shadows, but I can't see their faces. I hear some words."

"Words?"

"Something *like* words. *Rush ten line.*"

"What is that?"

"I don't *know!*" Chuck hit the passenger window with his fist. At least give me pain and blood and I'll be clear about that.

"Wait a second," Royce said. "Rushton. Maybe that's it. Did you know a soldier named Rushton?"

"I don't remember anybody named Rushton."

"Let's go see the doc, Chuck. This could be major."

"No."

"Come on—"

"No!"

"Okay," Royce said. "That's it. Let it go for now."

"I can't get any closer."

"Okay, that's all, Chuck. Take it easy."

"Drive me to Studio City."

"I thought you wanted—"

"Somebody I need to see. Now."

24

"Hey," Mooney said.

Sandy looked up from her cubicle desk. "Nice greeting," she said.

"You talked to Samson without me?"

"I was down there, they OR'd him," Sandy said. "I took a shot."

"You don't think to call?"

"No time." That was a half truth, maybe even a quarter. Sandy hadn't wanted to call him because his presence and attitude put Samson off.

"So he give you anything?" Mooney said.

"Not really."

"Then it was something." Mooney made wiggly fingers at her, like he was asking for money.

"Nothing that helps with Nunn," Sandy said.

"What else?"

Sandy swiveled in her chair, faced him. "You really don't like this guy."

"Got nothing to do with it."

"I mean, you're anxious about him."

"Why shouldn't I be?" he said. His eyebrows creased downward. Then he did his Bogart voice. "He's good. He's very good."

Actually, it wasn't a bad Bogart at all. Mooney could also do other oldies, like Edward G. Robinson. But it seemed like he would pick odd times to do them, like when he wanted to annoy her.

"I don't know that he's good in that way," Sandy said. "He seems conflicted and confused. He has PTSD."

"He was a chaplain. A man of the cloth. What's he got to be PTSD'd about?"

Sandy opened her file on Samson. "Doesn't say. But that scar on his neck?"

"Yeah?"

"Maybe that's the reason."

Mooney cocked his head to look at the sheets. "Maybe we better find out."

"You want to question him again?"

"Yeah I do."

"He's got counsel. I don't know that he'll consent."

"You're the charmer," Mooney said. "Work your magic. But one thing."

"Yes?"

"Don't ever talk to him without me being there, okay?"

Sandy didn't like the cold thrust of his words then, but decided to let it pass. He was right. He should be in on everything. She was, in a sense, training him after all. Should show him the right way.

"Okay," she said.

"Thanks, Shweet haht," Bogart said.

25

As Royce drove he said, "Let me get you together with a guy."

Chuck rested his head on the back of the seat. "What guy?"

"Guy I know, uses hypnosis."

"I don't buy that stuff."

"Now's the time. I don't want to have to drag you in."

"For mumbo jumbo?"

"Exposure therapy, Einstein."

"What, I take my clothes off and run down the street?"

Royce said, "Your normal memories are filed away in the right spots in your brain. And they don't intrude on your day-to-day. But the traumatic memories aren't filed at all. They're scattered all around, and can pop up and go *bam* any time. So what this guy does is he brings the traumas up, helps you remember, has you look at what you can tolerate, face it, realize it's not going to kill you. Then they can get filed away in the right places."

"Can we not talk about it now?"

"You never want to talk about it. That's part of the problem."

"Just drive, okay?" Chuck closed his eyes, wondering if he should go ahead and get hypnotized. What could it hurt? God had apparently chosen not to perform a miracle of healing. Maybe some Amazing Kreskin would do the trick, bring some order to the flashes that even now flooded in, piecemeal. The...

•

...Marine Expeditionary Unit to which he was assigned was launching an operation to enhance security for the citizens of the Garmsir District of Helmland Province. Garmsir was a planning, staging and logistics hub of the neo-Taliban.

By the fourth week Chuck was settling into his duties— conducting chapel, counseling, caring for the wounded, honoring the dead with memorial services (and making sure the commanding general was at each one). Then came the night before the day it all, literally, exploded.

A gunnery sergeant named Dylan Bly came to see him. Needed to talk. He was going out on security patrol the next day, and wanted Chuck to know something. That part of the memory was clear. Dylan Bly's eyes were full of both fury and fear, or at least that's how Chuck remembered it.

And he also remembered going out on patrol with Bly, in a second Humvee. It was a chance for Chuck to get to another outpost to conduct some services. Also, he wanted to be near Bly. For some reason, he felt Dylan Bly needed him at that moment.

The Humvees turned into a dry river bed, often used in lieu of roads in this part of Afghanistan. Chuck remembered looking out at the sky and the mountains and then hearing the explosion. Later, he would learn it was an IED—improvised explosive device—so common in this theater of operations.

The lead vehicle, the one with Dylan Bly in it, was on fire.

What happened next Chuck had to learn from a report. His own memory of it was a series of kaleidoscopic colors and shapes, very little making sense.

They were attacked. Small arms fire from all around. Dylan Bly was lying out on the dirt, exposed. Apparently Chuck ran out to help him, tried to drag him to safety behind the flaming Humvee. But then what may have been an RPG—a rocket propelled grenade—blew up somewhere near him, the concussive effect knocking Chuck clean out.

He was literally in the dark after that. The shadow figures appeared sometime in there, when they'd cut his throat after an interrogation. Just before the rescue squad came.

Chuck learned later he'd been left for dead at a villa belonging to a local warlord named Abdul Asad Sajadi.

Shipped back to the states, and debriefed, he could not remember any more than this. It was also the time Julia started to feel like a stranger.

26

"You sure you don't want me to wait?" Royce said. He'd pulled up in front of the squat, two-story office building on Ventura, just east of Coldwater Canyon.

"I'll take the bus," Chuck said. "I may be awhile."

"I don't mind."

"Thanks for coming to court."

"Always happy to help the criminal element," Royce said.

Chuck tried to smile.

"Call me if you need me," Royce said.

Chuck nodded, got out and went through the glass double doors. The offices of *LAEye* were on the second floor. Chuck took the elevator and went to the secure door. It was open. Some security. In the reception area was a desk with no one behind it.

Even better security. Why not just put a neon sign out in front that said *Drifters Welcome?*

There was a door to the inner sanctum, also unlocked. Chuck went through. He'd been here a couple of times before.

It was a typical hive of cubicles, with the sound of keyboards and a slight hum from the ceiling lights. Julia had worked at a cubicle in the back, next to Octavia Butler. Chuck walked back, getting hardly a look from the staff, thinking how easy it would be to wipe this place out.

Octavia was at her monitor, back to him.

"Clinton did have sex with that woman," Chuck said.

She spun around in her chair. "Chuck!" She stood and hugged him. "How long's it been?"

"Since the funeral, I guess."

"That's right." She had soft brown eyes. Her skin was smooth café au lait, her hair plaited. Chuck always thought she'd have made a good model. But all she wanted to do was be an investigative journalist, like Julia.

"How's that novel coming?" Chuck said.

Octavia smiled. "Still trying to work out the middle. Writing a novel'd be easy if you only had to do the beginning and end."

"Life too," Chuck said.

"Can we go out for coffee or something?"

"This isn't really a social visit, Octavia. I need to ask you something."

"Sure."

"Julia was working on a story when she was killed."

Octavia hesitated. She looked at the floor as if trying to remember. "Something about alligators."

"Did she give you any details about this story?"

"Not really. In fact, she didn't say much of anything at all. It was kind of strange."

"Why strange?"

"She usually talked to me a lot about her stories. This one she was kind of tightlipped about. I figured she just didn't want

104

to say anything, but I remember thinking at the time that was a little odd for Julia."

A surge of electricity went through him. "Octavia, I really need you to help me think this through. Is there anything that you remember about this period in her life that raises any questions?"

"Questions like what?"

"Anything."

She bit her lower lip and sat on the edge of her desk. "I'm really trying to think here, Chuck."

That, or trying not to say something. Chuck had the impression she was defensive.

"When was the very last time you saw her?" he asked.

"I remember that. It was the day before she was killed. I saw her in the office."

"What time?"

"Afternoon, maybe around three or four o'clock."

"Did you talk to her?"

"Just a normal *Hi, how you doing?* Nothing more than that. I was working on something too. I remember when she left she leaned over my desk and gave me one of these." Octavia made a bye-bye motion with one hand.

"And then?"

Octavia said nothing, but Chuck thought he saw a desire in her expression, like words were on the edge, wanting to get out.

"What is it?" he said.

Octavia turned her head.

"Tell me," Chuck said.

"Chuck . . ."

"Come on."

"Dammit, why'd you have to surprise me like this?"

"Octavia!" The voice came from a doorway halfway across

the room.

"The boss," Octavia said.

"He can wait."

"Are you kidding?"

Chuck put a hand on her arm, hard. "Tell me."

"Don't do this," she said.

"Please."

She looked at him and the pain in her eyes was palpable.

Behind him, the voice said, "Hey."

He was late twenties, with shag-thick black hair. He wore Ivy League style glasses, and a white shirt with tie and blue jeans.

"Van, this is a friend," Octavia said.

"How'd he get in?" Van asked.

"Mind giving us a minute?" Chuck said.

"Yeah, I do," Van said. "We got work to do here."

"Five minutes."

"No. Good-bye."

Chuck wanted to grab the guy's shirt and explain in journalistic detail to his face everything that was happening, and then shake him into silent compliance.

He realized later he might have done it, but Octavia said, "Wait for me downstairs. I'll take a break in a few."

•

It wasn't a few. In fact, it was half an hour, and Chuck's rear end went through several iterations of numb on an iron bench outside the front doors. When Octavia finally came down, she looked frazzled.

"Your boss is a real law-and-order type," Chuck said.

She took his arm.

106

There was a walkway between buildings. The warm-bake smells from the pizza place next door filled the space. It made Chuck hungry and sick at the same time. He couldn't eat until he knew what Octavia was holding onto.

"Sorry about what happened," she said. "Van's a little intense."

"What about Julia?"

Octavia got a pained look on her face. "Chuck, how are you getting along?"

"What?"

"You and your brother."

"Why are you asking—"

"You still teaching at that school?"

"What aren't you telling me?"

She looked at the sky. "Chuck, I'm a journalist. I'm supposed to report facts. I have no facts for you."

"Opinion then?"

"What does it matter what I think? The thing is you and Julia were together, and now you move on."

"I don't need a Dr. Phil moment. Tell me what you think, and tell me now."

"That's just it," she said. "I don't know. I only saw him once."

"Who?"

"Chuck—"

"Tell me!"

"She was seeing someone!"

The force of the words cut the air, leaving a momentary silence in its wake. Chuck took in a deep breath. "What do you mean *seeing?*"

"You know what I mean," Octavia said. "Why'd you have to ask me, Chuck?"

He had no answer. His insides were tearing a jagged line from heart to throat. The bile-taste of betrayal burned in him. Never had he suspected anything like that. Not from Julia.

He had never lied to her, not once. He'd been many things—difficult, distant, withholding. But he had never deceived. He thought that was at least one thing he and Julia had in common at the end. But what if it wasn't?

Octavia's words came from a distance. "Chuck, I didn't want to tell you. Ever. Why couldn't you just leave it the way it was?"

He took Octavia by the shoulders. "Tell me what you know."

"Let go," she said.

"Please."

Octavia shook out of his grasp. "Like I said, I only saw him once. He was kind of a big guy, long hair, shoulder length. I didn't see his face. I saw his back. He wore a black vest with a big sun on it."

"A sun?"

"Big yellow sun. And Julia got on the back of his motorcycle. It was a Harley. I know that sound. When I casually asked her about it the next day, she told me it was nothing, just an old friend."

"How do you know she was *seeing him?*"

"I wish you hadn't come here."

"Just tell me!" His mind was playing tricks on him now, a face of Julia was laughing in a distant corner of his brain, his own face next to it, melting like candle wax under a flame.

"Chuck, come on, I—"

"You're no friend of mine."

"That hurts, Chuck."

"What about me? You think this is cotton candy?"

"All right," she said quietly, looking at the ground. "I don't have anything else to tell you but that, and when I asked her about it she got a look on her face, and there are just some things one woman knows about another woman, that's all. She was telling me to leave it alone and I did."

Chuck ran his fingers through his hair, hard, like a kid digging for sand crabs at the beach. "Did Julia leave any notes? Any computer files?"

"I think you got all that. You still have them?"

"Whatever I had is now toast."

"What?"

"My house burned down."

"Oh, Chuck . . ."

"Octavia, will you try to think? Think who might know who this guy was? Maybe some other staff writers or something?"

"I can ask around if you want me to."

"I want you to. Please."

She looked at him a long time then, her brown eyes at once sympathetic and foreign. Then she put her arms around his neck and rested hear head on his shoulder. "Chuck, why'd it have to happen?"

27

"He does not act as we did," Steven Kovak said. "He does not think things through."

"It's America," Zepkic said. "It corrupts everything, but nothing so much as clear thinking. Do you know this is not taught even in the universities?"

The two men sat on a bench near the waterfall at Disney's California Adventure. The sound of these waters always comforted Kovak. It reminded him of some of his happiest days, as a boy with his father at the Sopotnica falls in Serbia.

It also masked talk should anyone want to listen in on his conversations.

Kovak said, "I pray on my knees each day, but I find no peace where my son is concerned."

"What is it they say here? *Kids today.*"

Kovak was glad he had one friend in whom to confide. He could tell Zepkic anything. They had killed men, women, and children together, and such bonds were not lightly broken.

Zepkic was very much like the bear-shaped rock that overlooked them — strong, dependable.

"I was in the shop the other day," Zepkic said. "A young girl walked in. She was a pretty thing. If I had been twenty-one and living in Vienna, I would have asked her to go to the opera with me. I would have spent all my wages to buy her flowers and a bottle of champagne and for the tickets to the opera. That was how pretty she was. But when she opened her mouth, the worst sound came out. A high pitched whine, a nasal abomination, and every other word from her was *like.* 'Like, do you have any, like, old vinyl records? My boyfriend like, likes them.' This is the youth of America."

Kovak appreciated his friend's desire to lighten the subject. But it would not lighten. "One day soon he will kill recklessly," Kovak said. "That could be the end of everything. Yet I would like him to have what I have built. I will not live forever."

"And who would want to?" Zepkic put his beefy hand on Kovak's shoulder, a hand Kovak had seen choke the life out of an Albanian soldier in half a minute.

"Dragoslav is not ready, and I fear he never will be," said Kovak. "He is like his mother that way. She was headstrong."

"He will have advisors. You are well served by your men. You have chosen wisely."

"I sometimes wish one of them was my blood."

"Vaso?"

Kovak nodded.

"It goes well, the trade?" Zepkic himself was a dealer in antiques, freelance assassins, and false identities. Such as Steven Kovak's.

"I have concerns with distribution," Kovak said. "These American white boys are soft. I prefer them to the blacks and browns and yellows. They are more easily controlled. But they think they are cowboys. Outside of that, the enterprise has a solid foundation. I want to keep myself at the top, for strategy. I need to stay out of distribution and finance. I've got good talent in place. I've read all of Peter Drucker now, and am confident of the long term. The only thing that could go wrong is internal, some failure or treachery on the inside."

Kovak stopped when he saw a man and woman walking by. The woman was pushing a stroller. The father was holding the hand of a boy of perhaps five years. A Mickey Mouse balloon was tied to the boy's wrist by a ribbon. Kovak recalled the rough hand of his own father, held when he was that little boy's age. His father had taken him to the circus in Budapest. He had paid for that by selling several farming tools.

"You look tired, my friend," Zepkic said.

Kovak shook his head. "What do you think God requires of us?"

"What he has always required."

"And what is that?"

"To survive," Zepkic said. "Now come, let's go have something very sweet to eat."

28

Chuck caught the Metro rapid bus and got back to Woodland Hills in twenty minutes. The bus dumped him just shy of Topanga Canyon Boulevard. He walked to Ralphs. Stan was inside the door and beamed when Chuck came in. He held out one of the ad flyers.

"Good afternoon, sir," Stan said, giggling. "We have fine Mentos today, seventy-nine cents a roll with a Ralphs card."

"Not now, Stan," Chuck said. "When's your break?"

"Oh. Two o'clock. Want to get some chicken here like we used to and —"

"It's almost two now. Take your break."

"I can't, Chuck. I have to do it when —"

"It's fine."

"I'm not allowed, Chuck. I'm on door."

Chuck grabbed the flyers from Stan's hand. Stan jumped back a step. "Hey!"

"I have to talk to you now, Stan."

"Hello, Chuck." It was Mr. Cambry, who had come up

from the side.

"Hi," Chuck said. "Can Stan take his break early?"

"I don't want to," Stan said. "Honest."

"That's all right, Stan," Mr. Cambry said. "Your brother is here. Maybe he needs to talk to you about the fire. How's that going, by the way?"

Chuck shrugged. "No word."

"Stan tells me the police made some trouble for you."

"Oh yeah?" Chuck said. "Stan sure likes to bump his gums, doesn't he?"

Cambry frowned. "Chuck, you don't need—"

"There's no trouble. I'm free as a bird, see?" Chuck spread his arms. "Can I talk to Stan now?"

"Sure, sure. No problem." Cambry walked away, seeming a little miffed. So what? That was a store manager's job, wasn't it?

"I'm going to get in trouble," Stan said.

"No you're not. Come over here and sit." Chuck went to one of the tables near the coffee bar and pulled out two chairs. Stan, a worried look on his face, sat and folded his hands.

"What's the matter, Chuck?" Stan said. "You look like you're mad at me. Did the dirty cops work you over?"

"Listen, Mr. Memory. I need you to start remembering some things."

"Okay. I can do that! Let's do a game."

"Not a game this time. I want you to think about Julia."

"How come?"

"Do you remember her ever talking to somebody on the phone, or going to meet somebody when I wasn't around?"

"I don't think so, Chuck."

"Well think harder."

"You *are* mad at me. That's not fair."

Chuck closed his eyes and worked his jaw a little. "Just

help me out here."

"I'll try, Chuck. Honest."

"Remember back when she left?"

Stan wrinkled his forehead. "You had fights. But it was because of your post traumatic stress disorder, I know it. It's an ongoing reaction to psychological trauma, first diagnosed—"

"I know that, Stan. Think about Julia. Did you ever see her act strange when I wasn't around?"

"What kind of strange?"

"Any kind."

"I don't know," Stan's voice was thinned out, which was how his stress manifested itself.

"Let's keep this real simple," Chuck said. "Did you ever see her with any man, at any time, alone?"

"I saw her with the mailman."

"Anybody else?"

"No, Chuck. I don't think . . . I mean I don't remember that. Chuck, why are you asking me?"

"Did she ever tell you to keep a secret from me?" Chuck realized he was leaning forward, gripping the arms of the chair in both hands.

"Secret?"

"You do know what a secret is, right?"

"Chuck, you're making me nervous."

"Think!"

A sheen of wet formed in Stan's eyes, pooling at the bottom of his lids. Chuck closed his own eyes and took a deep breath. What a slime he was, treating his brother this way.

"Stan, I'm sorry. Really." Chuck let go of the chair arms and leaned back. "Listen, maybe this will help you. I just talked to Octavia Butler, do you remember who she is?"

"Yes. She is a writer for *LAEye* and she was Julia's friend."

"Okay. I saw her just now. She thought Julia might have been seeing someone, another man, who I didn't know about."

"Oh, Chuck!"

"I just need to find out, you understand?"

"Yes I do, Chuck. I hate that! It isn't fair!"

Chuck nodded. "Let's see what we can remember. Octavia said this guy rode a motorcycle and had a vest with a sun on the back. Did you ever see anybody like that around?"

Stan didn't say anything. He was looking at the ground, his brow deeply furrowed.

"Stan?"

Stan put up one finger. "Wait, Chuck. There's motorcycles and a sun."

Chuck sat up straight. "You remember?"

"Yes, Chuck."

"When?"

"In the Yellow Pages."

"What?"

"You remember when you wanted to buy a motorcycle that time, and you looked in the Yellow Pages?"

"No."

"We were sitting at the kitchen table and it was eight-thirty-three at night. And you opened it up and then you looked inside and I saw it. There was a sun and motorcycles. A picture."

"A Yellow Pages ad?"

"I think so, Chuck."

"Where's a Yellow Pages around here?"

"There's a pay phone outside the other door. The phone number on it is 818-883—"

"Wait here." Chuck stood.

"What about lunch?"

Chuck took out his wallet. He had a ten dollar bill in it. He tossed it on the table in front of Stan. "Get whatever chicken this'll buy."

Chuck went out the automatic door at the west end of the store. The phone booth had a hanging Yellow Pages. He leafed through it. The *Motorcycle* section had big ads for Barger Harley and Kolbe Honda. Smaller ads for . . . there it was. Sun Cycles in Tarzana. Complete with sun logo.

He told Stan to eat the chicken himself, save the rest, and went to the street to catch the bus to Tarzana. His car was still parked outside Wendy Tower's apartment. He would pick it up later.

This couldn't wait.

29

Sandy was wary of her Detective CO, Lt. Sean Brady. He was, on the surface, even-tempered and fair. Scratch a little below that, though, and you found the harder crust of the old boys' network. Which meant he wasn't going to go out on any low hanging limbs for her. Not that she expected him to.

She didn't expect anything from the department anymore.

"Have a seat," Brady said when Sandy entered his office, at his request. He was a shade over fifty, in good shape. Pumped iron three times a week before coming in. He had a salt-and-pepper mustache trimmed short to go with his closely mown hair.

"So how are things progressing on the Grant Nunn killing?" he asked.

"Working it." Sandy dutifully plopped in a chair and looked at the wall behind him. Framed photos there, including one of Brady with the mayor, who was flashing his legendary pearlies like some Miss California all aflutter about world peace.

Brady said, "There a connection with this guy Samson?"

"There may be," Sandy said.

"He was dinged on a drug charge, yes?"

"Felony manufacture, attempt."

"And you're going down to the courthouse and questioning him?"

"There a problem?"

"I don't want there to be."

"Doesn't have to be," Sandy said. She was not going to be pushed, those days were over. Come whatever hassle they wanted to shove her way.

"You're making inquiries into something that happened outside our jurisdiction."

Sandy said nothing, tried to read his eyes.

"I got a call from the Kern County Sheriff," Brady said. "You're pulling records on a DUI in Beaman?"

"Yes."

"Pretty far afield."

"I'm trying to make a connection. It wasn't just a DUI. It was a hit-and-run, and killed Charles Samson's wife."

Brady's face remained impassive. "I don't see anything that connects that to the Nunn killing, except that Samson talked to Nunn and just happens to have a wife who got killed."

"If I could just follow this through a little bit, maybe I can give you—"

"I don't want you crossing over. Samson's a defendant in a drug case. That's none of your concern. Or an old accident out of Kern County, either. I want you to stick to your knitting right here." Brady paused, then quickly added, "No sexist comment intended, as you know."

Ah, there it was. A little good-old-boy needle, framed so innocently.

Sandy stood. "How much flexibility do I have?"

119

"Stay focused."

"I need to tie up some loose ends."

"You don't have a lot of leeway." Brady stood now, walked out from behind his desk. "You hearing me?"

Oh yes, very loud and very clear. He was giving her the administrative stare down. She'd seen enough of that in her time. She looked right past him.

And saw another photo on the wall. This one of Brady with some other luminary or—

She recognized the man the in photo, but couldn't place him.

"Anything else?" Brady said.

"What? No. That's it."

She left his office, the man in the photo playing with her mind. She almost bumped into a young clerk, the skinny kid from UCLA, who made a move like a matador to avoid her.

And then it came to her.

The man in the picture with Brady was a younger version of the guy who ran Chuck Samson's school. What was the name again?

Hunt. Raymond Hunt.

30

Sun Cycles was a tight little shop on the south side of Ventura Boulevard. A large glass window showed off the array of motorcycles inside. Various makes, lined up like a macho dream of highway freedom, bar fights and chicks. Chuck went in and glanced at the bikes. Sunlight reflected off chrome, and the smell of new rubber and leather mixed with the slight scent of grease.

He leaned on a black and silver Street Bob, waiting for someone to come out on the floor.

"You picked a nice one." Chuck turned and saw a short, thick-chested guy in a black tee with a sun logo.

"She's got a twin cam 96" engine," Black Tee said. "Chrome, staggered shorty exhaust. Classic style. You could see James Dean on this. And here's the thing. I can get it to you for under fifteen, if you can believe it."

Chuck said, "If I ever decide to take my life in my hands, I'll come see you."

"You don't ride?"

"I'm actually looking for somebody."

Black Tee, who was maybe thirty, squinted at him. "Yeah? Who?"

"A guy who wears one of your vests, with the logo on the back."

Black Tee laughed. "There's only about five hundred of those guys."

"He has, or had, shoulder-length hair."

"That really narrows it down."

"Any idea?"

"Sorry."

"You the manager?"

The guy shook his head.

"Maybe I could talk to the head guy," Chuck said.

"You know, maybe you should call the store later, we got --"

"I'm here now."

"We sell bikes here."

Chuck said, "I have to find this guy, okay?"

"Why?" Black Tee said.

"I need to ask him some questions."

"I really wish I could help."

"Do you?"

"Listen, if you're—"

The front doors opened and a couple came in, mid-twenties, decked out in retro rebel. Blue jeans with uprolled cuffs, black tennis shoes, white tee shirts.

"Sorry you came for nothing," Black Tee said, then switched gears back to a tight smile and made for the couple. "How you doin' today?"

Chuck went to the counter and looked over, through an open door on the side. A messy office space, no one inside.

He looked back and saw Black Tee engaging the couple,

but also giving him the corner of his eye.

There was another door on the other side of the counter. It said *Employees Only.* Chuck hired himself on the spot and went through. He heard a faint "Hey!" from Black Tee that he cut off by closing the door and leaning against it.

He was in the garage area. A couple of denim-clad workers were tinkering on motorcycles. He felt the pressure of someone trying to open the door. The voice of Black Tee blurted through. The tinkering workers looked up.

Chuck scanned the area looking for someone in authority.

Black Tee shoved against the door again.

At which point a man with a thick mane of gray hair, carrying a clipboard, appeared from Chuck's right, where the garage opened up to the asphalt driveway.

Chuck waited for another shove then stepped away from the door. A second later Black Tee burst through and almost went sprawling.

"What the hell is this?" the clipboard man said.

Black Tee looked around like a cat who'd fallen in the toilet. "He just walked in here," Tee said, as if defending his watch.

"Who are you?" Clipboard said. He was about six-two. He wore a black, long-sleeved shirt with the same sun logo on the left side.

Chuck said, "I want to talk to the boss."

"What about?"

"Police matter," Chuck said.

"You a cop?"

"I'm working with the police," Chuck said. "Can I have a minute of your time?"

"No way," Black Tee said.

Clipboard said, "Go on back inside, Chip. I'll take it."

Black Tee looked like he wanted to rip Chuck some new nostrils. He made sure Chuck saw his face, then stormed back through the *Employees Only* door.

"Okay," Clipboard said. "Give it to me now and make it fast."

"My name's Chuck Samson. Yours?"

"Nevermind me."

"Fine. I'm looking for a guy who was seen wearing a leather vest with your logo on it."

"Seen?"

"By a witness."

"What's this police matter you're talking about?"

Chuck looked at him intently, decided he was the kind of guy you should just be honest with. He wasn't going to be manipulated or intimidated or faked out.

"My wife was killed last year. She was seen with this guy, he had long brown hair, rode a Harley, had the vest. That's all I know. My wife was blonde, wore her hair short, about five-eight. She was a writer for *LAEye*."

"You saying this guy might have killed her?"

"No, not saying that. Who killed her was a drunk driver. But this guy might have been with her."

"Sleeping with her?"

The words brought Chuck up short, a jab to the ribs.

Clipboard shook his head. "Don't know anybody like that."

"You seem pretty sure."

"I am."

"You don't want to think about it?"

"Nope."

"You're a real sport."

"Now you can leave."

Chuck didn't move.

"Or I can call a real cop," Clipboard said. "Your choice."

31

As he walked down the alley behind Sun Cycles, Chuck heard a guy say, "Wait."

It was one of the tinkerers from the shop. A lanky Latino, late twenties. He had a thin mustache that looked like it was struggling to put on weight. He said, "Keep walking."

Like he was afraid he'd be heard or seen from the shop.

"I think I know who you mean," the guy said.

"Tell me."

"Keep walking, huh?"

After a few hurried steps, Chuck said, "All right, what do you know?"

The guy didn't stop walking. Chuck kept up with him.

The guy said, "You're talking about a guy used to come in a lot. I worked on his bike. '92 FXR. Beautiful machine. Kept up nice."

"What's his name?"

"Easy, *cabrón.* We got to walk more."

"Why?"

"You'll see."

Chuck grabbed the guy's arm. "Just tell me."

The guy yanked his arm away. "Don't touch me, man. You want something, I got it, but you gonna pay for it."

So that was it. "How much?"

"How much you got?"

"Nothing. A couple of bucks."

The guy shook his head. "Not enough."

"Then we have a problem."

"I don't got no problem. I got a solution. Right around this corner there's an ATM. You got a ATM card?"

"How much you talking?"

"I think you want this name pretty bad."

"How much?"

"Six hundred."

"You're crazy."

"I know. That's what they call me."

"Okay, Crazy. You think I'm just gonna to give you six hundred dollars?"

Crazy smiled. "I think so."

"Make it a hundred," Chuck said.

"Forget it."

"How do I know it's worth more?"

"Oh, you gonna want to know. It's good stuff."

Chuck's stomach clenched.

"I'll give you a hundred. If it sounds good I'll give you another hundred."

"Have a nice day." Crazy started back toward the shop.

"Okay," Chuck said, knowing he was had. "I'll give you two hundred for it."

"Three," Crazy said.

"If it's worth it I'll give you another hundred."

Crazy shrugged. "Show me," he said.

Chuck got two hundred from the B of A ATM. After the bills were in Crazy's hands, he motioned Chuck to the bus stop overhang. "Okay, this is how it is. His name is Thompson. That's all I know. I never got his first name. He never talked to me, only to Russell."

"Who's Russell?"

"The boss."

"So Russell was lying to me?"

"Russell is a big fat liar all the time."

"That's not worth another hundred."

Chuck watched as Crazy thought it over. He wasn't that big, maybe street tough, but Chuck was emitting a barely repressed rage. He knew the guy could feel it.

"Okay," Crazy said. "I got one other thing to tell you. But you can't do nothing to me about it, because it's gonna make you mad. You hear what I'm saying?"

"Talk."

"The money."

Chuck hesitated. Then he got another hundred from the machine. He slapped it into the guy's mitt.

"Okay," Crazy said. "I only seen 'em together one time, right? Out back of the shop, okay? They were, you know, goin' at it."

The sound of blaring horn skewered the moment, went into Chuck's ears like a hot poker. He felt feverish

"What exactly do you mean?" Chuck said.

"You know."

"Spell it out."

"Makin' out, man. Tongues and everything. Get a room, I'm thinking."

Chuck closed his eyes, fought to keep steady on his feet.

"Easy, man," Crazy said.

"Get the hell away from me."

Crazy put his hands up and backed up a step. "Okay, okay. I know how you feel, man."

Chuck wanted to make him eat the money and then find out how he felt about it.

And he stood there alone for five minutes, maybe ten. Two, or was it three, buses stopped, loaded, unloaded. An ambulance went by, sirens blaring, Chuck wanting to be standing in front of it, then thinking what did it matter anyway? You live, you die, sometimes you die before your time, like Julia. Lying, cheating, you can do that too in life, can't you? Do it to someone who put his pumping heart in your hands every night, letting you hold it, the only one, the only one . . . and there won't be another like you, Julia, I won't let the beating heart go anywhere close to that you know, thank you, you lying, lying, lying . . .

32

Steven Kovak, born Svetozar Zivkcovic, looked at his son and almost wept. For his son, yes—for what he was not and never would be. But also for himself, for how he had failed to forge a will of iron in his only child.

But while there was time left, he would not give up. He had never given up on anything. If he could only get that through to his boy, his work on earth would be truly done and he would have peace with God.

They were on the balcony overlooking the dark Pacific. The stars were bright, the sky clear. Kovak enjoyed his pipe, but his son still looked lost in the muck of his own confusion.

"This country is the problem," Kovak said finally. "It always has been. Oh, maybe not at the very beginning. Or during World War II. But after that the country became meek, womanish. It has allowed women to take away its martial spirit, its grit. They raise girls, not boys or men. This is why their time of greatness is gone. It will not survive. And their weakness is our advantage."

His son's head moved slightly downward, as if listening through one ear.

"We must never forget who we are," Kovak said. "We come from a proud race. Deep inside us we have flowing the memory of the Turks slaughtering us in Kosovo. That was June 15, 1389. The day hell came. The day you must never forget. We learned what subjugation was then. The Turks, the Mohammedans, took our children and conscripted them. Their blood tax bled us dry. Their abuses of our women taught us to hate on a scale never before known. History is what we must remember, son, because that is what keeps us strong."

His pipe was cold. Pausing to relight it, he looked upon his son and loved him.

"I have never told you this," Kovak said. "Now is the time."

Dragoslav's head came up slightly.

"It was August, 1968," Kovak continued. "I lived with my mother and father, your grandparents, on a farm in Kosovo. We had fields of wheat and cattle. Then the Soviets invaded Czechoslovakia and that scared Tito, Prime Minister of Yugoslavia. He was not Serb. He was Croat-Slovene, and to keep power he took the side of Albanians in Kosovo. Who then began to drive all Serbs out. One day they came to our farm. They told us to get out or die. My father refused. They took my mother and cut her open in front of us. Then they hanged my father. I pretended to scream and cry, but by then I knew I would never feel such emotions. The will to power and life flooded into me, and I surprised one Albanian with a rifle by jamming a stick into his eye. I took his rifle and killed two men before escaping on foot. I was three days without food. I thought I was going to die. Perhaps I did die, for I saw a great light just before I woke up in the bed of a Serb woman who found me, and nursed me back to health."

He noted Dragoslav was listening intently. This was the time he had been hoping for.

"I was in an orphanage, but ran away a year later and joined the Army. It trained me well. I made a name for myself. I knew God was with me. The great light. I knew I had a destiny. In the early 1990s I came to the attention of Radovan Karadzic."

"Karadzic?" Dragoslav said.

"The very same."

"You never told me."

"The time was never right. It is right now. The world calls him a war criminal. They call what we did ethnic cleansing. That is no crime, not in the eyes of God. You need only read the Jews' book to know that. I am proud of what we did, and you need to feel that pride, too."

"I want to, Father. I do."

Kovak put his pipe down on the small table between them, and put his hand on his son's head. "Of course you do," he said. "Why then do you allow your emotions to take you away?"

"It's the alcohol," Dragoslav said.

"Yes," Kovak said. "In that you speak the truth."

"I want to stop," Dragoslav said. "I can."

Kovak took a handful of Dragoslav's thick hair. He gently pulled his son's head toward him and kissed his cheek.

Someone knocked on the French doors. Kovak saw it was Simo, indicating something in his hand.

He stood and opened the doors, went inside.

"Further information on the teacher Samson," Simo said, handing Kovak a folder.

"Ah. Dragoslav, come inside." He waited until his son joined them. "This concerns you as well."

"I'm sorry, Father, I—"

"No, say nothing. To apologize is to be weak." Kovak opened the folder.

His breath left him.

"What is it?" Dragoslav said.

"The hand of God," Kovak said.

33

Saturday, after a so-so night in the motel, Chuck got Stan off to work and walked to Wendy Tower's apartment building to get his car. She was waiting for him outside, leaning on the dented hood, reading a book. Chuck saw the cover when he got to her. *Savage Beauty.*

"Serial killer novel?" he asked.

She looked up, smiled. "Biography of Edna St. Vincent Millay. You know, *I burn my candle at both ends?*"

Chuck said nothing. Stared. Stared at the picture of the poet on the cover of the book. She stared right back at him.

"What's the matter?"

Chuck wanted to say something but somebody'd stuck a pitchfork in his brain. He put the heel of his palm against his forehead.

"Chuck, what is it?" Wendy said.

Still he could not speak.

"Sit down," Wendy said, taking his arm and practically shoving him onto the hood of his car. She sat next to him. "You

134

want to come inside?" she said. "You want me to—"

"I'm all right."

"You don't look all right."

"I am. I just . . . thanks for watching the car."

"Sure, but—"

"I'm fine."

"Then I'd love to," Wendy said.

Chuck shook his head like a boxer getting off the canvas. "What?"

"I could use a drive. And so could you."

"I have to go someplace," he said.

"That's the very point of a drive," she said.

"You don't want to be seen in this junker."

"Live dangerously, I always say."

"I mean, all the way to Beaman. It'll be—"

"Great. I've never been."

"Wendy—"

"I think you could use the company. Me too." She stood up from the car and he noticed how nicely her UCLA sweatshirt fit her form. How casual her beauty was. Not savage like the book said. But real in a way he hadn't appreciated before. Or, to be honest with himself, just hadn't been able to notice.

"What I'm doing," he said, "wouldn't be of interest."

"Try me," she said.

Maybe he should. Maybe he needed another set of eyes and ears to help him make sense of things.

More, maybe he needed someone to trust.

"All right," he said.

He got onto the 101 freeway at Tampa. As he merged into traffic, Wendy said, "How's your brother holding up?"

"A little restless at night," Chuck said. "But getting used to fine motel living."

135

"And how are *you* doing?"

"Now that's a complex question."

"So, how?"

"Maybe you should ask me what the capital of North Dakota is instead."

"I'm asking about you."

"Bismark," Chuck said.

"Now that we've got that out of the way . . ."

"All right," Chuck said. "You don't know that much about me."

"I know you're a good teacher," she said. "I know you were a chaplain in the military. I know that fits you somehow."

"Why?"

"Just a feeling. How'd you get into that line?"

Chuck wanted to give her a short answer, a quip, but found himself saying, "I went to seminary because I wanted to know if there were any answers to the crap."

Wendy said nothing but Chuck felt the nothing as if it was a sharp stick to the side.

"I had a friend, we were in a band in high school. Great athlete, too. He could've been the starting quarterback on the team, but he liked music more. So the football guys are getting injured and knee surgeries and all that, but Guy is playing the drums and we're getting high together and laughing all the time. And then one day he's eating a burger at Tommy's over on Topanga when a couple of gangbangers come in, and one of them has a baseball bat. They're looking for somebody, it was a drug thing gone bad, they thought it was Guy. So they . . ."

Chuck fought back the tears, fought them hard, wasn't going to let them out in front of Wendy, in front of anybody, the VA doctor could go suck an egg.

Wendy said. "I'm sorry I—"

"No," Chuck said. "They batted him around and he's a quadriplegic now. He can't play guitar anymore. He lives with his mother in North Carolina. Last time I saw him, before he moved, he begged me to help him die."

He paused, blinked his eyes hard.

"A couple years go by," Chuck said. "I get a letter from Guy's mom talking about Guy finding peace, God and all that. I thought, sure. Right. Good for him. My mom used to send me and my brother to Sunday School when we were kids. But that's about all the God stuff I had. Then I get another letter from Guy's mom. This time it's because Guy is dead."

He wiped his eyes with the back of his hand. Finish this thing, get it over with.

"I was messed up. High all the time. And really, really pissed off at God. But I realized I didn't know that much about who I was supposed to be pissed off at. So I went to seminary. You know why? Revenge."

He glanced over and saw Wendy's confused look.

"That's right. I wanted to find out enough to know how to be mad at God and let him know it. Then 9/11 happened. It took me a long time to wrap my head around that. Should I be angrier? But I found I wasn't. I found myself . . . wanting . . . connection. They had this chaplaincy program at the seminary. I went and signed up for it. It was make or break. If I didn't get some kind of faith through it, I was going to leave. But I got closer, and I graduated, and they made me a chaplain and I went over."

"Afghanistan, right?"

Chuck nodded. "My first sight of the place, it was like a part of the world where all the color had been sucked out, leaving nothing but browns. God forsaken."

He paused, gathering the memory, which was one he

could still access. "I was in Kabul for a week. I went to visit the children's hospital. I was told they needed help. I was met by the director of the whole hospital, a doctor named Yousufzai. He wanted me to see. He said, 'Please tell the Americans.' What I saw were children with broken bones and wounds being held by their parents on plastic chairs, waiting for hours to see someone. And babies lying side by side on warming tables, sometimes all day, crying, as their mothers waited for injections that might or might not help. A place too cold in winter and too hot in summer, with cracked walls and windows. They've been promised funds for upgrading the hospital for years, but nothing's come in. They are understaffed and tired, and can't do anything. That was my first look at the war's toll. It was on the children, not the soldiers."

Silence for a moment. Then Wendy said, "You were . . . your brother said you were . . ."

"I got captured. Worked over. Somebody sliced my neck. I got rescued. Everything about that's in bits and pieces."

"I'm sorry. You don't have to talk about it."

"This you need to know. I'm a case. A head case. A real head case for the VA until they stopped seeing me."

"Stopped?"

"I'm pretty rare anyway. Maybe they just don't know what to do with me. My form of PTSD has a past and a future element. As far as the past, I have what's called abrasive amnesia. It means there are random places where my memory was sort of wiped out, rubbed down. I can remember some things and not others. Some things I can sort of remember, but it's fuzzy. And I've got foreshortened future. It means I think the future is just this dark thing, no point to it. That's why a lot of the guys commit suicide."

There it was. The S word was out. And now a question

hung in the air between them.

"I guess I'm just too stubborn to kill myself," Chuck said.

"I don't think that's it," Wendy said.

Chuck snapped her a look, like, *How could you know anything about it?*

"It's because of your brother," she said. "You care about your brother."

She was probably right about that.

Wendy said, "Why did the VA stop seeing you?"

"A problem with the paperwork," Chuck said. "It happens more times than you care to know, Ms. Taxpayer. My buddy, Royce, has been knocking heads with them, for me and a bunch of other guys. It's them I'm burned about. I mean, I have my arms and legs. A lot of them don't."

They rode in silence for a time.

"One more thing," Chuck said finally. "You know about my wife, about Julia?"

"Only that she died," Wendy said.

"I got some news. A little kicker, if you want to call it that." He paused, feeling his stomach roil as if it was filling with noxious fumes. This was more difficult than he thought, but he pushed himself to say, "I think she was having an affair."

Wendy said nothing. And he wondered if he should have brought it up at all. What business did he have dumping this on her? But she asked for it, and it needed to be out, all of it, between them, once and for all.

"I think it was with some biker named Thompson," Chuck said. "That's about all I know. I guess I shouldn't be surprised."

"Why?"

"Maybe it was my fault." He took in deep breath. "Maybe I hid in my PTSD. Maybe I drove her away. Maybe I screwed it all up."

He looked at her. "And one more thing."

She waited.

"That book you're reading. Edna St. Vincent Millay. My wife had one poetry book. She read it a lot. It was a collection. By Millay."

"Oh," Wendy said, looking at the floorboard.

"So yeah, it hit me back there."

"I'm sorry," she said.

"Not your fault. But now you know. It's still hard."

She nodded.

"Maybe you shouldn't have come along."

"Wish I hadn't?"

He didn't know what he wished, or would wish, or would want in the next ten minutes. "No," he said.

34

"Good morning," Stan said to the smiling woman who came through the door.

She took a flyer and thanked him.

A nice old man with a walker with green tennis balls on it came in next, and Stan held out a flyer but the man waved it off. He didn't seem in the mood to talk to anybody. Stan said, "Have a nice day," and the old man grunted. Sometimes that's all people did, and now he knew it wasn't because of him, because he had done something wrong. It was because people could be having all sorts of bad things going on, maybe even their house had burned down.

He hoped not. Having a house burn down was a very sad thing, because then you had to live in a motel.

The next person to come in was Mr. Hunt.

"Hello Stan."

"Hi Mr. Hunt!"

Stan liked Mr. Hunt a lot. He was a good strong man who gave Chuck a job at his school when Chuck really needed it. He was always very nice, too.

"You're looking sharp as ever," Mr. Hunt said.

"Guess what? We have cling peaches on special today, and I know you like peaches."

"How did you know that?"

Stan smiled. "Remember that day when Chuck brought me to the school, before he started, and you gave us a tour of the school, and we went into the cafeteria and there was a can of Del Monte peaches on the counter? And you tapped it once on the top of the can and said, 'Love those peaches.' Remember?"

Mr. Hunt's mouth hung open just a little bit. "You are amazing, Stan. Just amazing. I think you should go on *Jeopardy.*"

"Oh no," Stan said. "I'd be too nervous. Alex Trebek makes me very nervous."

"All right, son. No *Jeopardy.* So how are you making out in your new digs?"

"You mean the motel?"

"Right. Which one is it again?"

"The Outside Inn, right across the street."

"You have a nice room there?"

"It's okay. Number 207."

"Only okay?"

"I don't want to live in a motel. I want to live in a house."

"Of course you do," Mr. Hunt said, then his eyes sort of drifted to another part of the store.

Stan thought he might be confused about something.

"Is everything all right, Mr. Hunt?"

"What?"

"Do you need something?"

"Oh yes, sure, that's why I came in. I'm looking for the salad dressing. I wanted some Newman's Own Italian."

"Newman's Own is good. It's named for Paul Newman, who was the star of many movies, including *The Hustler* and *Cool Hand Luke* and *The Sting.*"

"He's the one all right."

"Aisle six, Mr. Hunt. That's where you'll find it."

"Aisle six, huh? Well, thanks Stan, thanks a lot. Nice to see you. Remember, if you need anything, anything at all, you call on me. You and your brother. You can call on me anytime."

That was nice. That was a very nice thing. To be able to call on Mr. Hunt. Nice people are what make the world a good place, Stan thought. Mean people suck.

35

The stench of late morning beer was heavy in The Tall T. Chuck felt a momentary pang of regret for bringing Wendy in with him. This wasn't the place for an outdoor person. It was old school, functional only, a place for people to come, sit, and drink, and little else. Dark inside, with haphazard light-boxes on the walls advertising various beers, Coors having the most prominent position behind the bar, over the booze rack.

Two old guys sat at the far end of the bar, engrossed in a discussion. The bartender, a wiry guy in a blue tee-shirt, made his way down to Chuck and Wendy.

"Hi folks," he said. He had a small hoop earring in his left ear, and a genial smile under cautious eyes. "Get you something?"

"My name's Chuck Samson, and I'm here on business. I'll skip the beer and just leave a tip, in exchange for some information."

The bartender did a little hitch with his face, shifting into doubt territory.

"Let me be real clear with you," Chuck said. "I'm not a cop or a criminal. I'm a school teacher and I have a colleague with me who will vouch for that. I'm the guy whose wife was killed up here last March, by the drunk driving the truck. You remember that?"

The bartender shook his head.

"The guy was actually in here that night. A bartender named Renner was working. Know him?"

The bartender tapped his upper teeth on his bottom lip.

"So when does he come in?" Chuck said.

"I just serve drinks."

"Do you know?"

"That's all I do, okay?"

Chuck didn't realize he'd taken a step forward until he felt Wendy's hand on his arm.

Now what? Toss a few chairs? Break the mirror like in an old Western? Who was he kidding, playing PI up here in this stupid town where the ghosts were all in his head?

But ghosts there were. Julia had been here. And for reasons he didn't yet know.

"You say that was your wife?" a voice said.

Chuck whipped around and saw one of the old guys, now on his feet, heading toward him.

"Yeah," Chuck said, glancing at the bartender, who was full on biting his lips now, and didn't look pleased. The bartender took out a cell phone and walked to the other end of the bar.

The old guy was slim and balding, with the upholstered skin of the inveterate smoker. He motioned for Chuck to follow him outside.

In the light of day and scent of pines, the old guy pulled out a mashed pack of Camels, drew one out with his mouth and lit up with a Bic. "I knew the guy what hit her," he said after his first cloud of smoke issued through his nose. "Used to come in here alla time."

"You know about the accident?"

"Everybody knows about that. Bad thing that happened. Sorry about your wife."

Chuck nodded.

"My name's Ezra, like Ezra Pound, the poet?"

"Sure."

"And who's your friend?"

"I'd rather keep her name out of it."

Ezra's fluffy white eyebrows went up. "Sounds kind of mysterious." He took a long drag on his unfiltered cig. The acrid smoke of it wrestled with the pine tree scent, and won.

"I want to know everything you know," Chuck said. "I want to know what happened."

"I didn't see it, of course."

"Did you see Ed Hillary the night it happened?"

Ezra nodded. "He was here all right."

"Did you talk to him?"

"I did, but I can't remember all we talked about. One night kind of melts into another, if you know what I mean. I used to be an electrician, but that's not a job you want to have if you like to drink. It can be a—"

"Think," Chuck said. "What did Hillary seem like? Was he drunk?"

"Nah, Hillary wasn't a real heavy drinker. He nursed. Usually a beer or two, and then he went home. I was kind of surprised when they said he was so loaded he hit a gal. He must've got a bottle or something after, cause he wasn't reelin' when he left here."

"The bartender that night was named Renner."

146

"Biff Renner, sure."

"He still work here?"

"Yeah, comes in the afternoon. You won't get much out of him. He told the police same thing I told you. Hillary had a couple beers and left, and that's the last we knew."

Chuck looked at Wendy, feeling like he was coming up quickly to a dead end. She seemed to pick that up.

To Ezra she said, "Did you ever see the woman who was hit?"

Ezra shook his head. "Not that I can remember."

"She might have been with a guy on a motorcycle," Wendy said.

"We get a lot of those around here." He took another deep drag on his Camel.

"Hey!" A short man with olive skin, a smooth pate and bushy black mustache was coming out of the front of the Tall T. "You need to get going." He waved his arms like he was shooing away flies.

"They're just friendly folks," Ezra said to the man.

"I don't care," the mustache said. "You're trespassing. Go on."

"This is Bashmajian," Ezra said. "Owns the place."

Chuck said, "My wife was the one who —"

"I know all about it," Bashmajian said. "You looking for a lawsuit or something?"

"No."

"It don't matter. You don't drink, you're trespassing. You want maybe a sheriff to talk to?"

"If that's all that's bothering you, I'll buy a drink."

Bashmajian shook his head. "I got a right to refuse service. And that's what I'm doing. So go."

"What's your problem?" Wendy said.

"And take your girlfriend with you!"

"She asked you a question," Chuck said.

"Get going."

Chuck stuck his face in Bashmajian's. "You hard of hearing? Somebody asks a question—"

The bartender shot out to join them.

He was holding a shotgun in one hand.

Chuck looked at him. "You have got to be kidding me."

Bashmajian backed away from Chuck. "Now you go."

This was crazy. This was *Twilight Zone* crazy, paranoid central. Little town and a bartender with a gun? On *him?*

Wendy pulled at Chuck's arm. "Let's go," she said.

Chuck didn't move. No way the guy would shoot him over this. No way . . . unless there was more, a lot more.

Maybe he could make a quick move, grab the slimy little owner and use him as a shield.

Sure, and his real name was Jet Li.

Wendy pulled on his arm again.

He let her. He started walking toward his car.

"Come back anytime," Ezra said.

You can bet on it, old man.

36

After sixteen years on the force, six as a detective, Sandy Epperson knew what made a good homicide cop. Three unalterable things.

First, the determination of a pit bull.

Second, attention to details, especially the little ones.

And third, the ability to get complete strangers to tell you their deepest, darkest secrets.

It was about those three things, and those three things only. Not the posturing you see from TV and movie cops. And it drove her crazy every time one of these slapped cuffs on a suspect and immediately Mirandized them. You never did that. You want the arrestees to run off at the mouth, and it's all admissible if you don't question them. Give them the standard warning up front, and they could clam.

The real cop world was so much different, but it all came down to that trio of attributes.

Sandy Epperson knew she had them, and that's why she knew she was going to keep on the trail, wherever the evidence

149

in the Nunn case led.

Even if it led her to Kern County.

At her desk in the squad room, she opened up the murder book, the blue binder system she still favored. The goal was to get everything in one of the smaller binders. This one, though, was the larger size. Because this case wasn't going to be open and shut.

She flipped past the cover page to the chronolog, the time-line record of her and Mooney's activity on the case. She always put her notes in contemporaneously, unlike some of the younger detectives who waited until they got back to the station. Too many of them would get fuzzy on what they'd done, and have to reconstruct by memory.

Mooney was like that, only he kept little notes on his Blackberry. Sandy had to remind him he better print out and keep all those notes, as they were discoverable by the defense in a criminal case. The last thing you wanted in court was some lawyer claiming the police destroyed electronic jottings, without backup.

Sandy turned next to the link chart. The computer analysis company the LAPD contracted with had just provided the report that linked Grant Nunn's cell phone to recently called numbers. With a search warrant, easy enough to secure in a murder case like this, Sandy would be able to get the phone company records for each of those numbers. Then it would be a matter of shoe leather. Knocking on doors and finding out what connection these people had with Nunn.

That was another thing about real detective work. Some of the new school kids thought you could sit at a computer all day and solve cases. No way. You had to get face time. And you had to get it fast. People were much more likely to talk when the killing was "hot." The longer you waited, the more memories got fuzzy, naturally or for some other reason, like self-protection.

Yet somehow Sandy was convinced the real connection in this homicide was not going to be there, in that web of numbers.

The details of the killing kept moving around in her mind, begging to be brought into some sort of pattern. She was doing her best, but doubts kept blowing the details around like dry leaves.

For one thing, the time and location was odd. Nunn was killed sometime between 7 and 7:30 a.m. in the back of the Target parking lot. There were actually two large lots, one on either side of Target. On the north side, the lot stretched all the way to Vanowen Street, and was utilized by those going to the 24 Hour Fitness next to the store.

South of Target was another lot that went to Victory Boulevard. The west end of the lot backed up against a cinderblock wall and oleander plants, and was well removed from store fronts and backs.

It was here by the wall that Nunn was found in his car dead of a single gunshot wound to the back of the head.

What was he doing sitting in this location at that time? And after calling 911 and supposedly being on his way to work?

Something, or someone, had convinced him to drive there. And park.

To get popped?

Which would bring it right back to something connected with Charles Samson and the guy who pulled the knife on him.

Sandy scribbled a note on the legal pad she'd laid out next to the murder book. At the top she wrote *Samson* then drew a two inch line and wrote *guy w/knife,* connecting them. She drew a small line sideways from the knife guy and wrote *black Escalade, no plate.*

In the middle of the page she wrote *Nunn* without any

connecting lines.

On the left side of the sheet, in the margin, she wrote down times with notations.

6:30 – ?

6:35 – approximate time of knife incident

6:42 – Nunn's 911 call; Samson leaves scene in car (arrives Ralphs approx. 10 minutes later)

7:00 – Nunn drives to Target

7:15 – approximate time Nunn shot

7:30 – ?

4:00 – Samson's house on fire (Samson and brother at work)

The timeline didn't make any sense. The Escalade was gone, Samson was off to drop his brother at Ralphs. Nunn was supposed to be on his way to work. But instead he went the opposite direction, almost immediately after calling 911.

The house fire was a wild card. Sandy drew a line from Chuck's name to a ? she put on the page. From the question mark she drew spokes pointing to these terms: *Samson drugs, landlord, arson/set-up.* From *arson/set-up* she drew a dotted line, indicating weak but possible link, back to *guy w/knife.*

Finally, at the bottom of the page, she wrote the name *Raymond Hunt* and drew a line to Samson's name.

Then she leaned back and looked at the page. It was something she did well. Like at a scene. So many detectives depended on what SID told them, but never bothered to do the most important thing—step back and ask, *What is this scene telling me?*

As she did now.
Until her cell buzzed.

37

Chuck said, "It's Chuck Samson, I'm driving back from Beaman."

"What were you doing up there?" Detective Epperson said.

"I went with a witness, a teacher I work with."

"What is it you want to tell me?"

She sounded guarded but open. Chuck said, "We went into the bar where Ed Hillary was last seen, before the accident. They clearly did not want to talk to me, except an older guy who said Hillary wasn't drunk when he left. Which leaves open that question, doesn't it?"

"Did you get the man's name you spoke to?"

"Ezra. That's all I got. But he's a regular there. The owner of the place chased us off. May be worried about a lawsuit, or he may be worried about something else."

"Like what?"

"I don't know. Hiding something. But I just thought you

should know."

After a short pause, Epperson said, "You're playing detective now, Mr. Samson. I don't think you should do that."

Chuck heard a beep on his phone. Another call coming in.

"I'll call you later," Chuck said. "Can I?"

"Talk to your lawyer first," Epperson said.

Chuck switched the call.

"Yeah?"

"Samson?" It was a man's voice, one Chuck didn't recognize.

"That's right," Chuck said.

"Want some info?"

"Who is this?"

"Let me rephrase. I know you need some information. About your wife. And that guy on the motorcycle."

Chuck tensed, saw Wendy looking at him with concern.

"Interested?" the voice said.

"I want to know who this is."

"Not on the phone, man."

"Where then?"

"You know Lazy J Park in West Hills?"

"No."

"Valley Circle and Ingomar."

"So?"

"Meet me there."

"Forget it. I don't know who you are, and I'm not—"

"Relax, son. It's a wide open park, lots of kids and dogs. Nothing bad's gonna happen."

"Give me a reason."

"You're into something that's going to get you killed, is that enough of a reason? And by the way, it's the same thing that got your wife killed. And come alone. I'll know if you don't."

Chuck tried to swallow. Couldn't.

"Just show up," the voice said. "I'll find you."

"This is nuts. Why can't you just—"

"Three o'clock."

"What if I don't show?"

"You got one chance."

Chuck said nothing.

"I'll give you one more incentive," the man said. "Maybe you want to find out about your wife's criminal record."

Chuck's body cracked with cold lightning. "You're a liar."

"Am I? She was from Davis, right? Of course you know that. Her maiden name was Rankin. Julia Rankin. How'm I doing?"

The connection dropped.

"What is it?" Wendy said.

For a moment Chuck couldn't say anything. The *Twilight Zone* episode was continuing. It wasn't Wendy Tower in the car with him, it was Rod Serling.

"I'll drop you off at your apartment," Chuck said.

"Something's very wrong," Wendy said.

"You're a good teacher," Chuck said.

38

Sandy noted the call from Samson in the chronolog, then flipped to the interview statements section of the murder book. Four patrol officers had canvassed the immediate neighborhood as well as the businesses. No eyewitnesses, though a man from the Target garden department, unloading peat moss from a delivery pallet, said he thought he saw a blue sedan drive slowly by. He took no notice of it, though. He thought the driver was a Caucasian male.

Great.

And another thing. This section of the parking lot had no security cameras set up. Might the killer have known that?

"All work and no drinking," Mooney said from behind her.

"Where've you been?" Sandy said.

"You working the book?"

"No, arts and crafts. I'm thinking of doing a collage with all the body photos."

"Well you may want to add this to the design." Mooney tossed some pages on Sandy's desk. The autopsy report on Grant

Nunn.

She picked it up. "You've read this?"

"It's yadda yadda, cause of death one bullet to the brain," Mooney said. "But there is one thing more."

Mooney pointed to the section marked *External Examination*. "Blunt force trauma," he said. "Back of the head. Somebody knocked him out before he got popped. Maybe it was one of those homeless guys who sleep by the wall."

"Who packs a .38?"

"It's been known."

"That still doesn't explain what Nunn was doing there in the first place," Sandy said. "What if he was hit somewhere else, and then driven there?"

"That makes even less sense," Mooney said. "I've been thinking, what if it was Samson?"

Sandy shook her head.

"No, listen." Mooney slid a chair over. "I've been thinking about it. Samson drove away, right? While Nunn was calling it in."

"Right."

"What if Nunn follows Samson?"

"Why?"

"Thinks something's not right. Samson's route to Woodland Hills takes him by Target."

"And what, Samson shoots Nunn?"

Mooney smiled.

"What possible motive would Samson have for killing Grant Nunn?" Sandy said.

"Hey, what possible reason would Samson have for cooking meth? But he was."

"But," Sandy said, "Samson wasn't alone. He had his brother with him."

"Maybe we should have a talk with the brother," Mooney said. "Alone."

39

After dropping Wendy off, Chuck started for the far end of West Hills. On the way he got another call.

"Where are you?" Royce asked.

"On my way to see somebody," Chuck said.

"Somebody you know?"

"That's complicated."

"Chuck, I don't want you to get nervous about this."

"About what?"

"Something I'm going to tell you."

Chuck almost laughed the demented cackle of the guys who think they're Napoleon. "Nothing you say is going to make things worse."

"I was messing around on the computer," Royce said. "You know that text message you got? Said Samson s-m-r-t?"

"Yeah."

"I Googled those letters, to see what it came up with."

"And?"

"First off, it's the NASDAQ abbreviation for Stein Mart."

160

"I'm getting mystery texts from a store?"

"You can also find an *I Am So Smrt* Homer Simpson tee shirt."

"Hilarious. What's your point?"

"Here's the thing, Chuck. I went deeper. I kept going. And then I got to *smrt* as a word. It is a word. In Serbian."

"Serbian?"

"Chuck, it's the Serbian word for death."

Something popped in Chuck's ears, like a mosquito had flown inside his head with a cap gun.

"Chuck, you there?"

"What is happening, Royce? What the hell is happening?"

"Hang tough, will you?"

"What choice do I have?"

He clicked off and drove, and it felt like he was driving in a wind tunnel full of fog. Even in the daylight everything seemed to blur. He wondered if he might not have a stroke.

That'd be just great, wouldn't it? Then Stan could start taking care of *him.*

Snorting a derisive laugh at himself, Chuck continued on.

He got to Lazy J Park a little before three, his head still pounding with what Royce told him.

But that only raised a ton of other questions, each more bizarre than the last. Serbians? The guy with the knife. What had he stumbled into with a stupid rear ender? What did all this have to do with Julia and voices on the phone?

Maybe it was time to go to the FBI or something. Sure, and with all their available time they'd look into *nothing.* No way to find the knife guy. And the cops were all over him, suspecting manufacture of drugs.

Really? Or were they leaning on him, trying to get some leverage? For freaking *what?*

Chuck parked in the small lot and sat for a minute with the windows up. The sun warmed the car and he liked the feeling. Enveloped by heat. It relaxed him and that's what he needed.

He looked out the windshield to see if anybody looked like he was waiting for him.

There was a kids' birthday party going on near the swings, complete with parents in party hats, a couple of blow-up bounce houses, a clown doing balloon animals and, yes, an old wrangler with a pony giving rides. When these West Hills parents gave a party, they didn't just do cake and streamers. Nothing too good for little Madison or little Noah.

A few yards away, an old man walked his dachshund. The dog looked like a knockwurst with legs. Two teen boys in wifebeaters and low rider shorts swaggered in front of his car, laughing at some inside joke.

But no sign of anyone waiting to talk.

Was he crazy for being here? If it was somebody who wanted to do him harm, would he have picked this place? Wide open and with potential witnesses all around? Maybe he was summoned here to be watched, to see what he'd do. Somebody doing some serious chain jerking, like leaving strange text messages on his cell phone.

Chuck got out. He stood at his car a moment, trying to look conspicuous. When he got no response he started walking across the grass, toward the fence on Valley Circle.

He didn't have to look lost. He *was* lost. Nothing made sense, and the idea that he would soon be looking into the eyes of a clandestine acquaintance of his wife's was more than just a kicker. It made everything else seem open to dream-like interpretation.

Maybe he'd never been in the Navy, never served in Afghanistan, never had a brother named Stan. Maybe he was like one of those guys in a paranoid movie of the '60s. What was it? *The Manchurian Candidate,* that was it. The one with Frank Sinatra. The one about brainwashing.

Or maybe he was Jim Carrey in *The Truman Show.* Some god-like madman was pulling strings, and soon Chuck would bump into the end of huge set.

At the fence, Chuck found he was fighting for air. His lungs constricted. It wasn't just the heat, it was the pressure of unreality, the closing walls of an existential trash compactor.

Now was the time to pray. To try again. To reach up for the God who had once allowed Satan free reign with a guy named Job.

But as Chuck closed his eyes, behind him someone said, "You think it's hot?"

Chuck turned. The clown from the kids' party was standing there, frilly collar, fire-engine red hair, and all. Beads of sweat rolled down his white-caked cheeks, leaving gray streaks like ski tracks around his large, red nose.

"Try standing out here in this get up," the clown said.

"Is it you?" Chuck said.

"Is it who?"

"Never mind."

"I don't want the kids to catch me smoking." The clown reached into his polka-dot pants and pulled out a pack of Marlboros. Fired one up. Blew out a stream of smoke.

"That's better," he said. "I been making poodles and giraffes for an hour straight." He held out the pack. "Want one?"

"No thanks."

"Then I guess we better talk about Julia."

It was him. Oh Mary, mother of Jesus, this was the guy. Chuck almost burst out laughing, a crazy laugh, like this was just the last nail in his bizarre coffin.

"Yep," the clown said. "I'm the guy."

Chuck said, "What's your name?"

"Boffo."

"Come on, your real name."

"Boffo the Balloon Clown will do. And you are in way over your head."

Under the makeup Chuck saw two very serious green eyes. Even with the clown's bulbous nose and ridiculous wig shooting out at right angles from his head, his expression was not about to make a kid laugh.

Chuck said, "How come you know about my wife's past?"

After another drag, the clown said, "Tell me what you think you know."

"Your name's Thompson, isn't it?" Chuck looked for a tell, but the clown eyes didn't dance. "You knew my wife," he added.

"Check."

"You slept with my wife."

"Now you're the clown if you believe that."

"You were seen."

"By who? That little rat from the shop? How much he tag you for?"

Chuck said nothing.

"Three bills? Four?"

"Tell me about Julia," Chuck said. "You were the guy on the motorcycle, the one with the Sun Cycle vest."

Boffo smiled. "Never heard of that guy. But go on."

"Come on, man." Chuck felt like laughing in guy's face and punching it out. It was all too absurd.

"I didn't sleep with her," Boffo said.

"You were intimate. The guy saw you."

Boffo shook his head. "The *cholo* made up a story for you. You bought it. Literally. Which shows you're dumber than you

164

look. Which brings me back to my main point, that you're in over your head."

Chuck was starting to feel heat from more than the sun. "I'm sorry if I'm having a little trouble talking to a clown who calls himself Boffo."

"You wound me," Boffo said. "I take this business very seriously. Kids depend on me."

"What was your relationship with my wife?"

"I was her source," he said. "On a story."

"What story?"

"Oh, bigger than that alligator farm jive."

Some kids screamed joyfully from a blow-up bounce house near the parking lot.

"You know about that?" Chuck said.

"Boffo sees all, knows all." He took another puff on his cigarette then rubbed it on the bottom of his big, floppy shoe. "Listen to me," he said. "If I talk to you, you don't ever try to find me. If I see anything I say to you show up online or in the news, I will find you and make you feel pain."

"Not very clown-like of you."

"Deal?"

"Fine." Chuck was desperate for something, anything. Even this.

"What's my name again?"

"Boffo," Chuck said, feeling ridiculous.

"Good. Not anything else. Now Boffo was a CI for the DEA. Confidential informant. What's happening here, even around this very park, is trade in H."

"Heroin?"

"What did I just say? It's all over this Valley, all through the Westside and the Hollywood Hills, out to the Pacific Palisades, every which way you look. And the people behind it are the worst people you never want to meet."

"Serbians," Chuck said.

Boffo's painted orange eyebrows creased upward. "Very good. You're right about that. The old ethnic cleansers. A more dangerous form of life you will not run across. You remember Henry Fonda in *Once Upon a Time in the West?*"

"Afraid I don't."

"Let's put it this way. Henry Fonda was the coldest-blooded killer in the history of the movies in that flick. These guys are worse than Henry Fonda."

"Was that the story my wife was working on?"

"It's also why she's dead. And why you will be, too, you keep after this. My guess is they've had you on their radar even from before the fake accident that took her out."

Chuck's entire body, despite the heat, went cold. "What do you mean *fake?*"

"You don't have to be a genius to figure that out. It was a hit job."

"Are you saying she was murdered?"

The clown nodded.

Words hooked the back of Chuck's throat, caught in hot tissue and stayed.

"Listen a little more," the clown said. "There's dirty cops involved, too. Now the LAPD is a lot cleaner than it used to be, but that only drives the dirt deeper. Any cops question you?"

"Yeah," Chuck said, as if from a distance.

"What about?"

"They're charging me with making meth in my garage."

Boffo snorted. "You got to be kidding me. Meth is high desert manufacture. It's not a lemonade stand. How'd that happen?"

"I don't know. I came home and my house was on fire.

They say it was started with propane and other stuff I didn't have in there."

"You have been so set up. You and Julia both. Man, you've got to get out of here. Move. Flee. Get gone."

"I have a job. I teach elementary school."

"They got kids everywhere. Even in other states."

"Tell me about Julia. What about her having a record?"

"I checked her out. If I was going to be her source, I wanted to know who she was. Found an old fraud charge buried in the records. Supposed to be expunged. She never tell you about that?"

Chuck could barely shake his head. A secret like that? It couldn't be. Julia would never have—

Boffo the clown got a softer look in his eyes. "Pal, listen up. I'm really sorry your wife died. She was smart and tough. I don't know why she wouldn't have told you some things, but hey, I was in the secret-keeping business myself. And now I'm out of it, doing time at kids' parties."

"What can I do?" Chuck said. "What can I possibly do?"

"Start all over again someplace else."

"I have a criminal charge hanging over me."

"Yeah, bummer. You have a good lawyer? If you don't, I got some names."

"They're not clowns, are they?"

Boffo laughed. "See, that's good. If you can't keep a sense of humor, even in the bad times, you might as well pack it in." He clapped Chuck on the shoulder. "Well, back to the salt mines."

"Wait. What if I want to get in touch with you?"

"Unless you book me for a party, don't try. Remember what I said. I'll be all over this if you say anything. And it really pains me to say that, as a clown. We like to be friendly to everybody."

40

Chuck dreamed, again, about Nolan Ryan. It happened off and on, a whacked-out dream in a far corner of his brain.

Nolan Ryan, his boyhood hero, wearing his Angels uniform, on the mount at the Big A, only his jersey was too short and his stomach was showing. He had a rash or something on his stomach, but a nice tan otherwise.

He was pitching to Mario Lemiux, but Mario Lemiux was a hockey player . . .

. . . Mario, another sports hero. Pittsburgh Penguins.

But on a baseball diamond?

And he wasn't holding a bat. No. He had a doorknob and a fish and a kite.

He better watch out! Chuck could hear himself saying that. Mumbling that in his dream.

Watch out Mario! Nolan has heat.

Here comes the pitch!

Somebody in the stands screamed.

It sounded like a man. A young man. A scared young man.

Chuck jolted awake in a chair.

Another scream.

Where was he? The smell . . .

The motel.

Another scream. It was his brother, asleep but screaming.

Chuck bolted to the edge of the bed and shook his brother. "Stan . . ."

Stan jerked to a sitting position. "Help!"

"Stan, I'm here, it's okay."

Before Stan could respond someone pounded on the wall next door and yelled an epithet-laced warning to shut up.

The digital clock read 10:04. Chuck's head was soggy. He could hardly remember what had happened that day. Beaman with Wendy. Dropped her off. Meeting a clown. Oh yeah, the clown. Life was a funhouse with wild mirrors now.

"Chuck," Stan said. "The wolf man was after me!"

"It's okay. Go back to sleep now."

"No Chuck! The wolf man was after me and he almost got me this time because you weren't there. You weren't coming!" In the dreams, Chuck had always been a presence that kept the wolf man from getting Stan. Sometimes, Stan had reported, Chuck just showed up and the wolf man ran away. Sometimes Chuck threatened him with a silver sword. Once Chuck had even flown through the air like Superman.

"It's just your dream, Stan."

"I'm scared!" Stan started crying, one of his fire hydrant cries Chuck called them. They burst out like water from a busted hydrant, and Stan jammed his head into Chuck's chest, bawling into it. When he did that, as a kid, Chuck would just have to hold him tight until he calmed down.

Chuck held him tight. "Okay, okay, okay," Chuck said.

Another thump on the wall, and another warning.

"It's okay now, Stan, you hear me?"

"You . . . gotta . . . be there, Chuck. If they . . . get you in a . . . dream . . . you die."

"No you don't—"

"You wake up and you're dead!"

Chuck squeezed his brother harder, patted the back of his head, let the rhythm of his breathing calm his brother down.

Stan wriggled free, wiped his nose with the back of his hand. "This time . . . it was real, Chuck! Like it's . . . gonna happen."

"Werewolves don't happen, Stan. It's—"

"Yes they do!"

The guy next door hit the wall again.

Chuck jumped over to the wall and hit it with his fist. Again. And again. "Why don't you shut up now, huh?" he screamed. *Pound pound pound.*

"Don't, Chuck," Stan said.

"Stop telling me what to do!"

"Chuck, you're mad—"

"Do I look mad?"

"Yes!"

"Good call!" Chuck grabbed the nearest thing, a pillow, and threw it as hard as he could against the window. It plopped harmlessly to the floor.

Stan giggled. "You didn't break the window, Chuck."

"Want me to? Want me to dive right through it for you?"

"No, Chuck."

"How about a chair? Huh?"

"No, Chuck."

"Listen to me, Stan. Remember what I told you once? Werewolves are myths. You remember what a myth is?"

"A story," Stan said quietly.

"Yeah, a story. But in myths there's a hero, see? The heroes have to leave the castle and go into the dark forest."

"Why?"

"I don't know why! Because they have to rescue somebody, or go shopping."

Stan giggled again. "Shopping?"

"Sure! Maybe they need to go check the specials."

"You're being funny now, Chuck."

"But in the forest, see, there's werewolves. And the hero has to fight 'em. But he gets help. He has a teacher or a good wizard or somebody like that, who gives him a magic sword or silver bullet."

"Okay, that's cool," Stan said.

"Yeah, and that's what he uses to kill the werewolf. Now the point of the myth, see, is to tell us we can kill the monsters."

"Really?"

Really? Did he actually believe this himself? After what he'd seen in Afghanistan? After that guy with the knife? He would have killed me, and maybe Stan, if he'd wanted to. He was big enough, he looked amoral enough.

Was there anything one guy could do to stop bad things? When he'd been cut in captivity—he wished he could see who did it, at least see him, but his mind kept crushing that picture into dust—was he able to do anything about it? No, he had to be rescued. But what if there's no one to rescue you? What then?

But Stan had asked. *Really?*

He had to get Stan to believe it, even if he himself did not. That was the only way to get Stan through the night, and maybe his entire life.

Chuck said, "When the time comes, you'll be brave. You know why?"

"Why?"

"Because I'm telling you to, that's why. And you always do what I tell you, right?"

"Right."

"So now I'm telling you to go back to sleep. Okay?"

"Okay, Chuck. But what if I have the dream again?"

Chuck was drained. "Just tell yourself to be brave."

"I want you to be in the dream, Chuck."

"I'll be there," Chuck said. "As long as I'm not busy in some other dream."

"What other dream?"

"The one where I go shopping in the forest," Chuck said. "And I'm looking for DiGiorno's pizza because my brother's hungry and—"

A knock on the door stopped him. Chuck sighed. The complainer was upping the ante. "Just be quiet now, Stan. I have to tell this guy we're sorry."

Chuck went to the door. "I'm sorry," he said. "It's all right now."

"No it isn't," the voice said, and knocked again.

Feeling with his left hand Chuck made sure the chain lock was in place, then opened the door a crack. The muted illumination of night light—mainly the amber glow from the motel parking lot—backlit the inquirer. "Look," Chuck said, "it won't happen again—"

The door slammed into Chuck's shoulder. He heard the crack of splintering wood as he fell back. Stan screamed again, this time in fear of something very real in the room.

Two men, not one. And definitely not a disgruntled neighbor.

Chuck rolled to his knees and got up.

Stan issued a rat-a-tat of shrieks.

A voice said, "Shut him up!" The voice was tinged with accent. *Serbian* . . .

"Chuck!" Stan cried.

In the dimness Chuck saw the other man rushing the bed.

Chuck charged him. He got hold of the man's shirt and felt back muscles underneath as hard as bowling balls. Chuck pulled hard, tore fabric.

Then a snapping noise.

Something punched his kidneys.

And his entire body filled with electric shock.

41

There is something in the air this night, Sandy Epperson thought.

In LA, the evenings beat with vibrations of death. Everyone knew that. Especially cops. But every now and then there seemed to be more in the ether, the incipient anticipation of deep layers of evil.

Sandy believed in evil. She'd seen too much of it not to.

This was the city for violent, conscienceless acts. And there were seasons for it. Sometimes the evil came in waves, and you could feel it coming, like a surfer senses the swells.

As she moved through her kitchen in the little house in Tarzana, the one she'd managed to buy at just the right time, she left the radio on to 1070, the all-news station, and poured herself another cup of chamomile tea.

Outside her kitchen window, the darkness itself seemed to move, as if it were a sentient being.

The news had just reported a hit-and-run near USC. A nineteen-year-old student named Rachelle Anderson, a

174

sophomore from Scottsdale, Arizona, was killed as she walked across Jefferson Avenue at Hoover Street with a male companion.

A witness said a black sedan hit the two in a crosswalk. Anderson was thrown to the side and died at the scene. The man stayed on the windshield for five hundred feet, the witness said, until the car stopped and a passenger got out and threw the man off the hood. Then the car drove on.

It was the passenger tossing the man to the street that got to Sandy. Like they were clearing off a bird turd. Just that fast, and they left two human beings to die.

There just seemed to be more of that kind of cold, calculated malice lingering out there in the city this night.

But that wasn't all that troubled her.

The Chuck Samson thing was buggy in her mind, pulling at her from different directions. Not the least of which was the hit-and-run on his wife. Something stank there.

And something else didn't smell quite right—her partner's consuming interest in getting Chuck Samson nailed any which way he could. What was up with that?

Or was she just imagining things, hoping she could weave a scenario that would prove to the big boys just how good she was? Was that still it? Her consuming passion was to make her former captain, and all the suits downtown, eat their collective shorts for what they'd done to her.

It had started with Captain Ford Elias at North Hollywood station, a little over six months after the Twin Towers went down on 9/11.

Sandy was still in uniform and on patrol duty. Her watch almost over at 7:30 one night, she was finishing up narratives on her reports when the call for backup came in. A black and white at the Ford dealership on Lankershim needed help.

Sandy and her patrol partner, Jeff Simms, rolled Code 3, lights and sirens. On the computer screen Sandy saw comments on the call: *Vapor/mist seen coming out of ventilation system. 3 people down. FD at scene.*

FD was fire department, and the vapor in a building meant possible terrorism.

When she and Simms arrived, Captain Elias put Sandy on traffic control. She immediately set up a two-block perimeter each way, and directed other cops to establish the cordon.

She'd just completed a WMD course at the Academy, and was on top of it. And knew something else—her captain had made a mistake.

Elias had set up the command post in a black Yukon, right across the street from the contaminated building. Downwind.

She ran to the CP and found Elias, marking the whiteboard, talking to his assistant. "Sir," she said, "you're downwind, and the CP should be at least a hundred yards away."

He snapped a glare at her. He was fifty-five, short gray hair, close-set brown eyes. He always looked suspicious about something. "We know what we're doing, officer."

"Then we need to move this perimeter to the next major, sir. People are vulnerable."

"Too much of a hassle," Elias said, turning back to the board. "Stay as is."

"This is protocol—"

"Get out there. Now."

Fine! Let people get sick on his watch. Sandy wanted to pick up the whiteboard and knock him over the head with it. Now *that* would do wonders for her career.

Fortunately, DOT—the Department of Transportation team—arrived and took over traffic control.

That left Sandy at the disposal of Elias, who ordered her and Simms to go inside the building and secure it as a crime scene.

"But it's a hot zone," Sandy said.

"You're assuming," Elias said.

"I'm not going in without a HAZMAT suit."

"I'm ordering you to."

"And I'm refusing, until FD gives the okay."

Simms nodded. "I agree, Captain."

"Then this is down as a refused order," Elias said. "For both of you."

An hour later, FD in HAZMAT suits went into the building and came out, reporting garlic powder and cayenne pepper in the vents.

Someone had played a practical joke. There was no danger at all.

But who could have known that going in? And who knew the departmental hell that would follow Sandy a few short years later, because of this one incident? How the administration would side with Elias on everything. How they made her feel like hazardous material for the department.

Sandy shook her head, dislodging the memory. She didn't want to sit here and go through it again, beat by beat, as she sometimes did.

It was so hard, having a mind that wouldn't shut off.

And now that mind snapped back to Chuck Samson and, again, Mark Mooney.

Why did she keep thinking of Mark?

Sandy changed the radio to smooth jazz. She had to get calm. Get some sleep. Get away from the thought that there was something in the air this night. Something in the air . . .

42

Stun gunned.

Chuck knew that's what had just happened to him. As a boy he'd touched a live spark plug once, on a lawn mower, and it zapped and numbed his hand. That was how his whole body felt now, muscles cramping, and strangely, as his juiced brain normalized, it was like coming off a high.

But he was not high. He was low, in a dark motel room, on the floor, looking up.

Stan. Where was Stan?

Chuck was aware of the bed moving. He willed his arms to move, tried to get up from the floor.

Something slammed his chest and forced him back down. A foot.

"Don't move," a voice said. He knew the voice. The guy with the knife. Mad Russian. No, Mad Serb. A white spark crackled in the night. From the spark's location Chuck concluded it was an electroshock baton in the Serb's hands, and he was showing off his weapon.

Chuck heard a muffled moan. Stan. The other guy must've had something over Stan's mouth. His brother would be scared to death. Chuck tried to move again, but the foot slammed him back to the carpet.

"Where is it?" The Serb asked.

"Where is what?" Chuck said, his voice thick in his mouth.

"Where. Is. It?"

Chuck shook his head, then wondered if the guy could even see that motion in the dark.

"You maybe like another jolt?"

The weapon sparked and snapped again. And half a dozen thoughts banged against each other in Chuck's mind. The Serb obviously thought Chuck had information about something, and Chuck was supposed to know what that was. He wasn't dead, so the Serb and his ally weren't sure where to find whatever this thing was. They were also stupid. Breaking into a motel room to do their interrogation. Too many chances somebody would hear.

He sized up the Serb as being reckless and foolish. But he was a fool with a stun gun. And a knife. Chuck remembered the knife at the scene of the rear ender. This current scene would have to be played delicately.

"Sit me up," Chuck said. "Then we can talk."

The Serb kept his foot on Chuck's chest and snapped the electric prod again. "No, no, my friend. You will talk when I tell you to and stay where I put you. If you want to leave this room with all your fingers and toes, you will not play games."

Stan moaned again. Definitely a pillow was over his mouth.

Chuck said, "Let my brother go, he has nothing to do with anything."

"Ah," the Serb said. "You want your brother to be all right, yes?"

"Just let him go."

"Don't be stupid with me, huh? Just tell me where it is, and you know of what I'm talking."

"You got the wrong guy."

"Samson. Chuck Samson. I don't like the name *Chuck*. It is a stupid name. You are stupid—"

"Key word is *stupid*, I get it—"

The baton came down on his leg and zapped.

A fusillade of hot nails ripped up his body. Once in a pickup basketball game a jerk had thrown the ball as hard as he could at Chuck. It smacked him directly in the family jewels and doubled him over, creating pain just like this.

"Don't make me do that again," the Serb said.

Another voice, accented, said, "How long we got to keep this going?"

"You hear that, Chuck?" the Serb said. "We don't have all night."

Night. His motel neighbor, trying to sleep.

Chuck yelled in full voice, "THANK YOU SIR, MAY I HAVE ANOTHER!"

A moment of silence.

He yelled again. "THANK YOU SIR, MAY I HAVE ANOTHER!"

"Shut up," the Serb said.

And then it came. The pounding on the wall. The voice of his neighbor screaming invective and threat.

"We got to get out," the other one said.

Hesitation. The Serb was unsure. In the gloom, Chuck saw him looking back and forth, his hair flying like water spray.

"THANK YOU SIR!"

"Stuff his mouth!" the Serb said.

Chuck grabbed the Serb's ankle with his left hand, pulled, and fisted him in the balls.

Now it was the Serb who cried out.

Flailing in the dark, Chuck had momentary freedom. He rolled left, away from the Serb's body, which fell toward the window. Chuck got to the foot of the bed, stomach down, and pushed himself up.

And saw a big mass of humanity pressing down on Stan.

Chuck jumped onto the bed, took one bouncing step and threw himself on the back of the big man. He got his left arm around the guy's enormous head, then slid it down to the neck. It was a tree trunk. But Chuck managed a choke hold and pulled for all he was worth. Which wasn't much at the moment.

The big man stood up straight and turned around, like a dog getting ready to lie down. Chuck held fast to the throat but knew this was only a temporary solution. Mad Serb was no doubt recovering, and he was the one with the baton.

"Stan! Get out!" Chuck yelled.

He sensed but did not see his brother getting out of the bed. A moment later the door flew open, and that Chuck did see. The lights from the liquor store sign on the other side of the motel seeped in, yellow and red.

The hulk spun around again and chugged his legs backward, crashing Chuck into the wall. Tiny sparklers gave a little Fourth of July party behind Chuck's eyes.

But he saw a blur run outside, unmistakably Stan. And then he heard Stan's startled scream.

Because there was someone else at the door now, shouting, "What the hell are you doing in here?"

The neighbor?

The Serb pounced at him, his baton crackling.

Chuck let go of the big one and ran to the door, not quick

enough to keep his neighbor from getting lit up. His body hit the walkway at the same time Chuck smashed into the Serb with his shoulder.

The Serb grunted and jammed waist first into the iron rail. Chuck sent an open palm smack to his right ear, a blow causing disequilibrium when delivered right.

From the hollow thwacking sound, Chuck knew he'd delivered right.

Mad Serb fell to his knees.

The walkway, up on the second story as it was, shook. Chuck knew in a flash it wasn't because of the fallen Serb. It was his thug partner, loping toward the door.

Instinctively, Chuck jumped to the right, his back to the room. And the big guy flew into the rail at the exact same spot the Serb had gone down.

Chuck saw with a glimpse that Stan, in underwear and tee shirt, was only a few feet away, his eyes wide.

"Let's go!" Chuck grabbed Stan's hand and turned him, and started running toward the stairway.

He heard the Serb's voice shout, "Shoot the legs!"

43

"I'm in my underwear Chuck!"

"Don't think about it!"

They reached the bottom of the stairs, and were in the parking lot. There was a small retaining wall on the edge of the lot. On the other side of the wall was another parking lot behind some office space. All Chuck knew was they had to get out of sight, fast.

"Over the wall," Chuck said, pulling Stan toward the barrier.

"I can't, Chuck! I'm in my underwear!"

"Stick with me."

"I'll get scratched!"

But Chuck was already boosting his brother on top of the four-foot wall. Stan's wiry body was as taut as an anchor rope.

"Jump over," Chuck said.

"My knee hurts!"

Chuck heard the sound of scuffling feet echoing through

the stairwell. Without a second thought he jumped onto the top of the wall and sprang off it like a cat. But he landed like a dog—with a heavy, splay-legged thud. He quickly recovered and pulled Stan off the wall, as a parent would a scared child.

They were now crouched in back of a cigar store and a Verizon cellular outlet. The small parking lot was empty. There was a breezeway between the two stores. Chuck took Stan by the wrist and pulled him toward the arch.

"My knee is bleeding, Chuck! I need a Band-Aid."

"I'll get you a bunch of them."

"Why are those men after us?"

"Later."

They got to the breezeway. Chuck pushed Stan's back against the wall, peeked around.

He saw nothing, but heard muted voices talking animatedly, like angry blue jays. Then the sound of car doors slamming and tires burning rubber.

They would be coming, driving all around. How hard would it be to spot a couple of guys on foot, one of them in his briefs and the other in tee-shirt, jeans, and no shoes? And without cell phones. He had to get to a phone. Call the cops. Maybe Sandy Epperson.

If they kept to the back of the stores, hidden from the boulevard, maybe they could find a place that was open, get in and make a call. They couldn't stay here. A side street was only a few yards away, and the Serbs could easily search the adjoining areas.

"Can you move?" Chuck said.

Stan said, "My knee hurts. It's bleeding!"

"We have to duck into the alley."

"What if we step on glass?"

"I don't see any glass. Come on."

"I'm scared, Chuck."

"Come on." Chuck again took Stan by the hand and pulled him toward the side street.

Just as a set of headlights careened around the corner, coming right at them.

There was no way out. Nowhere to run.

Stan yelped.

As a very nice silver Jag sped right on by. A youngish brunette in fully loaded makeup looked at them like they were splashes of graffiti.

"Hurry," Chuck said, leading Stan across the street and into the alley.

They were behind a coin laundry now. Up ahead a few cars were parked. Chuck remembered. There was a sushi place that stayed open late. He'd been there before.

With Julia.

They'd have a phone there.

Chuck's feet were starting to get raw. He could only imagine how Stan's were. But Stan wasn't crying about it. Maybe his little brother was getting a little tougher. Or maybe he was just too scared to think about anything, including sore feet. He hadn't mentioned his knee in the last twelve seconds.

Chuck kept hold of Stan's hand and ran on.

He couldn't let this be the end of things. After everything he'd been through, this could not be the way he died, with his brother at his side, failing to take care of him like he'd always been able to do.

He couldn't get gunned down in an alley. What would his kids think, his fifth graders, being told that their teacher was murdered and that's the way it was and isn't it such a sad day, kids?

He made for the door of the sushi place, bright red under a

sconce.

Be unlocked.

It was.

Chuck practically threw Stan inside, followed, slammed it behind them.

There was a small, dark passageway, and two cloth sections hanging at the end. Chuck pressed through them and almost knocked over a Hispanic man with a load of dirty dishes.

"Phone," Chuck said.

The man just looked at him.

"I want to use your phone," Chuck said. "You have a phone?"

The man shrugged. Chuck wasn't buying the can't-speak-English act. The guy just didn't like what he was seeing, and who could blame him? One shivering thin guy in his underwear, led by a guy with a scarred neck and no shoes.

"Owner?" Chuck said. "Owner, owner!"

The Hispanic turned his back and walked to the industrial sink and put the dishes in it. Like Chuck and Stan didn't even exist.

"Maybe you better wait here," Chuck said to Stan.

"Where you going?"

"To find the manager or the owner or—"

"Hand up!" The voice was high and screechy and trembling. Chuck turned and saw the business end of a double-barreled shotgun aimed right at his gut. Behind the gun was an old man with a weathered, Japanese face. He wore a bandana with a red sun between two Japanese characters. He was small, but his eyes were big.

"I need a phone," Chuck said.

"Hand up!"

"We're not here to—"

"Blow head off!"

Stan said, "He's going to shoot us!"

"Hand up!"

A younger man, who looked like a larger rendition of the shotgun guy, complete with matching headband, came in from the restaurant side. He was holding a revolver. He said, "You better put your hands up. My dad's fingers aren't as steady as they used to be."

44

Chuck said, "It's not what you think."

"No move!" the old man said. The double barrels of the shotgun trembled, fixed on Chuck.

"Okay, Dad," the young one said.

"Talk to them, Chuck!" Stan said.

"This is a mistake," Chuck said.

"Call cop," the old man ordered.

The son said, "Would you two sit on the floor, please?"

Chuck felt Stan shaking, put his arm around his shoulder. "Would you tell your father to put the firepower away? We were being chased, we *want* the cops to come."

The son frowned.

"Call cop," the father said.

"We've been having break ins," the son said. "So just sit down on the floor and we'll make the call." He motioned with his revolver.

Chuck sat, pulling Stan down with him. They parked on the hard floor and leaned against the wall.

"Watch 'em, Dad," the son said.

The old man nodded once, hard.

"Would you mind having him point that thing at the floor?" Chuck said.

"No floor!" Dad said.

"Might be a good idea, Dad," the son said. "Just lower it a little."

"Only little!"

The son disappeared through twin curtains.

And now, waiting, Chuck felt something he hadn't in a long time. It traced a sharp line back to Afghanistan, and the security patrol that was attacked. In that whole fight, which he could barely remember, one thing did stay with him—an inner tearing. It felt like the sharp talons of a predatory bird, clawing out from inside his ribs.

There was a myth like that, Prometheus. The guy who stole fire from Zeus and gave it to man. So Zeus chained him to a rock and a bird pecked out his liver. Only Zeus made the liver grow back, so it could be pecked out again the next day, and forever.

Only this bird was inside Chuck. In everything that had happened so far, the bird hadn't come back.

Now it had.

At least the dad wasn't pointing the weapon at Chuck anymore. It was more toward the Hispanic dish washer now, who hadn't moved at all during the last few minutes.

"Go on, back work," the dad said to him. Then to Chuck: "You two big trouble."

"Are we going to be all right, Chuck?" Stan said.

"Sure. When the cops get here, we'll straighten it all out."

"I hate being in my underwear, Chuck."

"Be glad you don't sleep buck naked."

"That's gross, Chuck."

Gunfire.

The sound of glass exploding.

The old man spun around. The shotgun went off.

More shots from the front, a scream.

Then silence.

The old man took a step toward the curtains.

Another shot exploded.

The old man went down, flat on his back, his head hitting the floor with concussive force.

For a second the only sound was the hot water shooting out of the sink where the dish washer once stood.

The curtains rustled, as if a soft wind were blowing them. And it stopped everything cold in Chuck's mind, because the soft movement of them looked exactly like the curtains that danced in the hotel room on his honeymoon night. They got a beach view room, he and Julia, and she went outside to the balcony, and when Chuck came out of the bathroom he turned off the lights and there was a single candle in the room. Julia had lit the candle and Chuck could see the curtains—same color as these in the sushi joint—could see them swaying gently, gently, and Julia came back into the room, through the curtains, like a ghost passing through a wall.

But through these curtains in the sushi place came a man. He wore a black workout suit and a ski mask. His right hand held a slate-gray submachine gun.

45

Forget about sleep, girlfriend. Sandy almost said it out loud.

She was sometimes kept up by hard cases, but it wasn't just that. The whole Elias thing flooding back to her memory was a big part. Six months after making detective, and going to Central, Elias was transferred over. And began his systematic campaign to break her down.

Sexual innuendo, racial slurs, all in private. And the one time she tried to record him he'd caught her. And then her complaint to Internal Affairs, and her Protective League lawyer advising her to take the deal—transfer to the Valley, and no liability anywhere.

"Anywhere," Sandy said out loud now. Oh boy, when you start talking to yourself, it's time to work.

She opened the Mac laptop on the dining room table and sat down for some research.

She accessed a newspaper database that was not open to the public. A joint project of the Los Angeles County Library and the LAPD, this was the most complete collection of local newspapers in existence, anywhere. From as far away as Barstow, and as near as downtown, the database covered every kind of newspaper, print and digital, from paid subscriber to free handout. It was an amazing thing that even Sandy Epperson was in awe of.

She typed in a search request on the name "Edward Hillary." All she knew about Hillary was what she'd read in the report on the Beaman hit-and-run. He was a retired cop. She'd never met him, but that wasn't odd in a department as large as the LAPD.

She got a ton of hits, some alluding to *Edmund* Hillary, the first man to reach the summit of Mount Everest. She limited her search criteria by date, going back only ten years.

Scrolling through the squibs revealed an Edward Hillary who played a doctor on *One Life to Live* for several years. It was easy to ignore those items.

An Edward Hillary was valedictorian of La Crescenta High School in 2006.

No help at all. There were probably still some people who flew below the Internet radar, who didn't have a database presence. Maybe a barfly named Hillary was one of these.

Then she stopped cold.

Two names, together. Two she'd never expected to see.

In a pdf document was a page from the *Los Angeles Daily News* nine years ago.

She opened the doc, and confirmed that an Edward Hillary was being honored with several others for a gift donated to a prestigious private school.

One with that other name attached to it.

The Raymond Hunt Academy.

The place Chuck Samson, whose wife died at Hillary's

hand, taught fifth graders.

Oh yes, girlfriend. Forget completely about sleep.

46

Chuck came to, face down, smelling oil. He was aware that his hands were taped in front of him, and that he was in a semi-fetal position. The right side of his head throbbed. He remembered the blow then, a gun butt, and knew it wasn't as bad as it could've been.

Vibration told him he was in the back of a moving vehicle. From the layout, apparent by instinct and feel, it was probably an SUV of some type. And the shifting of his weight meant they were on a curving road. Winding their way somewhere, at a slight incline. Maybe a canyon road. If that was so, maybe they were heading toward the ocean. This could be Topanga or Las Virgenes. Or they could be heading up into a mountain range, like the San Gabriels. Or—

Where was Stan?

Chuck rolled onto his back.

"Don't move," a deep, accented voice said.

Chuck wondered why he wasn't dead yet.

"Where's my brother?" Chuck said, his voice thick and

dull.

A jab to the ribs sent fire to his bones. Had to be the barrel of a gun. "Shut up," the voice said.

•

This is the worst, Stan thought. This is the worst it's ever going to be. They're going to kill Chuck and they're going to do the same thing to me. That's why they have me tied up and they put another thing in my mouth and they won't let me talk. They won't let me find out where my brother is. They won't let me wiggle around. They hit me. I'm in the back of some truck. They're taking me somewhere. I hope they take me where Chuck is. If they do anything to Chuck I will bite them. I will do anything I can to hurt them. Maybe I'm going to die but I will not die until I hurt them because of what they're going to do to Chuck.

Dear God, save me and Chuck.

I hope I don't pee. I don't want them to see me pee. I want to get them. I have to. I can't be scared anymore. Chuck needs me. I hate mean people. I hate them. I don't like these things in my mouth, I don't like to be tied up, I don't like what they're doing to me, but if I cry or pee they're going to hurt me more. I have to be smart. I have to. I can't be scared, Chuck told me not to be scared. I have to try, I have to.

I have to plan.

Dear God, help me have a plan.

•

A team of the worst people he'd never met. That's what Thompson—Boffo—had told him. No doubt, that's who had him.

But what did Chuck have to do with heroin trafficking?

And what was his next move? Do something nuts, like try to kick out a window? Jump into the back seat and roll around with the gunman?

As kids, he and Stan had a game with dandelions. One of them would blow the spores into the air and the other would try to grab as many as he could before they floated away or hit the ground. Chuck got to be pretty good at it. In fact, back in his fighting days, Chuck unleashed a one-two combination he fantasized was as fast as Muhammad Ali in his prime. It wasn't, but it was pretty fast.

Maybe he should make a play for the guy's gun and do some shooting.

Sure, I am Jean-Claude Van Damme. I am Chuck Norris. And this is a movie.

You jerk.

He thought of Stan again. Stan, who was no doubt going crazy. Stan, who would be out of his skin with worry. Stan, who would be wondering if the wolf man had caught up with his big brother.

If Stan was even still alive.

Once, they'd gone to a summer camp in the Angeles National Forest. In cabins and everything. Their mom was committed to giving them some semblance of a normal childhood, once the old man had taken off.

This camp had a big meadow in the middle, and the second day they got a big game of Capture the Flag going. Stan played defense, keeping up a constant chatter and asking Chuck please not to leave him.

Until Chuck told him he was going to go for it.

It was almost the most beautiful play in Capture the Flag

history. Chuck was Barry Sanders, his favorite running back, going this way and that, avoiding the destructive tag. He was twenty yards from home when he got flanked.

Changing directions yet again, Chuck slipped and went down and got multiple slaps from the enemy.

And heard Stan screaming, really screaming, not far away.

Later, Stan would admit he thought the opposition was really and truly capturing Chuck, and going to put him in a real jail.

He longed for those days again because this was no game.

But longing wasn't going to bring it back.

But the hot hate was cooking his blood, maybe that would help. Maybe that would keep him sharp.

•

Stan screamed hard against the thing in his mouth. And kicked his legs. Somebody pulled out the cloth, and said in a scary voice, "What?"

"I have to pee!" Stan said.

"Hold it in."

"I have to!"

Another voice, the one Stan thought was driving, said, "I don't want him messing the car."

"Where you think we can stop?" the first voice said.

"There's a turn out coming."

"Keep driving. The others will wonder where we are."

"I don't want that stink in my car, understand?"

"Some cop drives by, sees it, he ask questions."

Stan said, "I can't hold it in! I can't hold it anymore! My sphincter!"

"What'd he say?" the driving voice said.

"I don't know."

Stan said, "The urethral sphincter controls urination!"

"What the hell?" First Voice said.

"I'm pulling over," Driving Voice said.

And Stan told himself not to smile. Because his plan had worked. Chuck would be proud of this plan. When they stopped and they let him pee, he would fake them out all right. He was a fast runner and he would run away from the car so fast they wouldn't know what to do.

It was a good plan, he thought. A very good plan.

47

"How are things back in Bosnia?" Chuck said.

For a moment the only sound was the hum of the SUV and a little wind whistling through one of the windows. Or maybe even a snort of breath from the gun guy.

The driver said, "Make him shut up."

"Don't you want to talk about the Serbian mafia?" Chuck said. "And the fact that you all smell like garbage? Don't you ever take a bath?"

"Now!" came the order from the front.

The guy with the gun cursed in another language. To Chuck it sounded like he had just been called a *naked cake*.

The big man's hand slapped Chuck across the face. It was a good smack, stunning him momentarily. Chuck tasted blood in his mouth.

But noticed that to get him across the face, the big man had to lean slightly over the seat. When he did, he held the gun in his right hand, poised on the top of the seat.

Chuck said, "Thank you sir, may I have another?"

The big man hesitated then called him something. It sounded like *furry check*. He leaned over to hit Chuck again. Chuck rolled slight left at the same time shooting his taped hands up toward the gun. The big man's blow glanced off the back of Chuck's head. Chuck got his hands around the barrel of the gun and pulled.

It went off.

A blast, and the shattering of glass.

The back window blown out.

The SUV swerved left.

Chuck twisted the gun upward and it snapped out of the big man's hand. He pulled it into him and rolled right, once over completely. The gun, probably a nine, was barrel toward him. With his wrists together he couldn't easily manipulate it.

The SUV swerved right. The light from an oncoming car, now laying on its horn, caught the form of the big guy in full, making him a lurking shadow.

Shadow dance . . .

A shadow that was now jumping over the seat.

•

I am fast, and the plan worked!

I didn't have to pee, and you are stupid, mean people, you are stupid.

Run fast! Because they have a car and guns.

There's a hill, my feet hurt, but I won't let them catch me!

I am fast, I am fast, I am faster than the mean guys who tried to catch me in junior high. I am faster than all mean guys.

The hill is full of trees and bushes and dirt, but I will be safe and they will have to give up chasing me. Then the cops will come, they will come in the daytime.

There are wolves in hills. In the dark. They could eat me. They could smell me and eat me but I will hit them with a stick now. I'm not going to be scared this time, even though I am. Chuck needs me, and I am not going to be scared.

I wish I could see some lights somewhere. Maybe a town or a gas station or a 7-Eleven. I will give even a 7-Eleven another chance if I can get in there and get to a phone and call the police.

Lights! The road. There's a car on the road. Coming this way. Up. I have to go up the hill. Up where maybe wolves are. Can't think about that. Have to get away, had to save Chuck. Have to be brave.

Teddy Roosevelt. He charged up San Juan Hill. July 1, 1898.

Rough Riders. Mom liked Teddy Roosevelt.

Do it for Chuck, and for Mom, and for Teddy Roosevelt.

The ground hurts.

Chuck, dear God, don't let them hurt Chuck.

Can't think about that. Even if I bleed!

Up this hill!

Lights on the road.

They're coming!

48

Chuck hit the asphalt and rolled.

Flesh tore off the palms of his hands. His elbow slammed into hard road. He heard the sound of his jeans tearing at some unknown spot.

But he was out. The jump through the shattered back window had surprised even him, so it had to be a shock to the Serbs.

He heard the SUV skid to a stop about thirty yards away.

Bright lights slammed into Chuck's face.

Another car coming, fast, right at him.

He realized he was lying in the lane of oncoming traffic.

Blinded now by the lights, engulfed by the roar of a horn, amplified by adrenaline pumping through his head, Chuck pushed off from the road and thrust himself backward, toward the darkness of the canyon he knew was behind him.

He thought, as he fell, that the car whizzing past was his last chance to be saved.

•

What would Teddy do about barbed wire?

Stan was stunned by the fence. He needed to get through it. What was it doing on this hill?

But he was in his underwear and didn't want to tear his skin. If he got bad scratches he could bleed to death! And that wouldn't do anybody any good, especially Chuck.

He looked behind him and saw dark gray and what he thought was the strip of road. Then on his right, way far off, the headlights of a car coming, he thought, his way.

Maybe he should run down and wave his arms.

But people weren't as friendly as they used to be. In the movies they would stop but now was different, everybody was afraid.

He was starting to hate fear.

For a long moment he stayed still. Dear God, tell me what to do. What am I supposed to do?

From the side he heard a crunch, like branches being stepped on.

When he looked there was nothing. For one second.

Then light burst out of the darkness. It was a beam, a flashlight, aimed right at him.

And a voice grunted, "There he is."

•

Down, falling like a sack of auto parts tossed in a pit. Only the sack was his skin, ripping.

Chuck closed his eyes so as not to get jammed by a stick or bush or rock. His arms, held together by heavy tape, were useless in front of him, and he thought for a moment he had dislocated both shoulders. The pain was as hot as fire in August. He rolled over completely three times, stuck his bare feet out to stall the descent. He saw stars in the sky and behind his eyes. Then darkness as he ended up face down, sucking dirt and weeds on the sloping bank.

In the silence, the momentary pause, he listened. He heard only a slight wind whipping through the canyon, and then another sound—a car driving slowly by. It was them. If he was right about where he was, this was a deeply chiseled ravine and he still had a long way to go down.

And down was where he'd have to go, because up was only them.

He pulled his head up and saw the red of taillights, only a few feet from where he must have gone over the side.

If they got out with flashlights he wouldn't be hard to find.

If he stayed.

Forcing himself to his feet, feet now shooting with razor blades, he started down. It was an obstacle course of hard scrub and dirt and rock. Of unseen flora in the dead of night. He took in a full breath and smelled ocean in the air.

Not looking back, he let gravity help him get as far as possible. His only plan was to go deep into this crack in the earth and stay hidden long enough not to be found. Then he could figure out which way was north, which was south, east, and west, and maybe find his way to a house or town.

But every step was an agony of uncertainty. There was no moon and the expanse below was little more than a gaping maw of black. Chuck saw the terrain in his mind, recalling the times he'd driven to the beach on one of these roads. The green bushy splotches that looked so innocuous from the road were hard reality now when he needed to escape.

At least he was getting farther from the road, from the red

lights, from the enemy.

Enemy. That's exactly what they were. It was Afghanistan, come to his city.

Rushton Line . . .

He heard Dylan Bly's voice, breaking through his brain mass like an explosive device. *I know where,* Bly had said. Chuck hadn't recalled those words before, but there they were now. Like one of those loose files Royce told him about. Here under the stress of escape one of them flopped open.

Rushton Line . . . Did Bly say that? What did he mean?

Chuck told himself to keep moving. But he was waist deep in something now, sharp branches of something pushing back against him.

He needed to get his hands free but there was nothing doing on that score. He'd need something sharp, like a caveman's flinty stone. No time to stop and look for that.

He had to keep going. Had to make it out.

Had to get back to Stan.

49

"You must approach him in just the right way," Steven Kovak said. "You understand that, don't you?"

"Of course," said the doctor. Yang Jing's practice was confined to Kovak and his own family and staff. He was well paid for this. He was well paid because he was good, and because he could keep his mouth shut. He had come recommended by Zepkic, and been trained and scared into submission by Zepkic, too. He was small and tidy, a graduate of the medical college at Chenzhou, and at fifty retained a slight, Chinese accent.

Despite his experience, Jing did not know as much of about the workings of the mind as Kovak did. This was Kovak's own assessment, based upon his years of breaking the will of prisoners.

"The questions must be softly posed," Kovak explained.

"Perhaps you should be the one," Jing said. He was wearing his usual suit and tie, which always impressed Kovak. Would that more professional people did that in America. It was a discipline that was breaking down.

"No," Kovak said, offering Jing more tea from the service on the table in the atrium of his home.

Jing put up his hand. "No thank you very much, sir."

"You've administered thiopental how many times?"

"At least a dozen, sir."

"With interrogation?"

"Only once, last year, with you. You also questioned the subject, I forgot his name."

"His name is best forgotten," Kovak said. "He no longer exists."

Jing nodded.

"You must understand context," Kovak said. "I am going to give you all the information you need so that you can question him in detail. And you will never talk of this again, after this night, on pain of death. Is that clear?"

Jing's Adam's Apple bobbed up and down. "I am ready to take notes."

Kovak crossed his legs and steepled his fingers. "He was a Navy chaplain, working with a unit of the Marines. This was in the same region where I began. And through hard work and enterprise, my partners and I put together several boxes of gold and international currencies, worth at least ninety million dollars. That is, as they used to say in America, a lot of hay. This was stolen from us, and we had information and belief that it was a traitor working with an American soldier named Dylan Bly, who was operating in what they would call an undercover capacity. He was, in short, attempting to put a stop to our enterprise at the point of origin."

"I see," Jing said.

"We set out to capture this Bly, but he was very

uncooperative, and died on us. But he did have an association with the man you will be examining tonight. This is the man I and my host, a great warlord—a great *man*—questioned. Our subject's mental condition was terrible back then, and we were unable to complete the examination. The man was taken back in a raid on my host's villa. But he has come back to me now, in what I can only conclude is the hand of providence."

Jing said nothing.

"You follow the way of the Buddha? Or the Tao?"

"I have no religion," said the doctor.

"In this you are quite foolish," Kovak said. "And you must keep this in mind as you examine our subject. He was a chaplain, a man of God. You must convince him that you are also."

"I will."

"Good. What I want is to know what became of the boxes of gold. This may have been told to him by the soldier Bly. I want to know who the traitor is in my network. It is a thin reed that we have, but I must believe that is why our subject has come to me at this hour. The infusion of this capital would be of great benefit to us, as competition is growing strong."

"I understand."

"I certainly hope you do," Kovak said. "There is competition among physicians as well."

Jing frowned. "I am not entirely certain I know what you mean."

"It means you can be replaced. There is an evolutionary component to —"

The soft vibration of Kovak's phone interrupted him. He answered.

It was Simo. "Something has gone wrong."

Kovak closed his eyes. "Dragoslav?"

"I'm afraid so, sir."

50

Chuck's arms itched like freaking crazy.

The canyon was filled with poison oak. Every SoCal kid knew that. Leaves of three, let them be.

No time to be discriminating.

His arms itched but he couldn't scratch. He'd have to put up with it even as he kept moving.

He was at the bottom of the canyon now, sliding in mud. A creek bed. But apparently he wasn't being followed.

Yet.

Calibrating his direction from the road, Chuck figured he was facing away from the ocean. He had to keep moving. What choice did he have?

But it was like walking in cold pudding filled with broken glass. Chuck had to be careful not to jam his foot on something sharp and cutting.

He tried not to think about anything else being underfoot. Like snakes.

Don't think about snakes.

Too late.

He tried to get into the minds of the kidnappers. They were up on what was probably a two-lane highway in an SUV. They couldn't sit in the road unless they found a turnout. Those were few and far between if this was a stretch of road typical of the area. They would probably drive back and forth for a while, or maybe call in some heavy lights.

They probably already reported to the head man, whoever was hiring them. Chuck was still convinced that he was to be taken alive.

Now he wasn't going to be taken at all.

He was going to find Stan.

Maybe he should just wait it out, wait out the night. But that didn't sit well with him. It would just get colder and colder. This was Southern California, so he wasn't going to freeze to death. But it wouldn't exactly be Zuma Beach in the summer, either.

And weren't there mountain lions out here, too? He seemed to recall a surfer last year, stoned out of his mind, wandering up the canyon and getting torn apart by a mountain lion.

Gnarly, dude.

There you go again, thinking about things you can't control.

How often have you counseled men in battle on that very subject? There are things out of your control, things created by the acts of evil men. You can only live in the present.

Live.

211

51

"Stop your carrying on," the man said.

The way he said it scared Stan, but he was not going to show him he was scared. That was what he wanted, and he was not going to give it to him. He would wait then. Wait for his chance. He told himself to be calm, even though his body was tight in that way he got.

They were in a small room with soft furniture. The room had no windows. It had a sink. A silver sink with a mirror and some cupboards behind it. Two men had brought Stan here and locked the door. The same two men who caught him in the hills.

Then this man came in. He had a blanket with him and draped it over Stan's shoulders. The other two men left.

"That's better," the man said. He was a strong man. He had a look of someone who was in charge. It was sort of like Mr. Cambry's face at Ralphs Fresh Fare, only much stronger. Maybe this man owned many stores or many homes like this one. Yes, that was it, this was a very rich man.

"You are not in any danger here," the man said. "We both

want exactly the same thing."

His voice was strong, yes, but also soft and reassuring. What was he up to? Why did he have men with guns take Chuck away?

"We both want to see your brother, don't we?"

"Yes!" Stan said, then told himself he was being too anxious. He had to control himself. This was a mean man.

"That's right," the man said. "I need to talk to him about a certain matter."

"Who are you?"

"I'm someone who knows your brother."

"What's your name?"

"You may call me Steven."

"I had a friend named Steven once," Stan said.

"There. And so you have again."

"You're not my friend."

"I'd like to be."

"Why?"

"The world would be a better place if people were friends, don't you think?"

Stan didn't like the way he was feeling. Steven was saying the right things, but they sounded funny. That's what tricky people do.

"I don't want to be your friend," Stan said. "I want to see my brother now."

"He's not here," Steven said. "But soon he will be. He will want to make sure that you're all right. In the meantime, you can help him."

"How come you have guns?"

"Do you see me with guns?" Steven held out his hands and they were empty.

"But mean guys with guns killed people and took us!"

"May I call you Stan?"

Stan didn't know what the right answer was. "I guess so."

"Stan, listen to me. Guns are used when there is danger. Your brother is in danger. I want to protect him. That's why I'm having him brought here."

Could that be right? Could he be telling the truth? Maybe there were other mean people with guns trying to get Chuck. But I'm going to wait for him. I'm waiting for Chuck.

Steven said, "Did you hear me, Stan?"

Stan said nothing. He thought about the specials. He thought about the prices. He better not miss any work because of these guys. They better let him and Chuck go.

"I need you to talk to me, Stan, because you can help your brother right now."

"I can?"

"Oh yes, by telling me some things about him."

"I don't think I'm going to," Stan said.

"Now, that's not being friendly, is it?"

"You want to hurt Chuck."

"Is that what you think?"

Stan nodded.

"Do you believe in miracles, Stan?" Steven asked.

How should I answer that? Stan wondered. It could be another trick.

"I'd like to hear your answer, Stan. Do you believe in miracles?"

"Uh-huh."

"Why?"

"Because God can do anything. He can save Chuck and me right now, so you better not be mean."

"I believe in God, too."

"You do?" But how could he, and still do mean things, like

kidnap people?

"Of course I do," Steven said. "You have to be blind not to believe. I look out at the ocean, and know that God is the creator of all things. If that is so, he can do as he pleases. He can perform miracles."

Stan remembered his mother said once that the devil can perform miracles to fool people. He folded his arms.

"You won't help me?" Steven said.

Stan shook his head.

"But you do believe in miracles?"

Stan said nothing. He just wanted the man to go away.

"I will perform a miracle for you," Steven said. "Will that help you talk to me?"

Stan stayed silent. He can't do miracles! He's fooling me!

Steven smiled. His eyes crinkled when he did. He stood up from the chair and walked to the door. There was a keypad next to it. He hit four keys and the door clicked open. He made a motion to someone on the other side. Stan hoped it would not be one of the men with guns coming in to watch him.

It wasn't.

And Stan almost screamed.

But he couldn't, he couldn't make a sound, because he was maybe going crazy, the devil was making him crazy right now, because a ghost walked into the room.

"Hello, Stan," Julia said. "It's good to see you."

52

And sometimes, Chuck thought, you just have to get mad.

He remembered in seminary, what they called the imprecatory psalms. The ones where David raged against his enemies, calling down wrath on them. And he was a king. He had it pretty good. He had an army, too. I'm a guy in bare feet in the wild at night and hands tied in front of him.

But rage is going to keep me going.

Serbian mobsters. On our shores. Cockroaches. Step on them.

How's that for an imprecatory psalm?

Chuck laughed, and was glad he still had that capacity. He was moving like a blindfolded man across a mine field. Each clump in front of him had to be felt with either hand or foot, the way a blind person would use a cane. But up top he did not see the lights of a car, waiting. He was a good distance from the point where he'd gone over the edge. Maybe they were gone now.

Maybe they'd be back.

Chuck stepped on something hard and sharp. He pulled his foot back before putting full weight on it. He bent over and felt around. His hands found the rock. It was about the size of a baseball, but flatter. One side of it came to a dull point.

Chuck picked it up and parked his butt. He set the rock point side up on the ground, between his knees. Using his knees like a crude vice, he held the rock in place and started working the duct tape against the point. All he needed was a tear, and he could do the rest with his teeth. But the tape had several layers of thickness to it.

He counted ten passes over the rock before he felt a rip. He tried rolling his wrists to get more play. The tape held firm.

This was going to take some time. But it wasn't like he was late for a train. Nah, I got nothing to do, boys, how about we play the tie up and try to escape game? Let's do it at night in the middle of nowhere, too.

He rubbed the tape on his crude cutting rock, the caveman discovering tools. Give me a flint and I'll make fire. Ugh.

Stay mad, Chuck. Stay mad.

Stationary, he was aware now of only the sound of the occasional car passing on the street above, and the *phtt* of tape against stone. The whole thing was rhythmic now. Maybe he'd invented a new sound. Duct tape jazz.

He felt a significant tear in the tape. This time his wrists *could* move. He got about a half inch more of play.

Then heard something moving in the brush. Something very close.

•

Sandy Epperson said, "Mark."

"What the hell time is it?"

217

"Time to talk. I found something."

"It better be Jimmy Hoffa." Mark's voice sounded thick and slurry on the phone. Sandy couldn't blame him for being mad. But if you want to be a homicide detective, you have to learn that sleep is a luxury. What better time to give it to him than now?

"Better," she said. "I found a connection."

"This can't wait?"

"It's hot on my mind." She knew Mark was well aware of that phrase. It was one of the first things she taught him—to talk to the partner when something is hot on your mind. In the initial phase of forming a case theory, it was the synergy of front burner thoughts and the partner's fresh input that could make all the difference.

"I got another word for what's on your mind," Mark said. "But go ahead."

"How about the Raymond Hunt Academy?"

Pause. "What, Samson's school?"

"Yes. From Ed Hillary to Ray Hunt, to—"

"Wait. Ed who?"

"Hillary, the guy who ran down Samson's wife."

"You still on that thing in Beaman?"

"There's a through-line there." The most important aspect of detective work for Sandy was the through-line. Even in the most complex cases you could always find a main thread, something that ran through the entire series of events. Almost always it was related to motive.

"What does this have to do with Nunn?" Mark said.

"Nunn connects up to Samson."

"You playing with Legos? Thanks. Now I'm up."

"Run through this with me," she said. "You want to make some coffee?"

"Nah, I'll just tape my eyelids open. Go on."

"A little over seven months ago, Charles Samson's wife is killed in a little town outside of Los Angeles County. It happens. But then it turns out that the guy who hit her, Ed Hillary, was not some random drunk driver. He was, in fact, a major donor to the Hunt Academy in Calabasas. He gave money to the school where Samson worked."

Pause. "Okay, you have my attention."

At least his voice sounded alert now. "Scenario one. What if Hillary was trying to kill Samson's wife? What if it wasn't an accident?"

"Motive?"

"Samson's wife was a reporter of some kind. She told Samson she was doing a story on alligator farms. Turns out to be bogus. So instead, she's digging into something involving Hillary or the Hunt Academy, or both. And Hillary doesn't want her digging any further."

"Might be something there. You have another theory?"

"Scenario two. What if somebody wanted Hillary dead too? And set the whole thing up to look like a drunk hit-and-run? The thing that troubles me about Hillary is that he had so much alcohol in him at the time. When you look at what he had at the bar that night, he was nowhere near what his BAC was at the time of the accident."

"What are you saying then?"

"That somebody may have poured booze down his throat and set the thing up."

"And who would that somebody be?"

"That's a question for Ray Hunt, don't you think?"

"Sandy, I think you and your famous gut instincts need to get some sleep, like me."

"Wait—"

"Good night."

The call cut out.

And Sandy Epperson cursed at her phone.

53

She wasn't a ghost! It really was Julia!

She looked almost the same. Her brown hair was a little longer, her brown eyes a little more tired. But her voice was exactly like Stan remembered it. He liked it before, but now it was just freaky!

"I'm so sorry you've had to go through this," Julia said. She sat in the chair where the man had been sitting only moments ago.

"But you're alive!" Stan said. This was not right, this was not how things happened. People can't come back from the dead, only in horror movies and Stan did not like horror movies. "How can you be alive?"

"Believe me when I say it's best you not know," Julia said.

She looked so sad. "Did you get kidnapped?"

Julia put her hand on his knee. He didn't like to be touched there, but he let her this time. "Be patient," she said.

Stan thought she might cry.

"But you were dead," Stan said. "I saw them put you in the

ground."

"We haven't much time. You can help Chuck."

"Where is Chuck? Is he all right?"

"Yes. He'll be right here soon, in this house. They just want to talk to him. If you'll stay nice and calm, it will all be all right."

"Where have you been, Julia? Chuck was so sad when you died. But . . ."

Julia nodded, her own sadness again all over her face. Poor face.

"Will you come back to live with us?" Stan said.

"Stan, it's best not to ask questions now. I just want you to know you have a friend here. I'm here. Okay?"

"But you played a trick on Chuck. Didn't you play a bad trick?"

"You don't understand."

"I do too! I hate it when people tell me I don't understand something when I do. I understand that you fooled us but I don't know how you did it. And I don't know why you did it, but it was mean. It was a very mean thing you did."

"I know," she said. She stood and went to the door, hit the keypad four times. The door clicked open.

She looked back at him one more time before going out. She looked like she wanted to say something else. But she didn't, and closed the door behind her.

•

The thing in the brush, whatever it was, was getting closer. Animal of some kind. But what?

Chuck did not move, not wanting to attract attention. He wondered if this thing—don't let it be a mountain lion, let it be a rabbit—had picked up his scent.

And he was still bound by the tape.

He'd been so close to getting free.

He tried not to breathe too loudly.

More rustling in the brush. Chuck estimated the distance at twenty feet. If the animal couldn't hear him breathe, it no doubt could hear the Salvation Army drum in his chest.

Chuck worked his hands, pulled, the tape giving way a little more.

The rustling stopped.

In his imagination he saw a huge lion, stopping, snout upturned, sensing prey.

This was it. He was dead meat. A meal.

With the added help of fresh, survival-mode adrenaline, Chuck drew his hands to his chest, as if getting ready to row for old Yale. He couldn't help grunting as he pulled as hard as he could.

The next second felt like twenty.

And then he was free with a snap.

He listened. Only silence, but it was filled with something palpable.

Slowly, as if the slightest disturbance in the wind would set the animal-thing charging, Chuck reached down for the sharp rock.

No further sound.

But unless the thing had wings it was still there.

He gripped the rock like his four seam fastball in Little League. The gesture made him remember the time he struck out Mitch Corwin in the championship game. And now Mitch Corwin was playing center field for the Milwaukee Brewers. The highlight of his athletic life was that day. He felt just like Nolan Ryan. He even wore number 30 like Nolan did on the

Angels.

Sometimes Chuck wondered if he'd ever get to feel that way about anything again.

Now, holding his breath, Chuck got to a standing position. The animal-thing was directly to his left, somewhere. It was now as if he were on the mound with a runner on base.

Then he heard it, a low snarl. It froze every joint in his body, yet at the same time blasted awake every nerve. This was not unfamiliar. It was just like facing Mitch Corwin with two outs back in the championship game. Now this, the ultimate contest.

Chuck estimated the distance. One thing he always had was a sense of sound. It started when he would listen for his father coming home, fearing the worst. It got so he could judge just how far from the front door his dad was. And from the creaking of the floorboards which direction he was going. If it was toward the stairs Chuck would try to get Stan and hide in the closet. Estimating distance was crucial if they wanted to keep their butt cheeks from a beating.

About twenty feet was just right for the animal-thing. The snarl gave him the direction. Chuck tried to imagine a big catcher's mitt and a strike zone. He brought the rock to the ready position at his chest. Then a quick lift of his left leg, a stride toward the target and his fastball. Down the middle.

He heard a thud, like the ball settling into the catcher's glove, followed by high yelp. A dog sound. And the sound of rustling again, moving in the weeds, but this time away from him.

No more delay. Chuck started clambering up toward the road. Whatever that thing was, a coyote no doubt, maybe it had cousins.

It was time to get out of this canyon and find Stan.

•

"How could you be so stupid, so reckless?" Kovak said.

"I did what I thought was right," Dag said. "I don't need to be told anything else."

Kovak folded his arms. They were standing in Kovak's office, surrounded by computers and maps and every manner of electronic device. Dag wanted to pull wires out and throw them through a wall.

"Is that so?" Kovak said. "Now you are someone who thinks he can engineer a traffic collision? You pull a knife on someone, and think you won't be seen? Setting fire to this teacher's house?"

"Yes!"

"What was the point of that?"

"To put all suspicion on him, don't you see it?"

Kovak shook his head the way he used to do when Dag was a child, the way it always made him feel like he wanted to crawl into the earth and die.

"Where is the teacher then? Simo has brought the brother, but you have managed to lose the teacher."

"That's not true!"

"Then where is he? Is he dead on the road? Is he walking around? Is he talking to the police?"

"We will find him."

"No, I will find him. You have no more to do tonight. Do not leave this house."

"I will go and come as I like," Dag said.

Kovak slapped his son across the face.

54

Chuck reached the guard rail and felt like he was Steve McQueen about to flee the prison camp.

He saw a haze of light about a half mile away. It was a long half mile and his feet were raw. His body felt like a medical school class slide on abrasions and their various forms.

The other direction was black night with a ribbon of road twisting around a bend.

A ribbon with some very bad guys cruising around.

He would use both sight and sound now. He would be able to see headlights coming from up ahead, and hear cars approaching from behind. Behind was the problem. Cars from around that bend would appear quickly, throwing hard light on him.

Steve McQueen indeed. McQueen was ultimately caught.

Maybe he could be Charles Bronson. Bronson got away, didn't he?

He touched down on the other side of the guard rail. The

shoulder of the road was only about a foot wide. Rocks, gravel, glass all over it, he well knew. His best shot was to walk on the asphalt itself, and that was not exactly rice paper.

He headed for the light.

•

Stay nice and calm. That's what Julia said. And Chuck would be coming to the house!

Stan wanted to believe it. Chuck close again. Chuck would know what to do.

But would they do something bad to Chuck? The man said he didn't want to hurt Chuck, but bad men lie, mean men lie.

But Julia was here. Right here in this room, and she said stay calm and I can't stay calm, how can they tell me that when they close me up in here?

They are bad men with guns, they shoot people, but they kidnapped us instead because they want Chuck.

I gotta help Chuck. He said he wouldn't leave me. And I will never leave him.

But how, how?

Think.

Stan went to the door and put his ear on it. He heard nothing but a low hum of some kind. No voices.

He closed his eyes and saw the house in his mind. He saw the way they had taken him in. From a dark garage through a long corridor with tile and fancy wood and nothing on the walls. Lights right in the ceiling. Then through a door and down some stairs, past a little office of some kind—through the slightly opened door he saw a computer on a desk and a map on the wall, on a big corkboard with push pins. Then into this room, this special room with no windows, and locked in.

Then he thought he knew what he could do. Yes, he could help Chuck. He could fool them all. He didn't care if they were wolves now. He was going to help his brother, yes he was.

If he could get Julia back in the room.

He pounded on the door. "Hey!"

He pounded again.

55

A set of headlights flashed behind Chuck.

He was ready, had planned the maneuver. He put his left hand on the top of the guardrail and hopped over, turning so he faced the now oncoming lights, prone. The rail was the perfect height to conceal him. He had only a foot or so of ground before it dropped off sharply. He held the underside of the rail with his right hand.

The lights went past without stopping.

Chuck went back up and over, on the road again.

His helplessness almost amused him. How dependent are we on cell phones? How does anyone learn resilience anymore?

And where is a cop when you need one? It would be nice if that detective showed up just about now.

The sound of another approaching car. Same direction.

Same move, this time Chuck's legs slipped and threatened to pull him down the canyon again. His right hand grab saved him.

The car sped on.

Chuck pulled himself up. This was like one of those

dreams where you run in the mud and can't get anywhere, but you have to, because someone's chasing you.

The pain in his feet and legs told him it was no dream.

He made up some good distance this time. The air was cold and moist. A slight fog blanketed the source of the lights up ahead, but he would be there in maybe ten minutes.

Ten long minutes that stretched out like a couple of hours.

Stay mad.

As he walked, he remembered staying mad at God. It started when Dylan Bly died and he had his own throat cut. It deepened when he got home and found Julia cold and his own mind fragmented. It softened when he got the job at Hunt and was working toward some sort of truce.

Hardened again when Julia was killed.

Now what? When was there going to be some kind of resolution? Or were questions the only things certain in this life?

Another car. This time coming out of the fog toward him.

How many of these were there going to be? At this rate he'd reach the township by next spring. Part of him wanted to take a chance and flag the thing down. But what were the odds of anyone stopping, even in this last bastion of the hippy movement?

A staggering, bleeding, barefoot specter wandering the canyon road?

Don't think so.

Chuck stepped over the guard rail again and took his now familiar position.

Face down, he muttered, "For what it's worth God, I'm willing to start over. Bygones and all that."

He even laughed. He was remembering a video he saw in high school, an old Burt Reynolds movie. It was about a guy who wanted to commit suicide. At one point he swims out in the ocean, far from shore. Then suddenly wants to live.

So as he's struggling back toward the beach. He bargains with God. If you'll let me make it, God, he says, I'll obey the Ten Commandments. Then he starts to list them.

I shalt not kill.

I shalt not commit adultery.

Then realizing he doesn't know any more, Burt says, "I'll *learn* the ten commandments!"

It really was funny because people tend to wait until dire straits, or any kind of straits, to cry out to God.

But that's what Chuck was doing right now. Only he didn't know what to bargain with.

He heard the approach of the car, and the stream of light spilling through the guard rail slat.

It seemed to him then that the car was slowing. Chuck looked through the bottom of the rail. The lights brightened and the crunch of tires on the gravel told him something not good— the car was on the wrong side of the road.

His side.

He kept his face down, sniffing dirt.

The crunch of the tires stopped.

Had they seen him hop the rail? What now, dive back down the canyon?

Chuck heard a door open, close. The engine kept idling. The sound of feet on gravel told him it was only one person. If it had been the Serbs, it would have been two, and they would be talking. And rushing.

A beam of light blasted through the rail. Moving. A flashlight.

The pool of illumination jumped the rail and poured over Chuck's head to the ground around him.

A man's voice said, "What in the hell are you doing down

there?"

Chuck didn't move.

"Come on now, get up."

It wasn't all that easy to. Chuck's body, coming off the flood of adrenaline, was wanting to dial it in for the night. He felt every joint protest as he got to his feet.

The guy was shining the light directly into his eyes. Chuck put his hand up. "You mind shutting that thing off?"

The light stayed. "What happened to you?"

"You a cop?"

"Ranger. You fall?"

"I need a phone," Chuck said.

"You need a lot of things it looks like," the ranger said. "You're bleeding."

"Take me in, will you?"

"In where?"

"Your office, wherever. People are looking for me."

"I don't want to get blood all over my car."

"These people have guns. They are serious. And not only that, there's a dead body right down there."

"What?"

"Will you just take me in before—"

Chuck stopped, headlights coming around the curve. He ducked behind the ranger's car. He heard the car speed on by.

"You *are* spooked," the ranger said.

"I need to get off the street. Now. I'll pay to have your cruiser cleaned. Just take me in."

Chuck went to the idling car. Opened the driver's door.

"Hey," the ranger said.

Chuck got in and slid over to the passenger side.

The ranger cursed. But he got in behind the wheel.

"You need to tell me what happened." The ranger was in

his mid-twenties, with long blond surfer-hair and an official ranger shirt, with arm patch. But he wore blue jeans and sandals below.

"I will. Get me to your station. I need to make a call."

"I don't know who you are," he said. "I ought to hold you."

"For what?"

"I'm not sure yet."

"Believe me. You got nothing. I'm going to call an LAPD cop. She'll tell you. Just get me there."

"Guys with guns?"

"Real guns."

"What do you mean, dead body?"

"Yes, dead," Chuck said. "Don't worry, I didn't do it."

"You don't look crazy."

"Just drive, okay?"

"I'm the one —"

"Please."

The surfer-ranger said nothing more. He drove into town. To the left was what the canyon people would have called a mall—less than a strip in the more populated areas of the county. A grocery store, a funky restaurant decorated in early '70s hippy chic, a bead store. The ranger station occupied the corner after that, at the intersection of three roads, including the main one.

The ranger pulled to a stop in front of the station house.

"Can I at least know your name?" he said, almost apologetically.

"Call me Chuck. You?"

"Chip."

Chip and Chuck. Sounded like Disney characters. A couple of chipmunks, one on the run from killers. A laugh riot.

The station house smelled of old coffee and incense. The

olive drab color was semi-military in tone, but the surfer poster on the wall confirmed the personality of Ranger Chip.

"You want some coffee?" Chip said, lifting the partition at the front counter.

"Just a phone."

"Right here." He motioned to a desk with a computer monitor, stack of Post-It notes, and a pink phone.

"Does it work?" Chuck said.

"My partner picked it out. She's sort of retro-Barbie."

Chuck fished Sandy Epperson's card out of his back pocket and punched the number. According to the Frisbee shaped clock on the wall, it was almost eleven.

After three rings she answered. "Epperson."

"Samson."

"Where are you?"

"Ranger station in Topanga. I got taken tonight. So did my brother. Stan is still missing."

"What happened?"

"Can you get out here? It's real. Guns, kidnapping, it has it all."

"Um, yes, sure. What's the address?"

"Let me give you to Chip."

He could only imagine Epperson's face as he handed the phone to Ranger Chip. Chip made some preliminary remarks, listened, then gave her the exact address and hung up.

"She's on her way," Chip said. "This is real, huh?"

"Where's the bathroom?"

Chip pointed to the back. "I'll get a first aid kit."

Walking back to the bathroom was itself an ordeal. Chuck imagined he looked like something out of a George Romero zombie film. It's what he felt like, anyway.

And when he got to the bathroom and looked in the

mirror, he confirmed it. Dirt and spots of blood gave his face a walking dead glint. His shirt was torn. Around his neck scar were fresh scratches, from brush and small rocks.

Chuck turned on the water and splashed his face. The cold felt good. A nice breeze flowed through the crack in the frosted glass window, carrying smells of the canyon. There was a roll of paper towels on a counter. Chuck tore off a handful and soaked them, dapped at his face and neck.

Okay, you're on the upswing now. God, thanks are due, but if you can hold back the animals and mobsters and watch over Stan, I'd appreciate that a great deal.

His feet were next. Open cuts, scratches, dried blood and bruises. Chuck sat on the toilet and started cleaning. He thought about Bruce Willis in *Die Hard.* The scene where he runs across broken glass. And didn't that whole thing start because Willis was in a bathroom when Alan Rickman and his crew took over the building?

That was part of it here, with thugs taking over civil society. You try to do your work and get along, but they intrude in some form or fashion. They—

Chuck heard the front door open. He peeked through the open door and saw Chip at the counter, back toward him.

He heard Chip say, "What can I do for you?"

And then Chip's head exploded.

56

As she got in her car Sandy reflected that the strain in Samson's voice was as real as a fingerprint. What you think of a suspect is often an accumulation of little details. Sometimes your initial impression is confirmed, other times realigned after multiple observations.

Samson struck her from the start as truthful, but hiding something. Something big. Mooney thought it was all a ruse, pointing to Samson's ultimate guilt.

She thought the opposite, and the sound of his voice was another piece on the scales of her intuition.

Mooney, of course, was one of the new breed who thought "gut instinct" was something you used for ordering food, not solving cases.

She'd just see about that.

Chuck had taught him. Back when Stan was six and he wanted to fight like Chuck. He wanted to be able to beat up the mean kids and there were a lot of them, oh yes. But Chuck said, Don't use your fists, use your mind. But my mind isn't like anybody's, Stan had said. That's the good part, Chuck said. Things stick to your mind.

Chuck was doing his magic then, and he was learning things, like memory tricks. Chuck taught him that trick about using pictures to make numbers. Like a duck is the number two, because if you look at a duck on the water it's sort of shaped like a two. It made Stan laugh the first time. And then you can think of a number three like some handcuffs. Opened up, they look like a three. Chuck had some toy handcuffs and showed Stan. That's what they looked like. Four, that was a sailboat. Five, that was a hook.

And then Stan started memorizing numbers and it was easy. He could do it almost without trying.

He could even tell Chuck to hold up cards, a lot of them, one at a time, and then he'd tell Chuck what cards he'd held up and even the order of them.

So he could use his mind like that and sometimes that made Stan feel good when he was feeling bad.

Like now, he was feeling bad, but he was also using his mind just like Chuck said.

Nobody was coming when he pounded on the door.

He'd make them come all right.

The sink worked. He could run water. There wasn't anything in any of the cupboards. It was like it was supposed to be a bar once, but it wasn't anymore. What kind of a crazy place was this? Maybe it was for torture. Maybe they tortured you here by running water over your face.

Now Stan was running the water.

He cupped his hands and got some. He went to the door and threw the water at the bottom of the door. He was going to make it wet on the other side.

They'd see that. They'd think things.

Stan left the water running, and took two more handfuls and threw them at the bottom of the door.

"That feels good!" he shouted.

And waited.

•

Pure survival instinct turned Chuck toward the bathroom window. He'd barely fit through.

The sound of the counter partition slamming mixed with the voices of two men. And the sound of feet heading toward the back.

Chuck palm-pushed the window sill.

It moved half an inch.

He looked back through the half open door and saw no one.

Then heard slamming and rooting around. He remembered seeing a back office, opposite the hallways leading to the bathroom. They were checking there, but it wouldn't take long for them to realize their prey must be elsewhere.

And there'd be only the bathroom left.

Chuck used the heels of both palms.

Another half inch.

The sounds in the other room stopped.

Push!

The window loosened, and shoved open with a loud bang.

The scuffling of feet in the next room.

Head first, Chuck thrust himself through the portal to his only chance of survival.

It was eerily familiar to the SUV jump he'd made earlier in the evening. He hit the pavement behind the ranger station and had a quick choice.

Two roads, one narrow and leading upward. That was to his left.

The other one curved slightly down, to his right. It had the sharpest turn and would give him more immediate cover.

That's where he ran.

57

As Sandy Epperson cruised by the sign for the Theatricum Bottanicum, Topanga Canyon's outdoor theater, she thought about how terrible most criminals were when it came to acting innocent.

You didn't need all that hokum about kinesiology and lying indicators, as if they were magic. You could just tell because most people were lousy actors. Maybe a DeNiro could fool you, but not these scenery chewers. Not like your Scott Petersons, who were so full of themselves they thought they could charm anyone into believing them.

Samson was not an actor and not trying to be one.

Neither was she. No, she was more adept at keeping under the radar.

•

Chuck plunged forward into darkness. Against the starry sky, the trees were grim shadows. He had to lean forward at the waist to keep on the road, looking at the ground just a few feet ahead.

There were homes on the right. He saw lights in the windows of two.

Then heard the engine of an oncoming car. In a flash he remembered an incident from his childhood. He was fourteen and walking home in his neighborhood one night. As neighborhoods went, his was fairly safe, but when a car passed him in the street and slowed, he sensed bad news. So he backed up a few steps, turned and ran down the first side street he came to, and ducked behind some trash cans lining a driveway. Crouching there, he peeked out and saw the car drive by. He was sure it was looking for him. He waited a few minutes, then ran all the way home.

Now he followed his memory and ran up a driveway on his right. There was indeed a side yard and large, municipally-approved trash containers. One of them was green, to be used for leaves and grass. He opened it up and felt around and came up with a handful of mown grass. He threw his leg over the rim and got in, closing the top over him but leaving a slight crack to look out of.

The car cruised by. Slowly. It had a bright side light pointed in the direction of the houses.

It continued on past this house. Chuck listened for the sound of it getting further away. As soon as he could hear only the crickets he thought he'd wait another minute, then get out.

Light splashed around the trash container. Almost as if an alien space ship were hovering above him and about to beam him up.

Chuck didn't move, still holding the lid open a crack.

He heard something slam behind him. In the receptacle he couldn't turn around and look. He held his breath.

The top of the trash can flipped open. Chuck was staring

into the double barrels of a shotgun. The shotgun was in the hands of an old woman. She was all lit up. She looked like some avenging witch from a Tolkien movie.

She said, "What in the name of the good God are you doing in my trash?"

Chuck closed his eyes. "Do you have a phone?"

"You think I'm stupid? You think I'm just gonna let you into my house or something?"

"Some people are trying to kill me."

"I might be one of 'em, you don't get on out of here."

Chuck shook his head, not knowing whether to laugh or cry. He was about to drop from exhaustion, a phone was in this house, but an old lady was holding a gun on him and talking hillbilly smack.

And he wasn't in any mood to explain himself anymore. He stepped out of the trash container, dusted himself off and put his chest on the barrels of the shotgun.

"Go ahead and shoot, or let me use your phone," he said.

She thought a moment, then made a gesture with the gun. "Inside," she said.

The house seemed to have no available space for moving around, save for a narrow corridor. Like an ant farm. Newspapers were bound and stacked and up against the walls. Cardboard boxes of various sizes, some open some closed, spilled out who knew what — clothing, dishware.

Granny Shotgun led him to the kitchen and pointed to a wall phone with the gun.

Chuck dialed Royce.

"Man, you got to come get me right now," Chuck said. "I haven't got time to explain. You free?"

Royce groaned, then, "What time is it?"

"There's all sorts of stuff going down right now and I just

need you to get me out of here."

"Stuff?"

"I'll tell you when you get here."

"Where is here?"

Chuck looked at the old woman. "What's your address?"

"I'm not telling anybody where I live," she said.

"Please!"

She was still holding the shotgun, lazily in her arms, so the twin barrels pointed at his feet. She shook her head.

Fine, wonderful, this was just what the doctor ordered!

Royce. He was the kind of guy who could sell responsibility to teenagers. Chuck said, "Tell this nice lady who I am and who you are, would you do that?"

"Chuck—"

He held out the phone to the woman. She said, "Just let it hang and step over next to Bobby Sherman."

Chuck followed her eyes to a faded poster of a guy dressed in gaudy '70s clothes, from thick-striped pants to puffy shirt.

Whatever.

Chuck let the phone dangle from its base and went to the poster.

Granny Shotgun picked up the phone and said, "Talk."

Chuck read her face as she listened. It went through a few permutations of canyon skepticism before melting into warm acceptance.

Next thing he knew she was giving Royce her address.

She hung up the phone and put the shotgun down, leaning in a corner. "Thank you for your service," she said.

Chuck said nothing, but managed a nod.

"You want a Fig Newton?"

"I just want to rest."

"I want to talk. I want to know what trouble you're in. I

243

want to use it."

"Use it? For what?"

"My show." She shuffled over to a desk, and Chuck noticed for the first time that she was wearing a bathrobe with no belt. He silently prayed he wouldn't get a glimpse of anything.

She came back and handed him a piece of paper. It looked like the first page of a script.

The Audacity of Nope

The new one-woman show by Henrietta Hoover

I take the stage from the left. A spot hits me.

ME: Get that light out of my eyes!

Chuck looked up at her. "I guess you're Henrietta Hoover."

"That's not just who I am, that's who the hell I am."

Chuck said nothing.

"That's my tag line," she said. "I stole it from *How to Succeed in Business Without Really Trying.*"

I have fallen into the rabbit hole, Chuck thought.

"You don't know about my stuff, I gather. Not a theater person, huh? I've done several pieces. I was written up in LA Weekly. I was nominated for Drama Circle award. But maybe that doesn't mean anything to you."

"I—"

"This show is about my embrace of atheism, which I was stating publicly before any of these cockamamie new atheists with their fancy books came along."

She made a gesture with her arms and her robe threatened to flash open. Chuck looked at the floor.

"Ma'am, I'm just hoping—"

"Don't call me ma'am! What do you think I am, some sort of schoolmarm?"

"I don't have anything against—"

"I come out on stage, see, and I say to the light, stay out of my face. I don't need you. And then I sing a song about the pointlessness of existence."

Chuck said, "Would you mind keeping your robe closed?"

She looked down at her exposure. "Do you have something against the human body?"

"I just, um, have my mind on other things."

"What other things? There is nothing more elemental than the human body. We do not have minds that exist outside of our bodies, we do not have souls. Do you think we have souls?"

This was beginning to feel like one of those conversations from high school, when he was baked at the beach with his band friends. But there was no choice except to talk on. He was going to stay inside until Royce came, and the main thing was to keep her from disrobing until that moment. Or maybe ever.

"Sure," Chuck said. "We have souls."

"Who made these souls?" Henrietta Hoover asked.

"God."

"Oh really? Out of what?"

"Ms. Hoover, I'd be thrilled to come see your show, but—"

"Listen! What if, just like particles of matter existing before the Big Bang, particles of unconscious consciousness existed right alongside them? And then when the universe all came together, these particles did, too?"

Make me a particle and float me out of here, Chuck thought.

•

Stan heard somebody knock on the other side of the door.

"What's going on, Stan?" It was Julia's voice.

"I think you know," Stan said. That sounded good to him. It was good and tough. He was going to fool them all right.

"I need you not to do anything foolish," Julia said.

"Just you wait and see!"

A moment's pause. Stan hoped she wouldn't go away. That would spoil his plan.

He heard beeping from outside and then the door clacked open. Julia came in and shut the door behind her.

"You're not being very nice, Stan," Julia said.

"Am too! You're the one who's not being nice. You have Chuck and you're going to hurt him!"

"Stan, listen to me. I won't let them hurt Chuck. All they want is to talk to him. It's very important. Can you understand that, Stan?"

He shook his head. Hard.

"No, I don't think you can." Julia came to him and made like she was going to hug him. Stan jumped back and gave her the don't-touch-me glare. Chuck said it made him look like a mad dog when he did that. Fine. Good. He was going to mad dog them all, starting with Julia.

She didn't look mad.

"Stan, I always thought you were the greatest kid in the world."

"I'm not a kid."

"I thought of you like that. Like you were my kid brother. You know there was an old song, and whenever I'd hear it I'd think of you, Stan."

"What song?"

"It's called 'Vincent.' It's about Vincent Van Gogh. Do you

know who he was?"

"He was a painter and there was a movie about him starring Kirk Douglas and Anthony Quinn."

"That's right. This song was about him. And there's a line in it that says this world was never meant for one as beautiful as you."

Stan frowned.

"I wish this world wasn't the way it was, Stan. I wish there was a place where you didn't have to go through all this."

"I don't know if you're a bad guy or a good guy, Julia." He felt like crying just then, but he told himself not to because that wouldn't be good for the plan.

"I don't know myself, Stan. But will you promise not to try to hurt yourself or do anything foolish?"

"Like what?"

"I don't know. I know you have some imagination. No one's going to get hurt if we all just stay calm. Okay?"

"How did you fool us, Julia?"

"What?"

"How did you do that trick where we thought you were dead?"

Julia looked at him a long time. "Don't think about such things, Stan. You just wait. You'll be with Chuck soon."

Sooner than you even think, Julia!

She turned and punched the keypad again.

And this time a picture zoomed into Stan's mind, just like he knew it would. A snowman was holding a cannon that fired a ball into a duck's butt.

The duck went *Quaaacck!*

•

Ray Hunt slumped at his desk in the study, the tightening in his chest threatening to throw his heart to the floor. He'd done some wrestling in high school. Got to the state championships as a welterweight. He was crushed in the semis by a kid from Stockton who squeezed all the air out of Ray's lungs.

Funny that picture should come to him now. Or maybe not so funny.

It was dark in the house. Ray liked it that way just before bed. Astrid, as was her custom, would have cracked a book upstairs in bed, read three pages, and dropped off to sleep. Ray would come up and remove the book from her stomach and flick off the light.

But until then he would sit with only the desk lamp on, writing in his journal. He wrote it out in longhand, with a Bic pen, the greatest pen ever invented, the best value. He loved the feel of it on the page and knew he would not ever consign his most intimate thoughts to the keyboard and the computer. He wanted them on paper, because someday he'd be dead and he needed this journal to be found.

It was his confession and his catharsis.

And Astrid knew nothing about it.

He couldn't bear it if she did, until he was completely finished. Astrid, whom he'd known since they were in junior high school. The woman of his long years, of the good times and bad. And there would never be another to take her place if she were to go before him.

But what if he died first? And what if then she found the unfinished confessions of Raymond Hunt? He could only hope that she would understand, as she always did when she heard him out. He would craft the journal as carefully as he could, as a closing argument of sorts. He'd once harbored thoughts of going to law school and becoming a great trial lawyer. Viet Nam changed his perspective on all that. He was too restless when he got home to wait three years for a sheepskin and a shingle. He operated under the impression that he could die at any time, and there was no time to waste. So he and Astrid started the Academy on a proverbial shoestring.

And to all the world he looked like a success. A clean, upright example of the American dream.

He started writing in the journal, and out came *The American dream can easily turn into a nightmare.*

A noise in the hallway startled him. Astrid? No, it couldn't be, she would have come down the stairs and immediately alerted him to her presence.

The cat? Not with that heavy a paw step.

He looked out the open door of the study. Only darkness, with a bit of illumination from his desk lamp spilling onto his wife's display case. Astrid was a collector of things beautiful and porcelain, and entirely uninteresting to Ray Hunt. But because they were hers, he was happy they were there.

The floorboards squeaked.

"Who is it?" Ray said, feeling immediately stupid, as if some intruder would say, *Excuse me for disturbing you, sir. I'm just taking your TV . . .*

But then a form stepped into the doorway, and the form held a handgun.

"Jimmy needs your help," Tommy Stone said.

Ray's blood vibrated. Somehow he knew this was coming. Tommy Stone, Jimmy's younger brother, was going to go crazy someday under his brother's influence.

"How did you get in here?" Ray said.

Tommy was taller and skinnier than his brother. Jimmy had been a student at Hunt until they had to expel him. He wasn't going to let Tommy in, but that was before the money issue. That was before everything started to go south.

"Put the gun away, Tommy."

"You're going to help Jimmy," Tommy said. His voice gave off the embarrassing squeak of the pubescent boy, even though Tommy should have been well over all that by now. His gun hand was trembling.

Ray Hunt said, "He needs more than my help." And then Ray knew there was only one way left. "Tommy, let's go to the police—"

"You took our money! You owe us!"

"You don't have to be part of this. You don't have to go down that road."

"Stop talking. Jimmy needs a lawyer, a good one."

"Think about it, Tommy, you're—"

"Shut up!"

Ray Hunt stood. His legs were unsteady. He put a hand on his desk.

"Sit down!" Tommy Stone said.

"I'm not going to do this anymore," Ray Hunt said. "I can't. I know your brother killed that girl, that witness."

"You better watch your mouth, old man."

"Help him."

"Shut up!"

"He needs to come in. You need to bring him in."

Tommy pointed the gun at Ray Hunt sideways, gang style. "I told you shut up!"

From behind Tommy Stone came a voice. "Don't do it, son."

Tommy jumped, turned.

Ray Hunt watched, unable to move.

"Put the gun down," the voice from the shadows said.

Tommy fired into the darkness. One shot. Another. Wild.

Ray heard his wife scream at the top of the stairs.

Tommy turned again to Ray. His face was as frightened as any Ray had ever seen. Tommy's hand shook like a cold, wet dog as he pointed the gun at Ray's face.

Blam.

58

When Sandy Epperson pulled into the small lot of the ranger station it was stuffed with two Malibu police cars and a sheriff's vehicle. She saw three uniforms and one white clad older man moving in slow circles inside. A team of unsynchronized swimmers.

Had Samson called the local cops too? He had sounded truly spooked over the phone. She only hoped he wasn't talking too freely without her being present.

One Malibu cop stood sentry at the door. Sandy flashed her badge and the cop, a clean scrubbed football player type, said, "Far from home, huh?"

"This involves a case I'm working," Sandy said. "What's going on in there?"

"You need to talk to Lt. Shriber." He pointed to a guy in plain clothes.

"Okay," she said.

"I'll get him." He went through the door. Sandy followed him in and stayed by the entrance. Cop etiquette demanded checking in with the other jurisdictional lead before stepping into a scene. But what kind of scene was this? Did they have Samson in a chair somewhere? The one called Shriber snapped to attention when the cop said something to him. He came from around the front counter and approached Sandy. "Who are you again?" he said. He was thin of body and of hair. What was left on his pate was slate-colored.

Sandy flashed her badge once more. "Where is Mr. Samson?"

"Who?"

"Samson. Charles Samson."

"Don't know what you're talking about. I got—"

"He's the one who called me. From here."

"And who is this guy?" Shriber asked.

"A guy I'm interested in. On another matter."

"That doesn't help me."

Sandy wondered how much to give him. The complete story? No, not relevant. She wanted to find Samson, and quick. "He's in some trouble. There may be people after him."

"You say he called you from here?"

"That's right."

"Interesting."

"Why?"

"There's a broken bathroom window. Maybe that's where your Samson slipped out, after shooting this young man."

Sandy was too stunned to say anything. Shriber motioned for her to come through the counter gate.

The victim was on the floor, blood pooled around his head. There was a crater where the back of his skull should have been.

"Samson did not do that," Sandy said.

"Yeah?" Shriber said, with an uptick in tone that invited her to continue.

"Samson's no killer. He called me, he wanted help."

"Maybe he made his own help. Describe this guy for me."

"Whoever is after him did this, most likely. There's no sign of robbery, is there?"

"I don't know. We're not through."

"You won't find any," Sandy said. "And the exit wound, that indicates a serious weapon, not your average handgun."

"I know that."

"Have you got a couple of cruisers out there looking for people with guns?"

"Not yet."

Sandy said, "I'm just going to look at that bathroom window if you don't mind."

"Now wait, this is a secured scene."

"It won't hurt to cooperate."

"I have a scene to observe if you don't—"

"Then you might want to observe the blood satellites." Sandy nodded toward the small blood spatters that separated from the parent upon impact with the floor. Crime scenes always told a story. Blood spatters were subplots.

Shriber looked down.

"The pattern is interrupted in the middle," Sandy said. "There's a slight smear. That's where your killer crossed over and headed toward the back, the bathroom."

"Samson maybe."

"To find the least favorable way out of this place?"

"Maybe somebody was in the front, spooked him. He looked for a back way out of here."

"There a back door?"

Shriber looked toward the rear and had nothing to say.

"Keep looking," Sandy said. She pulled out her card and handed it to him, then went to the front. As she went out she almost knocked over another woman coming in. Charging in, more like it.

"Detective Epperson, I presume?" The woman had short brown hair and was dressed like a professional, with navy blue coat over crisp white shirt.

"Yes," Sandy said.

"My name is Lucy Bowers. We have to talk."

Lucy Bowers? Where had she heard that name? Wait. She lived across the street from Charles Samson.

Or had, until she disappeared.

But she sure wasn't disappeared now.

When Sandy had been a little girl, and her mother found herself inside some hard situation, she used to say, "That's a fine kettle of fish."

Well, here is the kettle, Sandy thought, and I'm in it. And fishy doesn't even begin to describe the smell.

•

"You're not telling me you think there's a reason for all this, do you?" Henrietta Hoover had mercifully kept her robe closed but was now sitting with her legs crossed. Showing a little too much leg.

"Reason?" Chuck said.

"You think there's a deity who made us?"

Sitting on a hard chair, and knowing he looked like hell's own ambassador, Chuck did not continue the conversation.

"What's your line of work?" the woman asked.

"School teacher."

"How long?"

Chuck said nothing. He couldn't imagine having to listen to this woman's voice for an entire evening of theater.

"I'm gonna keep asking until you answer," she said.

"Why not let me ask you questions?"

That seemed to please her. Good. At least this way he'd control the conversation until Royce arrived.

"Where were you born?" Chuck asked.

"Pittsburgh," she said. "A good place to be *from*."

"They have the Steelers."

"They have jack, Jack. You married?"

Oh no. "I thought I was asking the questions."

She shook her head. "Not anymore. Divorced?"

"I never talk about my personal life on the first date."

"Life sucks," Henrietta Hoover said. "And then you die."

"That doesn't leave much to look forward to."

"There is nothing."

How many conversations like this had he had in Afghanistan? With young soldiers who'd lost limbs or knew they would? Who fought the inner ferret of fear every day?

In some strange way, those had prepared him for this moment.

And then it struck him. She was as much a victim of the battle of life as the soldiers were of the war in Afghanistan. Whatever had happened to her, she was lashing out and looking for a reason to live. As much as he didn't want to do it, his training kicked in and pushed the words out of his mouth.

"You're gambling with the universe," he said, "and you have limited information. Why bet against hope and meaning and beauty? Why go all in on that bet?" He was talking to himself now, as much as he was to her.

She was silent for the first time in a long time. Chuck couldn't read her face, but he imagined the sound of rusty gears inside her head. "Where are you going?" she finally said. "I mean, when your friend picks you up?"

"Anywhere that's not here," Chuck said.

"Something bad really has happened to you, hasn't it?"

"Best you don't know about it," Chuck said.

"Will you come back?" she said.

"Back?"

"Will you come back and visit me sometime? I haven't had a good conversation like this in a long time."

She seemed to sink into the chair, like loose change between cushions. In the dimness of the light Chuck could see hard lines on her face.

"Would you?" she said.

"Henrietta, it would be a pleasure," Chuck said.

She smiled.

"Maybe I will take that Fig Newton," Chuck said.

Ten minutes after the Newton, Chuck heard a car pull up in the drive. He peeked out the window and saw headlights, which were immediately shut off.

"He's here," Chuck said to Henrietta. "Thanks for having me."

"Stay out of trash cans," she said. "And don't forget to come back."

"I won't."

As he moved for the door she stopped him, and kissed him on the cheek.

He gave her a quick nod before she did anything else, then back through the narrow pack-rat corridor and out the side door.

Royce was out of the car.

"What the heck is this place?" he said.

Chuck said, "Did you see any other cars on the way in?"

"No. There were a ton of cop cars out at the corner, though."

"Gotta go there. I have to tell them what happened, and

start looking for Stan."

"Chuck what is—"

"In the car." Chuck hopped in the passenger seat. Royce got in and started up the car. As Royce backed out of the driveway, headlights on, Chuck saw Henrietta looking out the window at them, like they were a ship going to sea.

"Tell me now what is going on," Royce said, heading up the dark road.

"You were right about the Serbs," Chuck said. "I got the info from a guy who knows. It's drugs, Royce. Heroin. It's serious, because they've got Stan."

"No way."

"They came to the motel. The one I rear ended and another guy. They want something from me. He kept saying 'Where is it'?"

"Where is what?"

"That's just it. I don't know. He had a stun gun, a baton."

"This keeps getting better and better."

"You don't know the half of it. Stan and I got away, they chased us, we got held in a sushi restaurant and . . . did you hear any reports about a killing at a sushi place?"

"Killing!"

"These guys shot up the place. I can't believe this is happening."

Chuck closed his eyes, rubbed them. His head was buzzing. When Royce didn't say anything, but slowed, he looked up. "What?" he said.

"Look."

Royce's headlights illuminated a lightless SUV straight ahead of them. In the middle of the road.

"It's them," Chuck said.

"Hold on," Royce said.

He shoved his car into reverse.

This was crazy. Also their only chance. But it could mean death to both of them and he'd brought Royce right into the middle of it.

No time to think of that now.

Royce spun the tires as he turned. Chuck looked back and saw the SUV hit its lights and come toward them.

"I'm sorry," Chuck said.

"We've been through worse," Royce said. He gunned the car forward toward the deeper darkness of the canyon.

•

Stan listened at the door and heard no voices. Maybe it was now or never. Time to make a play. Time to show what he could do.

He could sneak! He got very good at sneaking as a kid. When dad was looking for him, or when bullies were around. He learned to sneak. He sneaked away from the Reilly brothers, one older and one younger, who were going to give him a super wedgie one day. He heard about it at school, and knew where they'd be waiting for him. He sneaked out by hiding in a bathroom stall with his feet up on the toilet so they couldn't see. Then he went out low between the buildings at the corner of the campus and hopped the fence.

He could sneak, and he would, and when they came back to try to find him he wouldn't be there.

Where he would be he didn't know, but he was going to find his way to Chuck for sure.

He closed his eyes and saw the duck getting shot with the ball from the cannon held by the snowman.

Snowman was an 8.

Cannon was a 6.
Ball was a 0.
Duck was a 2.
8-6-0-2.
He would show them.
He pressed the numbers on the keypad.
The door went *click.*

59

In the small inner office of the ranger station, Sandy Epperson said, "Okay, what is this all about?"

The woman placed an FBI credential on the table in front of Sandy. But the name was *Erica DeSoto*.

"Lucy Bowers is a deep cover name," DeSoto said. "There is more going on here than meets the eye, as they say."

"I'd like both my eyes to know what's going on."

"Suppose you tell me why you're here?"

"I'm here as an LA cop. We've been looking at a man named Charles Samson."

"For what?"

"Murder."

DeSoto smiled. It was one of those knowing, Fed smiles Sandy Epperson had seen before. She hated that look. It usually meant an investigation was being snatched away from her.

"Charles Samson is no more a killer than Paris Hilton is a law professor."

Sandy felt a rush of energy, the kind that confirmed her

hunch about Samson.

"And you know this how?" Sandy said.

"Listen," DeSoto said.

•

Chuck thought Royce might fly right off the canyon road. Down into some ravine. It was not easy negotiating these turns at this speed.

But what choice? Guys with guns and deadly intent behind them.

If we hit a cul-de-sac, Chuck thought, we're cooked.

"Maybe we should ram them," Royce said.

"Head on?"

"Why not? Give us the element of surprise."

This was what it had come to? This was the plan? It made a perverse sense, a head on crash. Because the whole bloody thing had started with a rear ender. That was LA for you, it all came down to cars.

"We could stop and make a run for it," Royce said. "In the dark, maybe we'd have a chance."

"Let's ram the hell out of them," Chuck said, surprising himself. But he was tired of running, tired of bad people having their way. Ram them and kill them, that was the only way. You can't avoid it in this world, some people just have to die and it's not going to be you or Royce or Stan, not if you have anything to say.

And if you flame out and die yourself, so what? You went down with a fight.

"Hey man, you ready?" Royce said.

"Yeah."

"I'm gonna turn around."

"Do it."

There was another curve and another little offshoot road. Royce turned into the road, stopped, backed up.

As he did, the headlights from the oncoming car hit them from the side.

The sound of popping. Only hard and metallic.

Gunfire.

Before Royce could make the turn, his SUV slumped left. Chuck registered this as tires being shot out. Royce tried to regain control but it wasn't happening.

More pops. Hitting the side of the car.

"Get out and run!" Royce said. He reached over and popped the glove compartment, took out a gun. "Now!"

"No!"

Royce said, "Do it for Stan. Go!"

No time, no time, Chuck pushed out the passenger door and started to run.

But his feet said No way, it was over, no more for them. Four steps, maybe five and Chuck fell to his knees.

The sound of feet, healthy feet in strong shoes, came closer, like swooping birds.

Two of them, strong armed, pulling him up. His feet on fire as they walked him back. Headlights

illuminating the road.

Royce face down on the road, not moving, another of the slime standing over him with a handgun pointed at his head.

"No!"

Chuck heard the shot as they shoved him into the back seat.

Guys got in on either side of him.

Dear God, forgive me.

Tears burned his eyes.

Royce, Dear God, forgive me.

60

"What happened here tonight is about a network of former Serbian soldiers," Agent DeSoto told Sandy Epperson. "There was also a wipe out at a sushi restaurant in Woodland Hills earlier tonight. We think that's their work, too."

Holy mother of pearl, Sandy thought. "But why?"

"They're running heroin here in the Southland. We think the leader is a man named Svetozar Zivkcovic. Ever heard that name?"

Sandy shook her head.

"You've heard of Radovan Karadzic then? He was in charge of the ethnic cleansing of Bosnia in the mid-1990s. He was caught in 2008."

"I think I do remember that."

"Zivkcovic was Karadzic's right-hand man, his chief assassin, his terror. He was reportedly in Afghanistan in 1999, in league with a local warlord."

"How did he end up in Afghanistan?"

"It goes all the way back to the Soviet occupation. I'm

265

telling you, nobody learns the lessons of history, do they? This area of the world has been the graveyard of every empire that tried to occupy it. The Soviets thought they were the exceptions. We did, too. No matter what force is there, an opportunity comes around for people to exploit weaknesses by force.

"The old khans, who controlled the Helmand Province, were targeted by the Communists in the early years of the Soviet war. Most of them were wiped out or fled the country. But that just created a power vacuum for new warlords to step in, hardened by the occupation and merciless. And smart. They trafficked in guns and cash and the most important thing of all, the poppy."

"Their chief export," Sandy said.

DeSoto nodded. "Their new axiom of power was, Who controls the poppy, controls the province. And the Serbs took notice. So Zivkcovic was dispatched to work with Abdul Asad Sajadi, a respected Mujahideen commander in Kandahar during the Soviet occupation. He provided training and weapons and strategy that helped bring down the Communist occupation. The Soviets called this war The Bear Trap. From 1989 to 2002, Zivkcovic and Abdul were a force in the region. They even got the CIA to buy back a cache of stinger missiles it had provided during the war. But they were solidifying their trade in opium. Abdul was assassinated in 2003, we think by the CIA."

"You *think*?" Sandy said.

"They never talk to us," DeSoto said. "But it's obvious. Anyway, he's got trade partners there. And his network is active here in Southern California. Maybe he's here, too. He would have come in before 2001 and the Patriot Act. He would be deeply invested, would have as tight a false identity as big money can buy. Then he probably goes to Europe as a businessman, legit, and slips untraced into Afghanistan. That, at least, is our theory."

"Okay," Sandy said. "But what about my guy, Samson?"

"We got a lead about him from one of our agents on the Afghan Task Force. We check all returning vets, routine stuff. But something clicked on Samson and it had to do with his wife. She was a journalist and was getting deep into a story about heroin in SoCal. So we rented a house in his neighborhood. We needed a home base and cover in the area anyway, and this was a good a place as any."

"Then you knew him. As a neighbor."

"As someone to say Hi to, yes."

"You know about his house on fire then. Who started that?"

"We think it was one of Zivkcovic's people. We think they made me, and I got out of there. Before this all happened."

"Surely you don't think Samson was into trafficking," Sandy said.

"No. But he works at a school that has a connection."

"The Hunt Academy?"

DeSoto nodded. "You ever heard of the Westies?"

"Oh yes," Sandy said.

"And James Stone?"

"Jimmy Stone, sure."

"How about Ryan Malik?"

Sandy nodded. "He's one of them, too."

"Dead. Got it from one of the Serbs. And that put the fear of Zivkcovic into young Jimmy. He came to us."

"Did you bring him in?"

"We're leaving him out. But if he cooperates, and keeps alive . . ."

"That's cold," Sandy said.

"It's a cold world, Detective. We have names. Two names

Jimmy gave us. One was *Dog* and the other was *Vaso*. That's it. That's as far as we were, until tonight."

•

When they took the hood off his head, Chuck saw he'd been walked into a palatial room with a huge skylight. The sound of a fountain running brought his attention to a small grotto of ferns and rock next to floor-to-ceiling windows. Two marble pillars supported an arch over the windows. One entire wall was built-in bookshelves but with a huge flat screen TV in the middle. The floor was dark burgundy tile. Chuck was no design maven, but thought it looked like his favorite Mexican restaurant back in Chatsworth.

Which was where he wanted to be right now, with Stan and a pitcher of margaritas.

The view through the windows was a postcard blown up to life size proportions—full moon, shining down on the ocean, seen through a clutch of palm trees.

It might have been the most mellow, most beautiful, most relaxing place in Southern California, if not for the two guys with weapons flanking him.

A man walked into the room as smoothly as a motivational speaker coming onstage. He was maybe fifty and in solid shape. His tight cotton shirt revealed a bull-like build. He had calm, intelligent eyes. He was not just an occupier of space. He was the kind who owned every room he entered.

This was the guy. The one behind it all. Chuck knew that as sure as he knew his own name.

The man waved his two gunmen out of the room. They obeyed quickly, like soldiers.

That's what they were. Serb soldiers. Right here in

Southern Freaking California.

"How do you like Alan Ladd?" the man said. Accent, but from one who was fighting hard not to have it.

Chuck fought the fuzziness in his brain, which wanted to shut down for the night. What did the guy just say?

The man walked over to the window, looked out. "It's beautiful tonight," he said.

"What do you want with me?" Chuck said. "Why all this? Where's my brother?"

"When I was a boy," the man said, "I was sometimes able to go to the cinema. Your American movies were a godsend. Old movies, not like the atrocious offerings being made today. John Wayne I liked, but most of all I loved *Shane.* Alan Ladd. Do you know the movie?"

Chuck wondered if he'd fallen into the Mad Hatter tea party, only the Dormouse was a crazy Serbian criminal.

"Shane is God come down from the sky," the man said. "He rides into a valley and brings order against the evil ranchers. He does his job then returns. He fights. There is a wonderful fight scene."

"Where is my brother?" Chuck said.

The man raised a finger. "Jack Palance plays the gunfighter who comes to kill for the evil rancher. Shane works for the good homesteader. But you see the point, don't you?"

Chuck said nothing. What do you say to someone who is talking about movies at a time like this?

"It is because the fate of people is very often not in their own hands," the man said. "They are at the mercy of the forces that are stronger than they. That's when you need a Shane on your side. I will be your Shane."

Chuck opened his mouth to speak but his muscles, even those in his jaw, were starting to betray him. He was standing, barefoot, on the cold floor. He was sure he'd fall at any moment but willed himself not to. Don't lose consciousness. Keep your mind on the cold. Keep awake. Keep—

"My name is Kovak," the man said. "I am in the manufacturing business. I support my community, and families. I am very much a believer in the family."

Talk to him. Keep awake. "Sure. So much so that you kill innocent men?"

"God tells us that none are truly innocent, Mr. Samson. I'm sure you have many questions. But you are here to answer only one. For me. I know you may need some help, and I am going to offer it to you."

"I'm not going to say anything until I see my brother."

Kovak nodded like a priest with a penitent. "I understand. I do. You are a good man. But I must know first how much you remember. You see, you know where something of mine is, and my only question to you is going to be, where is it?"

"I don't know what that means, what any of it means."

"I know," Kovak said. "That's why I am going to help you remember. Bear with me for just a little while more, and all will be well."

•

Now where?

Think!

Stan felt the mist of the night air, the ocean air, on his skin. He was in the back of this big house. Wow, it was big. It was one of those big houses he saw sometimes on TV, when there was something about rich people and where they lived.

This was where they were going to bring Chuck.

A rich guy with guns must live here.

He'd have to be extra good and sneaky to avoid the guns.

They'd had him in a little house in the back. It was next to a swimming pool. They kept it dark out here, so that was good. He could sneak around in the dark.

And they had lots of plants and trees and stuff all around the pool. It was like they wanted a jungle here. That was good, because now he could hide. They might not check on him for a long time.

He had to get help. Get somebody to come help rescue him and Chuck.

But how?

Think!

He saw someone moving at the back of the big house, on the other side of the swimming pool. Coming out of big doors.

Quick.

He ducked down behind a big rock. They had some big old rocks out here in the back. Everything about this house was big. Stan could hide good. He could always hide good. He could squeeze into places Chuck couldn't because Chuck was too big and not wiry, like him.

Watch them. Watch and see if you can see Chuck in there.

The man who had come out of the back of the house was walking to the other end of it. There was a door there. He opened the door and then a light came on. The man in there looked kind of big. Kind of scary.

He sat down at a desk.

And then there was a glow. The guy was sitting at a computer. A big man at a computer. Maybe I can get a rock and hit him on the head. Like in *Braveheart*. He liked that movie. It was the one with Mel Gibson. That was a movie about Scottish people a long time ago who threw rocks at their enemies. They were good rock throwers. And rocks could really hurt.

271

Stan remembered when some kids threw rocks at him when he was walking home from school. They hurt. Chuck found out who they were and took care of them. Now it was time to take care of Chuck.

But there weren't any rocks around that he could see . . . just these giant ones. And if he blew it the big guy would probably shoot him. And then maybe go shoot Chuck.

So maybe wait. Just wait.

No. That wasn't good enough. Chuck was in trouble.

Maybe a tree branch. Stan looked around in the moonlight—he was glad there was moonlight—and saw that there was a tree of some kind a few yards away. He tiptoed through some ivy or something to the tree. But there were no branches he could reach.

Dang it!

Come on, Stan, *Think.*

He heard a noise. It made his body go on full vibrate. Chuck once called him a live wire when he got scared. That's what he felt like right now. His body humming. He listened.

Something moved in the bushes. What if it was a bear or something? That would be bad. He didn't want to get eaten by a bear! Not now. Not knowing he was so close to Chuck.

More rustling, closer, faster.

He wanted to scream, but he couldn't do it or he'd give himself away or maybe they'd hear him and kill Chuck.

Don't move. If I move it'll hear me. It'll get me.

Sound above him. Like a helicopter.

But it was in the tree. Something was moving in the tree.

Oh no. It was going to jump on him!

He covered his face.

But then one last burst of sound and then nothing.

Stan opened his hands and looked at the sky. Against the

moon, the big bright moon, he saw a couple of flying things. Birds? Or maybe bats?

Flying things going away. Gosh, if he could only get Chuck on a flying thing, a plane, they could fly out of the country forever and live where Julia and these bad guys could never find them.

Stan tried to calm himself, slow his breathing. And as he did he looked back at the room.

The glow was still there, but the big guy was not.

61

They took Chuck up some stairs, the Kovak guy and one of his men and some wispy Asian dude following, holding an old fashioned doctor's bag.

It was this guy Chuck feared most.

Up in a second-story room now. The soldier opened the door and pushed Chuck inside.

The room was dim, the recessed lighting kept low. A large bay window gave the same ocean view as below. This man sure liked his moonlight. Maybe he was a werewolf. Maybe a silver bullet was what we needed here.

Or any weapon. And an invading army.

There was the chair in front of the window. The soldier took Chuck's arm and set him in the chair. There were large flat arms on the chair with leather restraints. The soldier put his hand on Chuck's throat and pushed him back against the chair. Kovak secured the restraints around Chuck's wrists.

"I'm afraid this is necessary," Kovak said. "You will understand. No harm is going to be done to you."

"I believe everything you say," Chuck said.

"There is no need to be skeptical. I'm a man of my word. All you have to do is give me what I want and I will let you see your brother."

"I have one question for you," Chuck said. "Will my brother and I be able to leave here alive?"

"Why don't we take this one step at a time? It's very important that you relax. Isn't that right, doctor?"

The Asian man said, "Yes, that would be very helpful."

He placed his black bag on the table and opened it.

●

Stan sat in front of the computer.

Okay, now think! Do it. Think.

What was her name? The cop. The nice cop.

Epperson, that was it.

And she was from Topanga. That's what she said. Topanga station.

Stan Googled *police Topanga station.*

Got it! Top hit.

It had a phone number. He'd call!

No phone in here, in this little office slightly off the pool.

Now what?

Think, Stan, think before they come back.

There were two pictures on the website. Tim Barasco and Harold Peters. It said they were Captains.

Captains were good.

But there were no phones!

Wait a second, wait. What's that? A link. A link on that Captain's name. Barasco.

Click.

There he is again. His picture. And stuff about him.

Tim Barasco began his career as a police officer in 1988. He promoted to Sergeant in March 1993 and to the rank of Lieutenant in February 1999. After promoting to Captain in April 2005, Captain Barasco was assigned to Southeast Patrol Division as the Commanding Officer, where he led a very successful effort...

Come on, that doesn't help.

Wait. Under his name.

Leave a Message

Click.

A box came up. He could type into it!

A door slammed.

•

The doctor prepared a syringe and spoke softly. "It will go much better if you do not fight. You will feel warmth in your arm and then in your head. It will be as if you are dropping into a nice sleep, but you will not be asleep. Is that clear?"

Chuck said nothing. He would give them nothing. He would go to sleep. He would black out. He would . . .

The doctor swabbed Chuck's left arm at the elbow.

Don't give them anything. Nothing.

Nothing.

"Little sting now," the doctor said.

And then it was warm, in his arm.

•

Gotta hurry!

Stan typed.

*help us tell detective epperson me and chuck are
at this big house by the ocean they got us*

"Hey!"

A guy coming in the other way, through the other door, running at him.

Send, send, hit send!

62

A dim light flicked on in the back of Chuck's brain. The figures standing there in the shadow dance, two of them, he saw the faces. Yes, for sure, it was the same, it was this one, Kovak, and another, darker. The darker one had deformed feet. Like rocks.

"The feet . . ." Chuck said.

"Ah!" Kovak said happily. "You see them."

"See what?"

"Try to hear him," Kovak said.

"What do I hear?" Chuck said. His voice was thick and slow.

"Just listen."

"No," Chuck said.

"And?"

"My brother."

"I like you," Kovak said. "I like you very much. You may be able to save your brother. Would you like to do that?"

"Where?"

"You give me something first. That's all I ask, will you do

that for me?"

Stan. Need to see him. See him. "Yes," Chuck said.

"Good," Kovak said. The Kovak in the room with him now. The Kovak in his memory was also talking. Chuck could hear his voice, *"Where did he say it was? The truck. Where did he say it was?"*

And then in his brain two men fighting. Men in uniforms. Sports uniforms.

The dream. The weird, strange dream. Only not a dream now, in his mind now.

"You see something," Kovak said, Kovak in the room. "What is it?"

"Nolan Ryan," Chuck said, unable to resist the questioner. "Mario Lemiux."

Chuck's eyes were heavy, like he wanted to sleep. But it was clearer in his mind. Nolan Ryan and Mario Lemiux. He could see them now.

Nolan Ryan, his childhood hero, wearing his Angels uniform, on the mound at the Big A, only the uniform top was too short and his stomach was showing. He had a rash or something on this stomach.

He was pitching to Mario Lemiux, but Mario Lemieux was a hockey player . . .

Kovak shook Chuck's shoulders.

The images in Chuck's head scrambled, then coalesced again, stronger.

Kovak said, "What are you talking about? Save your brother."

"No," the Asian doctor said. "Too hard."

"Shut up," Kovak said.

Rush ten line . . .

"I see it behind your eyes," Kovak said.

"Rash," Chuck muttered. "Nolan Ryan has a rash tan line."

The doctor said, "He's delirious."

"No," Kovak said. "He's got something. He's *got* something."

Someone pounded on the door.

Kovak went to the door, threw it open. Chuck heard voices. He thought he heard someone muffled, like he was gagged.

The door opened wider.

Stan!

Gagged. Eyes pie shaped. Hands restrained behind him.

Pushed inside by someone.

Someone Chuck knew.

Yes. The guy from the accident. The guy who rear ended him and pulled a knife. The Mad Russian.

Every nerve in Chuck wanted to jump up and tear into everybody, but he couldn't move. Lethargy enveloped him, made everything feel slow around him.

"And so here he is," Kovak said. "Your brother, safe as you can see. He's scared, a bit nervous—"

Stan broke free of the Mad Russian and ran at Kovak with lowered head.

And got him right in the stomach.

Kovak grunted as he went down, hard, on his back. Stan on top wiggling and trying to get up.

Mad Russian grabbed Stan by the shirt and yanked him up like a laundry bag.

"No!" Chuck managed, his tongue feeling like two tons.

Mad Russian threw Stan against the wall.

Stan hit, went down, didn't move.

God, oh God, let me out of here. Give something to kill with.

Kovak was on his feet. Blue fire in his eyes.

He advanced toward Stan.

God, oh God.

Kovak stopped before Mad Russian, took one look at Stan, then slapped Mad Russian so hard he hit the ground.

"Incompetent!" Kovak took a step toward the downed soldier.

Crablike, Mad Russian scurried backward.

And then the room's lights started flashing. Alarms split the air.

Kovak leaned over and picked up Mad Russian the same way Mad Russian had picked up Stan.

He threw Mad Russian out of the room.

He waved at the doctor to follow.

The doctor seemed like he couldn't get out of there fast enough.

He's going to leave us here. Me and Stan.

Stan, who still was not moving.

Kovak went through the door, closed it.

Chuck could not hear a lock. The alarm pierced his hearing.

He wanted to cover his ears, couldn't do a thing.

Alarms and flashing lights going on in the room and in Chuck's mind.

63

Remember!

Afghanistan.

Kovak was there. And so was the man with rock feet. Deformed feet. Dressed in Afghan clothes.

Warlord.

A villa. He'd been taken to a villa.

Chuck closed his eyes. The alarms going off made it hard to think.

They tortured him, he knew that. He knew because he'd been debriefed after, and that cut on his neck, didn't happen by accident.

It was coming back.

A truck.

Something about a truck.

Dylan Bly.

Something Dylan Bly said about a truck.

Chuck opened his eyes

Stan wasn't moving.

The door opened.

No.

It couldn't be.

No.

It was.

Julia.

I'm gone now. Crazy. It's over. I'm gone, crazy . . .

But she closed the door and came to Chuck.

She unlatched the restraints.

No, he was still crazy.

It could not be her.

"Chuck, get up," she said.

"Dear God!"

"Get Stan up. Hurry."

Chuck grabbed her shoulders. "Tell me what this is!"

"They're coming," Julia said. "Cops and who knows what else. We've got to get out the back way."

She sounded like Julia. She looked like Julia.

She *smelled* like Julia.

Chuck tried to talk, couldn't.

"Get Stan," Julia said.

Yes, Stan on the ground.

I *am* crazy. I must be. This can't be happening.

Stan started to roll over.

To get from where he was to Stan was a matter of ten feet, no more. But those ten were like a slog across a muddy football field at night. Half his mind was trying to make sense of Julia being alive, and that half was sending signals down his spine, to his legs, to his arms, distress signals, trying to put the brakes on movement. The other half was getting to his brother, and then getting out of there, somewhere.

And Julia was letting them.

How, *how?*

283

On his knees, Chuck ripped at the duct tape on Stan's wrists. It wouldn't budge. He leaned over and used his teeth to create a tear, then ripped it off.

He untied the gag.

Saw Stan's glassy eyes.

"Stan, hey."

"Chuck?"

"I'm right here."

"They're mean."

"Can you get up? You hurt?"

"I'm mad now."

"We need to go."

"Julia's here!"

"I know." Chuck looked up but Julia was gone.

64

Alarms still sounding throughout.

"This way!" Stan said.

Chuck followed his brother, down the hall, down stairs in the back.

Where was Julia? What was going on in the rest of the house?

Why can't we stop this, slow it down, like a replay on ESPN?

His head felt like a football kicked for a fifty-yard field goal.

Down the stairs and out through a back door with leaded glass. A pool was there and vegetation and the moon bright enough to bathe it all in silver.

"Here Chuck!" Stan was at the wall next to a rounded door. Stan tried to open it.

It didn't budge.

Chuck grabbed the latch, tried it. Nothing. Stuck or locked.

"Look out," Chuck said. Then gave it a police-breaking-the-door-down kick. And got a pain shooting up the leg.

"That only works in movies, Chuck!"

"Stay back!"

He gave it another kick, blood returning to his head, heart pumping. He would get them out, get Stan out, and then he'd think about Julia. He needed time!

Another kick.

A fourth.

The door moved a little.

I am Chuck Norris. And this *is* a movie.

Chuck gave it everything he had.

The door cracked open.

"You did it!" Stan said.

Chuck took him by the arm and led him through the door to a broad expanse of open hillside.

Where a dark figure was waiting for them.

In the moonlight, Chuck saw the glint of a knife.

From the silhouette and the hair he was sure it was Mad Russian.

Who lunged forward, knife out.

Chuck readied his hands.

Just as Stan jumped in front of him.

And took the blade in his gut.

•

Sandy Epperson couldn't help thinking back to the time they had that shooter up on Beachwood, right below the Hollywood sign. He'd parked his trailer up on the fire road, about a hundred yards from the nearest house.

But he was sending rounds into the back of the homes all along the ridge with a high-powered rifle. Killed a dog and almost a toddler.

By the time they'd gotten a command post together it was hell on the hillside as this guy had unlimited ammo and a perfect spot to let it go. Stark hill behind him, narrow road in front that couldn't be accessed. Three SWAT snipers couldn't draw a bead on him because of oleander overgrowth.

It was like this guy had planned it all out. He wasn't some crazed vet with too much beer and Doxepin in him. He was sending a message or making a statement or just taking it out on the world.

The standoff took four hours to resolve. It was night when it finally ended under helicopter lights and a SWAT drop from the hill.

It was amazing what one guy in the right position could do. Sandy thought about that now as police and sheriffs and FBI came together on another, much tonier hillside.

The guy in the trailer turned out to be a petty criminal turned actor who'd been turned down for a one-line part in a Bruce Willis movie.

But this one, if they were right, would be a fish much bigger. Moby-Dick size.

All because of a message that had been auto-forwarded to her phone and traced by Agent DeSoto's partner using a tracking system DeSoto referred to as "Bowser." Sandy didn't know if that was an acronym or a dog name, but it didn't matter. They were converging on a location now, and doing so with extreme care and reinforcements.

Driving up the street behind DeSoto's unmarked car, it seemed to Sandy just like Beachwood again. There was no Hollywood sign this time. A big moon was out instead, like a sign that said "Welcome to Malibu."

65

Chuck's fist caught Mad Russian directly in the nose. He could feel the cartilage crunch. His only thought was to create as much immediate pain as he possibly could, put an end to his life if need be, but at whatever cost incapacitate him.

Because he still held the knife.

Stan was on the ground behind him.

Chuck felt every move as if it were orchestrated, all of the techniques he'd learned as a Navy chaplain training with Marines, and all of the old dirty fighting tricks he'd picked up along the way.

Curling his fingers into a fist and sticking out his thumb, Chuck jabbed at Mad Russian's left eye. In the dimness it could not be precise but as it landed Chuck knew it was a pretty good guess.

Solid contact.

Mad Russian cried out, brought a hand up to his face as he stumbled backward.

He couldn't be allowed to recover. When an assailant had a

knife it did the most damage when it slashed. Every advantage had to be taken when he became distracted.

Like now.

Chuck put everything he could into a kick between Mad Russian's legs.

And missed the bulls-eye.

But Mad Russian took another step back.

Had this been a one-on-one street fight, Chuck would have run away. That was, after all, the first rule. You get away from someone with a blade. Only a fool stays and tries to disarm a knife attacker.

But he could not leave Stan, and Stan could not run.

Somebody was going to die on this hill.

•

Sandy knew from bitter experience that there was nothing more difficult in a SWAT situation than expedited neighborhood securing at night. You had two simultaneous problems to handle, and either one of them could explode out of control at any moment.

First, there was the danger itself, the "hot spot," be it shooter, hostage taker, or armed resister. Or, worse, a number of resisters with weapons and ammo.

Second, you had to protect those in homes, the potential gawkers and looky loos, but also the folks just sitting inside having a relaxing time by their windows. Anyone in the line of potential fire had to be notified and usually evacuated.

It was worse when you weren't sure of the terrain. Even with the command post vehicle provided by the Sheriff's department, and its monitors of neighborhood layout, getting to the homes in real time and as quickly as possible was the challenge.

There was another problem—the low ground. Snipers always worked best with "elevated advantage." That wasn't going to happen here.

As Sandy was thinking about all this she got a call from Agent DeSoto.

"We've been made," DeSoto said.

66

Three things happened simultaneously in Chuck's brain.

The first was his next move, seen as if projected on a screen. Mad Russian was back against a retaining wall or small hedge—Chuck couldn't tell in the light—and it was going to be just like the old schoolyard prank. Guy gets behind another guy, on all fours, and a third pushes the hapless victim backward.

This would be one push, and it would have to be now, and it would have to work.

The second flash in Chuck's mind was Julia's face. It held a grim, mocking look. It was a nightmare face.

Third, he heard Dylan Bly's voice. He was talking about a truck . . .

Chuck put his hands out like battering rams and charged. Flush contact with his chest. And as the knife hit Chuck's chest, Mad Russian fell over a hedge. The momentum of the hit thrust Chuck forward, and he fell, too, following Mad Russian over and on top of him, and they began to roll.

•

Sandy Epperson, Los Angeles Police Department detective, was trained like all police officers to handle a weapon. Her choice was the Beretta 92F, which had been standard issue before Chief Bratton took over in 2002. Bratton favored the Glock, but Sandy stuck with her Beretta—and a backup Smith & Wesson .38.

She'd only had to fire the Beretta once in the line of duty, and that had been two warning shots at the corner of Western and Santa Monica when two utes (she did like *My Cousin Vinny*) did not attend to her order to stop. She fired in the air— not SOP she would later learn before a board of inquiry—but it did get them hitting the ground so she could effect the arrest.

The brass was not happy with her, but the Korean liquor store owner brought his entire family down to the Bradbury Building and practically laid siege to it on Sandy's behalf. Nothing further was done, not even a reprimand.

Now, out of her car on the road in the Malibu hills, Sandy had her weapon drawn again and was prepared for what might be coming down the hill toward her.

This was her position now, for better or worse. She and the entire ad hoc team would have to do what they hated most— make the best of a bad situation.

That's when she heard the roar above her head.

•

Chuck Samson had never head butted anyone, even in his dreams. He knew it was a risky move and done clumsily could cause as much injury to the butter as to the buttee.

He knew it had to be the rim of the forehead. A Marine once told him that if your head was a cigar, the strike point should be where you cut the cigar, just below the rounded edge. Not the part of the forehead you slap when you forgot your car keys. Just above that.

But then there was the target. It couldn't be the teeth or you'd get cut.

And it couldn't be the forehead, or you'd get your own bell rung.

That meant the nose again, and that's where Chuck, now atop Mad Russian on the ground, aimed.

Keeping his teeth clenched, he hit pay dirt with a satisfying thud. Clean, like hitting a pitch with the fat part of the bat.

He didn't have to guess about the damage. Mad Russian was hurt. It was just a matter of how bad.

Now he had to get the knife.

If there had been something around he could have picked up and used as a club, Chuck would have done it. But there was no time to look.

There was only time to bite.

Chuck pushed upward then reached out with his left hand and covered Mad Russian's right. He brought his right hand over and gripped Mad Russian's forearm just above the wrist.

Then Chuck dove into that fleshy middle like a starving man taking his first bite of corn on the cob.

The Mad one screamed as Chuck tasted blood.

And felt the Mad hand loosen.

Chuck swiped with his left hand and made contact with the knife handle. He scraped the weapon out of Mad's grip like one would get rid of a tarantula.

He heard something roar over his head.

Chuck brought his elbow up and brought it down toward

Mad's windpipe. But Mad heaved upward and Chuck made contact with the chest only, and not at full force.

His attacker issued a guttural cry like a wounded animal. It turned into a raging scream and all his muscles seemed to tense at once under Chuck.

From the feel of him, he was massively strong. Stronger than Chuck for sure. A cold-blooded killer he'd be if he was at full strength.

He could not be allowed to get to full strength.

Then Chuck's world turned upside down.

67

A helicopter?

Sandy instinctively squatted because it was buzzing so low.

Not a police chopper. Too small.

It was a private rig, big enough for two people.

And she knew it held the two people they needed most.

Of course, that kind of knowing was called a *hunch,* and that did not cut it in a court of law.

Powerlessly, she watched as the copter headed out to sea.

*

Somehow the Mad Russian had enough strength to turn Chuck completely over.

And put his right hand, his iron hand, the one that had grabbed Chuck that day of the rear ender, around Chuck's throat.

Chuck felt the air leaving his body as he sensed the downward angle to his right.

They were on an incline.

Roll baby, roll.

He tried. But Mad Russian was on top of him, astride, using his body weight to press down on Chuck's windpipe.

And he laughed. The Mad one actually laughed and Chuck saw his teeth in the moonlight as if he were some werewolf or crazy kid pretending to be a werewolf to scare his girlfriend.

Chuck tried to roll with the incline. Couldn't.

His body was cut off from the oxygen he needed with his heart beating fast and his lungs screaming for air.

Not going to make it.

Stan. Run. If you can.

Flying in from the left, hitting Mad Russian full on. It was a human battering ram. The grunt and scream of the ram could belong to none other than Stanley Charles Samson.

And all three started rolling, rolling like snowballs in cartoons, gaining speed.

Then the feeling of lightness, of air.

The spinning mass of humanity, downward in the night and light and the sea air filling Chuck's nostrils, and Chuck thinking this is the last thing I'm ever going to smell.

Stop.

Hard.

Jarring his head.

Something sharp, deadly, impaling.

Ripping through flesh. Fixing him in place.

The world going darker.

The moon fading to black.

68

It was almost light when Sandy Epperson got back to her house and she wanted nothing more than to throw herself into bed after merely kicking off her shoes. No time for niceties. She needed to sleep. After the adrenaline rush of the raid, the alerting of the Coast Guard to be on the lookout for a chopper, the gathering of bodies and victims off the hill, she was ready to get at least ten hours of sleep.

And then she got a call from her partner. She almost ignored it. Let it go to voicemail. A fat lot of good he was doing last night.

But at the last second she decided to give it an answer just to get it over with.

"Who's your hero?" Mark Mooney said.

"What is it, Mark?"

"You need to get some work done," he said.

Sandy fought back a curse trying to explode from her throat. "I've been a little busy."

"Oh really? Playing SWAT? I hope you had fun."

"Tell me what this is about and fast. I want to go to bed."

"I had to shoot a kid tonight."

His voice had suddenly changed, from joking to deadly serious.

"But he was about to shoot somebody else," Mark said. "One Raymond Hunt."

Sandy's head went even lighter, like it was floating off her neck. "Tell me what this is about, tell me now."

"That's what I'm doing. Raymond Hunt accepted drug money to fund his Academy. Our Jimmy Stone was the go-between. His little brother went to have it out with Ray Hunt at his house tonight. He was about to shoot him, and I got him in the wing. I'm very good."

Sandy said nothing. Her eyelids felt like overfed St. Bernards.

"And I got a complete confession out of Hunt," Mark said. "The whole set-up. It's going to make me look like the smartest kid in school."

"Wait a second," she said. "Wasn't I the one who told you that? And you told me basically to shove it."

"You don't sound happy."

"I'm dog tired, Mark."

"Then you rest up. Until our meeting with Brady."

"Meet with Brady? Why?"

"You can congratulate me."

"Why?"

"You'll find out. Night, sweetie."

The call dropped.

And so did Sandy Epperson, onto the sofa. She was thinking what a snot Mark Mooney was when she lay down. She was thinking he was going to get the nod to Robbery-Homicide, the elite unit, when her head hit the pillow.

She thought of nothing more, but in the thickness of sleep

she dreamed. She was in an ice cold lake. Underwater. She couldn't breathe. Her father was trying to get to her. His hand was in the water but he couldn't quite reach...

•

The park was beautiful.

It wasn't like any park Chuck had seen before. Not a real life park, so he knew it was a dream. But he also knew this was more than a dream because he wasn't dreaming, he was dead. He was seeing a vision in death.

Right?

He asked himself that question. He could hear himself asking if he was dead, right in the vision. His voice coming out of him.

He was seeing the park as if he was standing right there on the ground. Not himself. That would have been more like a dream, Chuck reasoned.

I can reason. I'm thinking.

This is a good sign.

In the park there were two figures, on the other side of the park, on the other side of the green grass.

Oh yes, old friends.

Nolan Ryan and Mario Lemieux. Only this time looking at Chuck, smiling, waving to him to come over and join them.

But if I go, where will I be?

Come on! they shout.

I have to find my brother, Chuck says in the vision.

"Your brother is all right."

That voice didn't come from the vision!

Open your eyes, Chuck.

"Your brother is going to be fine." The voice is a woman's

voice. Chuck knew that voice.

"Stan . . ."

"Yes," the voice said. "He's downstairs."

"Where?"

"Hospital. Santa Monica."

Open your eyes!

Light.

He was not dead.

Alive.

And she was Detective Sandy Epperson.

He was hooked up in a bed and alive.

"You're going to be all right, too," Sandy Epperson said. "You'll need a lot of time to heal, though."

Voice thick like it was coming out of tar pits. "Want to see Stan."

"As soon as you both are able. You've been in here two days."

"What . . happened?"

"Later. When you're feeling better."

"No. Now." He was coming back and he wanted to know everything. He wanted his mind working again.

"You and your brother only helped bring down the most vicious heroin trafficking network we've ever had. Nothing major."

Okay, good. Funny was good.

"And you," Detective Epperson said, "managed to kill the son of Svetozar Zivkcovic."

"Who?"

"Also known as Steven Kovak, the man whose house you were in."

"How? We fell."

Epperson nodded. "It was nasty. Dragoslav Zivkcovic, also

known as Dag the Dog, fell right on top of a Manzanita. Branch went right through him, through his heart, and through your side. You two must have looked like shish kabob."

Chuck felt the tightness of the bandages around his body.

"We got Kovak," Epperson said. "He tried to get to a boat by way of a two-man chopper, but went down near the Channel Islands. Coast Guard picked him and his chief guy out of the drink."

"My wife—"

"That's enough for now. You need to rest."

"No. Where is my wife?"

"You're going to see her," Sandy Epperson said. "But not yet."

69

Two days later Chuck told the nurse on duty that if he didn't get to see Stan right now he was going to rip the tubes out of himself and sing opera.

They wheeled Stan up to Chuck's room.

"Leave us alone," Chuck told the nurse. When she hesitated he sang the opening of *La Donna É Mobile* and she left.

Stan. He looked skinnier in his white gown, and his broken arm, in a sling, was like a stick in a handkerchief.

But his smile was a hundred watts.

"I did it, Chuck," he said. "I fought the Wolfman."

"That you did," Chuck said.

Stan pulled up his gown. A massive bandage was around his middle.

"You can put your gown down now," Chuck said.

"I wanted you to see."

"I saw. Believe me, I saw."

Then Stan put his hand out. Chuck took it. Stan squeezed it hard. "I won't leave you, Chuck. I'll be there when you need me."

Chuck said, "I know that, brother. I know."

●

Another two days, and Chuck was going to start doing show tunes unless he got out there. He wanted to see Julia, and they weren't telling him anything. Sandy Epperson said the Feds were in control and just hang tight.

He decided he'd start with *Oklahoma*.

The nurse—he was starting to think of the head day nurse like Nurse Ratched in *One Flew Over the Cuckoo's Nest*—told him to wait, he'd be having a visitor.

Another shock to the system.

It was Lucy Bowers.

His neighbor.

Or was it? She said her real name was DeSoto and she started spilling the strangest undercover story he'd ever heard outside of an NCIS episode.

Unbelievable.

But the end was the kicker. They had Julia in custody. And she wanted to see him.

●

Thirty-six hours later, Chuck walked into the federal building in Westwood. Agent DeSoto met him in the lobby and took him by express elevator to the top floor. There were interview rooms up there, and she walked with Chuck to one near the end of the brightly lit corridor.

She paused. "Before you talk to Julia, there's someone else who wanted to see you."

"Someone else? Who?"

"Does the name Vaso mean anything to you?"

Chuck shook his head.

Agent DeSoto opened the door. A man in an orange jumpsuit was seated at the spare interview table, his head down on hands shackled to a metal ring.

He looked up. And Chuck had to fight to keep his sutures from ripping out of his body.

"Hi Chuck," Royce Horne said.

70

"Mr. Horne has given us a confession," Agent DeSoto said. "He's waived his right to counsel."

"Didn't order a mouthpiece, Chuck," Royce said, smiling slightly. He had three or four day's growth of beard. He was trying to look like he always did, secure and in control. But there was the slightest bit of vulnerability in his face.

"And he wanted to talk to you," Agent DeSoto said. "We have consented, as long as it's understood this conversation will be recorded. You can have a seat, Mr. Samson.

Chuck quietly pulled back the government-issue chair and sat down across from Royce. He was trying to keep his head from exploding.

"I'll be right outside the door," DeSoto said, and left the room.

Royce started with a smirk and a light tone. "You remember the first time you saw Afghanistan, Chuck? I know what came to your mind. God forsaken, that's what you thought. It's like a world where all the color got sucked out. A world from a bad fairy tale. How did God even make such a place? You haven't given up on God, have you, Chuck?"

Chuck said nothing.

"What do you owe Uncle Sam, Chuck? You were a chaplain, not a soldier, but you went through the fire like the rest of us and when you came back, what do they do? They run you around because your DD214 is incomplete, through no fault of your own, mind you. So the VA says sorry, dude, can't do anything more fer ya. The grass doesn't grow and the money does not flow from the United States Treasury. Not for us. Not for the soldiers. It's always been that way, Chuck. You, of all people, deserve better. So do I."

"What are you trying to say?" Chuck said.

"That world with the color sucked out, I saw it, too. I knew then that's the world we all live in, no matter where we are. Then a warlord—a warlord, Chuck, isn't that the funniest thing you ever heard?—he showed me some color. It was the color of money. I was a liaison. With Sajadi and his network. You never knew I was there, Chuck. You were too busy counseling soldiers. I was busy talking to Sajadi. Now, this villa, Chuck, I'm telling you. A compound with huge guard dogs, iron gates, and an inner garden, like something out of an old Steve Reeves movie. There he was, Asif, in his flowing robe to cover his grotesque thickness. Somebody made him special slippers, with the fronts curled up like a genie. A genie, Chuck! I almost laughed. He carried a Kalashnikov assault rifle with a gold-plated forestock. The strutting peacock. Zivkcovic was there and it was nothing more than a matter of money. They offered me the deal of a lifetime. All I had to do was keep a few secrets, and bring a few people in. And why not? We all know we turned a blind eye to the poppy fields, to the warlords, to the drug mafia. We let it go, because the money was flowing to the farmers, and they were happy, and the Taliban was underfoot. But look what happened after we pulled out and NATO came in. How long did that prosperity last? What good did we really do, you and me? So you see, Chuck, nothing in this world makes sense unless the poppy grows and the money flows."

Chuck said. "You're telling me you were part of this drug business from the start?"

"What you don't know about Dylan Bly is that he was a ghost. An infiltrator. A CIA man. He was there poking his nose into things a little too deeply. The day before he died he and an Afghani named Daood killed two of Asif's thugs and stole the equivalent of $20 million in gold and paper kept in two trunks. Daood was about to be taken in by us, but offed himself with a gunshot under the chin. I was to bring Bly in for questioning. I saw him talking to you that night. Yes, I was spying on him, and you. I knew it was something heavy, from the body language. Do you remember what he told you, Chuck?"

The words echoed in Chuck's mind, as if from deep within a cavern. "He said he was afraid of dying."

"The next day, the security patrol went out. You came along, probably because of Bly. Am I right? Then we got to the wadi, and Bly's Humvee hits an IED. Only it wasn't an IED on the ground. It was under the Humvee. I put it there. And used a remote."

Chuck said nothing, tried to picture it.

"Bly was not supposed to die. But you jumped out and ran to him like some hero and Bly ended up dead, by a bullet that was meant for you, Chuck. They were shooting at you. They stopped shooting when they saw me. Do you remember what happened to you in that river bed?"

"RPG they said," Chuck said. "Concussive blackout."

"Wasn't an RPG, Chuck. It was me. I beaned you one on

the head."

"You what?"

"To save your life, Chuck. To get you out of there. I was supposed to bring in Bly, so we could get him to talk. The idiot ends up dead. That left only you, Chuck. We took you instead. How much do you recall about what happened to you?"

"I remember the rock feet."

"Asif Sadaji. He had deformed feet."

"I remember the smell of his breath. I don't remember much after that."

"Then you don't know that I was there. I was watching. I hope you believe me Chuck, but the reason you have all your fingers and toes is because I made that a condition of the questioning. They didn't have to go along with it, but they did. Asif and Zivkcovic. You see, I felt bad about what you had to go through. No matter who I was in bed with, I didn't want that happening to an American at their hands."

"I'm touched," Chuck said. "But if you were there, why didn't you get caught when they got me?"

Royce smiled. "Who do you think got you out? Who do you think sent the alert? We were all long gone when the rescue team arrived. I convinced them not to kill you, Chuck. You were the only one who could tell us where the gold was. I was going to get at you later. But they took you back to the states before I had a chance."

Chuck was silent.

"Then, when you showed up in LA, and came to the VA, I knew the day would come when you would have to be questioned by Zivkcovic. His new identity was well established, even though he secretly went into Afghanistan. On business. Isn't that a gas, Chuck? On business! I worked my way up to be his right hand. That didn't take much, considering what a lousy excuse for a son he had. I didn't let them know about you being in Los Angeles, because I was stringing them along. I was planning a little coup, for the right time. And I was getting some help."

"From who?"

"Hold onto your chair, Chuck." Royce looked like a kid getting ready to tell his mother he ate cookies before dinner. "Julia."

Royce paused, his eyes filling in the blanks.

Chuck's words were a whisper. "You and Julia?"

"Things happen at home when guys are off playing war. It's an old story, Chuck. But she never said anything bad about you. She never—"

"Shut up!" Chuck gripped the chair arms. "You say her name again, I'll throw this chair through your teeth."

Royce sat back, as far as the cuffs would let him. "That's not like you, Chuck. Not like a man of God."

"You better not say his name, either. Unless you're crying out for mercy."

"Maybe he'll give me a break, Chuck. Isn't confession good for the soul?"

"Why did you confess?"

"I'm tired, Chuck," he said, and smiled. "You want to hear something funny? Killing people makes you tired. You either keep juicing yourself up or sleep it off. I just want to sleep. God must respect that, right Chuck? Besides, I was doing some good, looking out for you the way I did."

"You did what?"

"The day you rear ended Dag's car—I mean, the day he caused you to do that—I was watching. I had been tailing him that day, because I knew he had in mind to try to prove himself to his father. But he was going to jeopardize everything, and it was part of my job to keep a reign on him, try to keep him from blundering into something that would drag you in. I'm the guy who called you, Chuck. Remember? *She can see past the grave?*"

"What . . . you?"

"To keep you from getting in too deep, Chuck. I was *protecting* you. I wanted you all to myself."

Chuck shook his head, blood rushing behind his eyes.

"And then I had to pop that guy who stopped to help," Royce said.

"You did that?"

"Sure. He could ID Dag. That's when things started going crazy in my head. Chuck, it was like . . . did you ever watch the old Ed Sullivan show on tape? My dad had 'em. There was a guy I saw once, a plate spinner. He got a bunch of plates spinning on these long sticks and he had to keep them all going at once. Sometimes it looked like one of them would fall, but then he would run over and get it going again. That's what my life has been like and you know what? I'm kind of glad that's all over. I just wanted you to know that your life isn't over. I want you and your brother to live."

"What about her death? Julia's death?"

"The Feds know all about that—" he looked up at the camera mounted on a ceiling corner—" Right guys?"

"You're talking to me now," Chuck said.

"It was Hillary. Had to get rid of him. And it was a way to get rid of Julia, too, so to speak."

"I saw her body."

"On a monitor. You spend a little money, and have a guy named Vaso visit you, a coroner might do some neat tricks for you. Another one of those plates, Chuck."

"Spin to your grave," Chuck said. "I'm done." He stood.

Royce shook his hands hard, jangling the shackles. "I want you to forgive me, Chuck. You have to. It's your calling!"

"I'll work up to it," Chuck said. He started for the door.

"Chuck! I have to know. Where is it? Where did they bury the gold?"

"Why would I tell you if I knew?" Chuck said.

"I can't do anything about it now. I just have to know."

"You let them cut my throat to find out."

"We weren't going to let you die. I wouldn't have let them kill you."

"You're a prince."

"Where is it buried, Chuck?"

Chuck pointed to his left temple. "In here. And if I ever dig it out, I'll send you a postcard."

Royce smiled, a forced one from the look of it. "Deliver the news personally," he said. "I'm going to need visitors."

71

"She's in the next room," De Soto said. "Look, if you want to wait—"

"I want to go in now. Are you going to record it?"

"We have to."

"Not this time. Please. I think maybe I'm owed that much."

Agent DeSoto paused, took out her phone. She turned her back and walked a few steps away in the corridor. She was back in thirty seconds.

"Go ahead," she said.

When the door clicked behind him Chuck thought for a moment it was his own heartbeat. Because Julia was at the table, in shackles, just the way Royce had been. Her coveralls were blue. Her eyes, once beautiful to him in ways he could hardly express, were now empty rooms with the lights out. No electricity running through the house.

Her lips were dry and cracked.

And Chuck had to keep reminding himself that this was real.

He sat.

Julia tried once to make eye contact with him. He saw a flicker of candles in those empty rooms before she turned her head away.

And sobbed.

He had never seen her cry like that. She'd always had a command of her emotions, a strength. He'd admired that about her, even though it sometimes seemed like a hard shell. Now what? Here in a federal interview room? Should he comfort her? Why? After what she'd done to him? And Stan? Should he hit her with something sharp to make her pain match his?

How about walk out and leave her without another word?

And then he found himself saying, "You have a lawyer?"

Julia, head down, sucked in breath behind her sobs. There was a box of Kleenex on the interview table, the only other object in there. No doubt for times just like this, from suspect or witness.

Chuck snagged a couple. He reached over and gently tipped up Julia's chin. She turned her head away. "No, Chuck."

He turned her head back. "Let me." He dabbed her eyes gently, then under her nose. He crumpled the Kleenex into a tiny ball and tossed it on the floor.

Julia took a few deep breaths. "Public defender," she said.

"You need a good lawyer."

"She already cut me a deal," Julia said. And now she looked at him.

When she did, Chuck felt a wave beating against his chest. He wanted it to come crashing through and cover her and drench her with regret. Instead, he closed his eyes to dam it up, and said, "What happened, Julia? How . . .?"

Julia took in a deep breath. "How well did you know me when you married me, Chuck? We didn't know each other at all. You didn't know much about my past. You didn't know what I was capable of."

"I just knew I wanted to be with you."

"And I thought getting married to you could save me."

"From what?"

She looked down at her cuffed and folded hands. "I'm not a good person, Chuck." She paused for a moment that stretched out until Chuck spoke.

"Is that it?" he said. "That's your excuse?" He snapped the words with a whip-like bitterness. It felt good for half a second. Then he thought, maybe she deserved one click off the reel, one inch of slack. But only one.

Julia said, "You know that book of poetry I had? Edna St. Vincent Millay?"

"Oh yeah. Burned up in a fire. Sort of fitting, isn't it?"

"I deserve that."

"Who knows who deserves anything?" Chuck sat back in the hard chair and folded his arms. He felt like a piece of beef hanging upside down in a big meat locker. Powerless to move, to think, to do anything but wait for someone to unhook him.

Julia.

He had loved her powerfully, but maybe brokenly, too, and that was the tragedy of it.

"Can I tell you something about it?" Julia said.

"About what?"

"The book."

"It's your show." He said this tiredly. His energy was fast draining, the way you crash after a caffeine high comes to a rapid conclusion.

"It was the one book that spoke to me when I was growing up," Julia said. "Her sonnets were a lifeline for me."

"I don't know anything about your growing up," Chuck

said. "Or sonnets. You never let me in."

She laughed then. Short, sharp, jarring.

"Why are you laughing?"

"There's a sonnet in that book that's my favorite one. I've got to tell you the first line. *This door you might not open, and you did; So enter now, and see for what slight thing you are betrayed.*"

"Touching," Chuck said, his mind chopping up the word *betrayed* into several mental pieces and scattering them around.

"That's the way I kept you out, see?" Julia said. "I had this door I didn't want you to open. I didn't want anybody to open it. I thought it would drive you away. I thought if we got married I could keep the door closed. But there is a crack in the door, there's a big crack and the door is flying off the hinges. You want me to tell you about it? It's not particularly interesting. Other girls have been abused. It's not like I'm unique. It's not like I deserve any breaks. But I just want you to understand. I just want you to see . . ."

"See what?"

"That it wasn't your fault. I don't want you to go away thinking any of this was your fault. You don't deserve that. And Stan doesn't deserve that."

"Stan especially."

"I'm not in any way excusing myself," Julia said. "I didn't want to get involved with him."

"What's the matter? Can't you say his name?"

Her eyes flashed for a moment, and Chuck saw in them something of that past she had hidden from him. He didn't know what was in those murky waters, and he didn't want to. He did not want to feel sympathy for her.

"I'm sorry," she said. "I hate myself for what happened. He told me how much money we'd have. He told me we would get away from the whole world. Do you want to know something, Chuck? Getting away from this world is something I've wanted to do since I was six years old. The world is ugly. Reality is ugly. I wish I could have stood by you, but I'm not that good."

They sat in silence. Chuck started to feel the talons grip his brain but he fought them back. He was not going to fold in front of her. He was not going to give her that.

But part of him saw the wreck she was, and was sorry for it, sorry for himself, too, because he had loved her and once felt like Fred Astaire in her arms. And all that was gone now, exploded like an IED on a dusty Afghan strip of hell.

The tears were coming down her face now, soundlessly.

Tears like those of some of the rough, tough soldiers he'd counseled alone on dark nights of the soul. Tears of hopelessness and fear.

"Julia," he said.

She looked up at him. And then said, "I'll miss you. And Stan. I'll miss you doing those magic tricks, too. I'll miss Stan's laugh."

Chuck felt a jarring in this head, like a drunk kicking a locked tavern door. But it opened. Light came out.

"What is it?" Julia said.

Astonished, wordless, Chuck stared at her, more light flooding in.

He stood.

"Don't go," Julia said.

"I have to."

"Will I see you again?"

"I don't know." He tried to see the future. Couldn't. "I just don't."

"Chuck!"

But he was out the door, calling for Agent DeSoto.

She came out of an open door and into the corridor. "What is it?"

"Get your team together, and somebody to record what I'm about to tell you."

"What? What are you—"

"It's going to blow your ever-loving federal mind."

•

Ten minutes later they were in a conference room on the third floor: three FBI agents, an Assistant U.S. Attorney named Cheryl Magnussen, and a stenographer.

"It's like this," Chuck said. "There's a truck with some untold millions of dollars in gold in it. Ditched. A soldier named Dylan Bly was dying, and told me where it was. He knew I did memory tricks."

The faces in the room tried to look like they understood.

"Here's the trick," Chuck said. "Nolan Ryan has a rash on his tan line. He's pitching to Mario Lemieux, who is holding a knob, a fish, and a kite."

The faces in the room began to get restless.

"Listen, it corresponds to numbers! Nolan Ryan was number 30. And Mario Lemieux was number 66. I see their uniforms. That makes their numbers stand out. But then the crazy phrases are numbers, too. Each digit has a sound associated with it. A one is a *d* or *t* sound, because it looks upright. A two is an *n* sound, because it has two legs. A three is an *m* sound because it has three legs."

"Is he serious?" AUSA Magnussen said to DeSoto.

"Let him finish," DeSoto said.

"Four is *r*, because it ends in *r*. Five is *L* because when you hold up five fingers, your forefinger and thumb form an L

317

shape."

"He *is* serious," said Magnussen.

"Six is a *ch* or *j*. Seven is *k* or a hard *g*. Eight is *f,* because it looks like a handwritten *f.* It can also be *v* sound, because it's close. Nine is a *p* because it looks like a backwards *p*. It can also be *b*."

"Can we get to the point here?" Magnussen said.

"This is what it is," Chuck said. "Nolan Ryan is 30. His phrase translates to 461252. Mario Lemieux is 66. His phrase is 298671."

"So what?" Magnussen said.

"It's latitude and longitude! 30.461252 by 66.298671. That's somewhere in Afghanistan, ma'am, and it may just be a huge boatload of drug money in gold."

A long pause clenched the room in its fist.

Without taking her eyes off Chuck, Magnussen said to the stenographer, "Did you get those numbers?"

72

Detective CO Brady put his hand out, indicating Sandy should take a seat.

It's the hand of death, she thought. I'm out of here again. Didn't follow protocol. Good excuse to get the axe out and—

"Detective Epperson," Brady said. "I'd like your side of the story."

"My side of what story?"

Brady did the little drumming thing with his fingers on the desk. Oh so theatrical. Sandy wanted to rap his knuckles.

"The Raymond Hunt story," Brady said. "Did you know that Ray Hunt and I knew each other?"

"As a matter of fact I did."

Brady frowned. "How?"

She felt really petty, but said it anyway. "Oh, by observing things. You know, like that picture on the wall behind you?"

Her CO looked behind, saw the picture, turned back and smiled. "You think you're pretty smart, don't you?"

Sandy shook her head, and was reaching for her shield to throw it on the desk when he added, "Because I do."

"You what?"

Brady picked up the desk phone, punched a button, said, "Send him in," and hung up.

A moment later Mark Mooney entered the office, his puffed out chest with him.

"What is this?" Sandy said.

"That meeting I told you about," Mark said.

"Your partner," Brady said, "got the Raymond Hunt confession all clean and neat."

"That's what he told me," Sandy said. "He must be a super detective."

"He is. He was trained by one of the best."

"Excuse me?" She looked at Brady first, then Mark. Mark was smiling. He went to the corner of Brady's desk and sat. "I was just telling Cap that I really don't want you to get a big head or anything."

"What does that even mean?" Sandy said.

"Gut instinct," Mark said.

Sandy waited.

"The other night when you called me to give me your theory about Ray Hunt, after I hung up, I don't know, I got a little gut instinct myself. I thought, Now what would Detective Epperson do?"

He smiled.

Sandy did not smile.

"So I thought I'd go have a little talk with Mr. Hunt. At his house. At night. Catch him when he's not expecting anybody. And when I got there, the door was open. And Jimmy Stone was inside threatening our Mr. Hunt. It's what we detectives like to call serendipity."

"That's a big word," Brady said. "Even for you."

"Especially for you," Sandy said.

"What I'm saying, partner, is that you da man."

"I don't want to be da man," Sandy said.

"But you are," Brady said. "And we can't have that around here."

"What?"

"I'm going to give you two days to clean out your desk and hand your files over," Brady said.

"But—"

"And then if you need help moving it all to your new office at RHD, I'll give you hand."

"Not me," Mark said. "I've got work to do."

"Wait a minute," Sandy said. "What just happened?"

"You're gonna be one of the best," Mark said. "Try not to blow it."

Ten minutes later she was back at her desk, still numb, picturing how her mom and dad might have looked if they'd been here to hear the news. They would have liked this kettle of fish.

Her phone buzzed.

"Detective Epperson," she said.

"Chuck Samson."

"Mr. Samson. Well, how you doing?"

"Better than most, not as good as some."

"Maybe that's the best that can be said for any of us. The Feds treating you right?"

"They love me. That's not why I'm calling."

"Oh?"

"You still have an unsolved case, I believe," Chuck Samson said. "The killing you tried to pin on me."

"You mean Grant Nunn? Look, we never really thought—"

"You were doing your job. I'm good with that. I also know who did it."

"Excuse me?"

"You want the guy who killed Grant Nunn, don't you?"

Instinctively, Sandy grabbed a pencil. But she tapped the eraser end on her desk. "Mr. Samson, you have a theory?"

"No, I have the guy. Or I should say the Feds do. Agent DeSoto, you know her, she's the one to contact."

"This is for real?"

"It's all recorded down at the federal building."

She used the pencil to write *DeSoto* on a piece of scrap paper. "I'll follow this up." She paused. "What about you, Mr. Samson? What are your plans?"

"Teaching," he said.

"Where?"

"Same place."

"But I thought, the administrator . . ."

"The parents came together to save the school. The school board voted to change the name to Academy of the Hills. All the teachers are staying."

"That's great. I'm happy for you. And for the kids."

"You keep holding that thought, Detective."

"Done deal, Mr. Samson."

73

Los Angeles Times

State Department Denies Rumors of Gold Cache in Afghanistan

Afghani Government Asking Questions

The State Department today issued an unqualified denial of rumors that a cache of gold has been recovered in a desolate area of Afghanistan known as the "Iron Stove."

"I can state categorically that these rumors are false," Assistant Secretary of State Erik Pappalardo said. "We do not withhold information like that from the Afghan government, and certainly not when it comes to something like gold."

But the Afghan liaison to the State Department, Aarif Chowdhari, told reporters he believes the gold does exist and that is "has been stolen from our country."

74

"I'm glad to see you looking so well, Stan," Mr. Cambry said.

Stan was back inside Ralphs, his domain, his world, his place, his work. He loved it here, and he was back. He was sore. He was bandaged. He was told not to do anything too strenuous. But this was work! "Mr. Cambry, I'm sorry I missed work. I really am."

The boss smiled. "All you have to do is call in. Let me know what's going on."

"There was something going on all right."

"Nothing bad, I hope."

Stan was about to tell him. The words were on his lips, bubbling up from his throat. But then he saw old Mr. Manchester coming in with his cane. "I'll tell you about it later, Mr. Cambry. I have to see the specials. People are gonna want to know about the specials!"

Mr. Cambry gave him a slap to the shoulder and Stan walked to the door and grabbed a specials flyer.

Doritos were $1.88!

Oh boy, he was going to tell Chuck about that for sure. Chuck *loved* Doritos.

75

The auditorium was packed.

Chuck Samson, sitting in the back row, had Wendy Tower on one side of him and his brother Stan on the other. He looked again at the program. It had a whale on the front, a drawing, and the whale was singing.

"It looks like opening night box office will be boffo," Wendy said. Then added, "Why are you looking at me that way?"

"Remind me to tell you about Boffo the Clown," Chuck said.

"This I've got to hear," Wendy said.

"Oh yes, you do," Chuck said. "How about at dinner tomorrow? The two of us?"

She smiled. "I can go for that."

Stan leaned over to Chuck and whispered, "Are you going to hold her hand?"

Chuck gave his brother a gentle rap on the leg.

Stan giggled.

It was the way Stan used to giggle, at home, when he and Julia and Chuck had lived for a few brief months of happiness. Thinking of Julia then brought the same dull ache to his stomach, but it was not as bad now, not like when he'd first seen her in federal custody. He had gone to visit her once more, just before they shipped her off for a short prison run. She'd cooperated with the feds and her deal gave her two to four years.

He told her then the hardest thing he'd ever had to tell anyone, that she couldn't be part of their lives anymore. That he would pray for her safety and her health and her ability to start a new life on her own. She looked hurt, even stunned. Maybe she'd hoped for too much.

Which stunned him, too.

He left her something, cleared with the detention unit. A paperback edition of the sonnets of Edna St. Vincent Millay.

He had looked up that one she mentioned. The one that started *This door you might not open, and you did; So enter now, and see for what slight thing you are betrayed.* He'd read the whole thing several times, and two other lines jumped out at him.

One was about the room that was uncovered behind the door. It held nothing. It was only "cobwebbed and comfortless."

That was the room in Chuck's mind where memories of Julia were shelved now.

And at the end, the poet says she seeks another place.

Both of them, Chuck and Julia, would not dance together again. They each had to find another place.

And for Chuck, it was right here, right now, at this school with the new name, next to his brother, and next to Wendy Tower.

The lights came down. The curtains parted and the crude set, made up to look something like a ship, appeared in all its handmade glory. The quest for the white whale was about to begin.

Chuck reached for Wendy's hand.

ACKNOWLEDGEMENTS

This novel would not have been possible, in its present form at least, without the incredible help of some very cool people, including: Cindy Bell, Emily Bell, Mike Berrier, Rich Bullock, C. J. Darlington, Teddi Deppner, Jennifer Lindsay, Richard Mabry, Carrie Padgett, Mark Young.

ABOUT THE AUTHOR

JAMES SCOTT BELL is the author of the #1 bestseller for writers, *Plot & Structure,* and numerous thrillers, including *Deceived, Try Dying,* and *Watch Your Back.* His novella *One More Lie* was the first self-published work to be nominated for an International Thriller Writers Award. Under the pen name K. Bennett, he is also the author of the Mallory Caine zombie legal thriller series, which begins with *Pay Me in Flesh.* He served as the fiction columnist for Writer's Digest magazine and has written highly popular craft books for Writer's Digest Books, including: *Revision & Self-Editing for Publication, The Art of War for Writers,* and *Conflict & Suspense.*

Jim has taught writing at Pepperdine University and at numerous writers conferences in the United States, Canada, and Great Britain. He attended the University of California, Santa Barbara where he studied writing with Raymond Carver. He graduated with honors from the University of Southern California Law Center, and has written over 300 articles and numerous books for the legal profession. He has had three feature screenplays optioned and is on the faculty of Act One, the Hollywood screenwriting program.

A former trial lawyer, Jim now writes and speaks full time. He appeared as an expert commentator on *Good Morning America,* CBS radio, and in *Newsweek* magazine during the O. J. Simpson murder trial. He lives in Los Angeles.

For more see his website at www.JamesScottBell.com

He blogs about writing and other subjects every Sunday at www.killzoneauthors.blogspot.com